I0461140

Flat Earth

A novel by Martin Holman

Worcester
Holman House Publishing

ISBN: 9780983732969

Cover design by: George Norman Lippert
Printed in the United States of America

Part 1

Now and Then

As a dog returns to its vomit, so a fool repeats his foolishness.

Proverbs 26:11

To the love of my life, Carie Marie, for always being there for me and our four gifts from God.

I love to tell stories. I love to tell stories about my life and the lives of interesting people who do interesting things. I tell stories that make people laugh, cry, or want to think deeper about life and love. I like it when my stories make them feel differently about who they are. I won't bore you right now with who I am. After all, that's not the more interesting story.

September 2, 2010

Now

Grace Dumais worked six days a week and felt depressed every single one of them, plus one. Her life was in shambles, and a wide gap was developing between her and her husband of five years. Declan Dumais tried to take control of all the problems at home by building schedules and giving short "motivating speeches," but those speeches and his faulty perspective were tiny Band-Aids on large bullet wounds.

Declan's confidence stood taller than his actual height. Wiry and short with a tiny nose, ears, and a tight Marine haircut, he looked like an athlete. His job as a PE teacher did nothing to dispel that myth.

These days, Grace never quite did her hair or looked like she wanted to impress anyone, but in college she twisted the heads of men faster than a praying mantis. Her hair was dark brown and bouncy, but her attitude had lost its former pep. She seemed taller than her husband of the same height.

Each day felt like a blur. Declan went to work teaching at the elementary school and Grace watched the boys. After work, Declan came home and spent time with the kids so Grace could get a bit of sleep. Then she woke up around 10:00 pm and drove to work at a nearby gas station for 11:00. The station was in a rough part of town near Great Brook Valley, a collection of housing projects in Worcester not far from their house in Shrewsbury.

Declan slept and she worked till 5:00 am. At five, she drove home to start cooking Declan's breakfast. He'd laid out the ingredients the night before to ensure she made the things he wanted to eat. After all, he was a Phys. Ed. teacher, and needed the appropriate body fuel.

Two days a week, Declan went to the library to study after work. Simply being in his home office wasn't enough. He told Grace she could hire a sitter if she wanted, but mentioned funds were tight so she had to be careful spending too much. On those Tuesdays and Thursdays, if she didn't hire a sitter, she watched the kids, went to work and slept very little.

When my wife, Marie, heard about this new schedule, she had Grace bring the boys to our house. Grace cried for an hour when Marie presented the offer. My wife asked me to mention this to Declan in hopes his pride would get in the way of requiring us to watch the kids with that regularity, but when I did, he thanked me and said it was for a good cause.

Declan chose Tuesdays and Thursdays to study because of the Flat Earth Group. His friend Adam Starr held private "Flat Earth" meetings at the Shrewsbury Library those days, and Declan wanted to hear what others had to say. More importantly, he wanted to share with others what he was learning during his private study times after.

Seven people attended the group every week, and Declan enjoyed the discussions. Adam was the leader, with his bright white hair and his resemblance to the professor from Gilligan's Island. Every time he spoke with his British accent it seemed like the wisest, most eloquent thing anyone said that day. Declan wrote everything down.

Lou, or "Sweet Lou" as everyone affectionately called him, was the self-professed "Lieutenant" who took the lead each time Adam could not make the meeting. Everyone liked Sweet Lou, but didn't respect him the way they did Adam. Lou was bald with two patches of hair on either side of his head, light strings crossing over the "bald head sea" from one side to the other. He had a pot belly and rosy cheeks and early on Declan hoped he played a Santa character during the holidays (the handlebar mustache needed to be replaced by a beard, though, for the sake of appearances).

One of two women in the group was a gruff, heavyset woman named Jenny Cruze, a "wicked cool name" Declan thought to himself the first time he was introduced to her, though the coolness, in his opinion, ended there. She spoke in a deep southern drawl that made Declan wonder what made her move north. Each time she spoke his name, he laughed to himself.

"Is that what you think Dee-Eclan?"

"Dee-Eclan, please come over here and help me with this."

Then there were the twin brothers who looked like they still lived with their mom. They either loved the polyester pants they received from their grandfather or they bought them at the Goodwill store for that cool throwback style. When it came to Mike and Gary Barnsworth's clothing, neither was true. They looked malnourished, hardly said a word, and Declan later learned they did still live with their mother.

The sixth member seemed a little out of place among the misfits. Amber Starr intensely studied and talked about every aspect of Flat Earth theory. Whereas mostly "scientific types" attended these kinds of meetings including her father Adam, Amber, five foot three and in Declan's mind a twin of Shania Twain, participated as much as anyone else. At twenty-five, the group designated her the "baby." When she spoke, however, every eye fixated on her.

Declan's attitude toward her was no different. He found himself smitten by her confidence. When the group dismissed for the evening, he longed for her to stick around and talk to him about the theory, or whatever else was on her mind. He couldn't tell whether she had an interest in him. She knew he was married, but Declan had been hit on enough times by the moms at his school to know that didn't always matter.

After a few months, smitten by infatuation, Declan wanted to make a move on Amber, yet understood the consequences if he stepped into such a thing. He believed in God, and even claimed to love him, but Grace was going crazy and in the last year his connection with Amber felt so strong. He convinced himself that God wanted them together. If it was not reciprocated, it would end up making things awkward at the group, and ruin some good friendships. To say nothing of what would happen if Grace found out.

So, he continued wanting her, but doing nothing about those desires. That left him unfulfilled and longing, but in the end kept him safe from making a stupid decision. This routine worked everywhere except the shower.

I guess it's wrong to say he did nothing because Declan threw himself into his Flat Earth "studies." He went to the library every Tuesday after work, met with the group at seven, then studied on his own until closing at ten.

Declan liked to stick with what he could control, and tonight's meeting topic was figuring out why the United Nations had a vested interest in keeping people from knowing the truth about the shape of the Earth. In 1959, seven nations placed flags down in Antarctica, as well as resources to make fight over the land a real possibility. America and the Soviet Union, the two superpowers at the time, agreed on a peace treaty called the Antarctica Treaty on June 23, 1961.

Declan wondered why the two worked together for such a treaty since the Cold War had raged on in the late Fifties. The two countries suddenly became friends on this topic and spearheaded the push to fight for the treaty to be enacted and enforced.

The three major tenants of the treaty were: The countries would ensure that the legal status of the continent's independence remained unchanged; that scientific cooperation continued; and that all exploration done in Antarctica was for peaceful purposes only.

People traveled to Antarctica all the time. Cruises and tours to breathe the fresh Antarctic air, provided they had $10,000 to drop for the vacation. People regularly mocked Flat Earthers for arguing that the UN kept people from visiting the seventh continent. This was a silly debate and many in his group often wondered who spread these types of idiotic points when it came to arguing for truth

Though Adam started a few groups in the local Massachusetts area, and loved to spread the "plain truth" about how the world really worked, he believed the official "Flat Earth Society" was a government-planted organization that spouted off "idiot science" to make true Flat Earthers look crazy. When Declan studied, he made sure to look at credible and scientific sources only.

For instance, though people could go to Antarctica on guided tours, those tours only traveled to sixty degrees latitude, essentially the coastal areas of the continent. To go beyond that required being part of a scientific community. Even then, it would be easier to be chosen as a Chick-Fil-A owner/operator than be approved for a research project on Antarctica.

It was possible, however. One must fill out State Form DS 4131, and that form must be approved. The EPA must then verify the visit complies with the Title 40 Code of Federal Regulations, or CFR. Finally the NEPA must prepare an Environment Impact Statement. That statement, Declan found out, would cost him - or anyone who wanted to research the tundra - $250,000 to $2,000,000. Not to mention, no one except government scientists had ever been issued a research approval beyond 90 degrees latitude. So no, Antarctica was not exactly an open country for anyone wanting to investigate.

Should one try to navigate their way into the interior, they would be arrested. UN troops ensure it security, and US Marshals have jurisdiction to arrest anyone caught on the continent without government approval.

Declan looked at his watch. He had to be home by at least 10:35 so Grace could get to work, and the library was closing soon anyway. He leaned back in his chair and rubbed his rubbed his face. On nights he wasn't at the library he usually stayed in his home office or played with the boys. Communication had frozen between him and Grace as she continued to struggle. He knew the remedy, but she never listened.

* * *

Grace's eyes wanted to shut. They were, in fact, shutting as she drove the boys to the mall one afternoon while Declan worked, or studied, or whatever he was doing during whatever time it was right now. She didn't want to go to the mall, but the kids had been rambunctious and staying at the house felt like more of a problem than a benefit. Why couldn't he just come home? She thought to herself. Why couldn't things be like they were before? When he wanted her and she craved his body touching hers? Now she hated when he touched her. Every few days or so he came home and tried to control her like some whore. He did his thing, and then went into that damn office to study.

Now she felt tired and lonely. The mall wasn't where she needed to be right now, but it was where she was going. A few weeks before, she'd ordered new credit cards. Grace figured she could use them to get some new clothes and start feeling more confident about herself. Walking into a room where every guy shifted their eyes from their girlfriend to her no longer happened. It wasn't that she'd gained much weight over the years.

In fact, in some ways she was smaller than her college days, but the soul had ways of exposing a lack of confidence as much as the body did.

She parked in the same lot she'd parked the last time she visited the Solomon Pond Mall, four years ago, but this time much closer to the door. When she decided to come here earlier, in the chaos of the kids around her, she'd forgot about her last visit and the balding, bearded man smoking outside of the entrance. As she walked in with the boys she could see him again in her mind's eye, and hated him. She hated his stench. She wondered if he'd tried it with anyone else.

For a moment she considered turning around and going to a different mall, but it had been a while and this was the most convenient. Grace breathed a sigh of relief when she stared through the TGI Fridays window and did not see her old "friend" – she couldn't remember his name - but silently thanked him for paying attention enough that day to save her from what could have potentially been disastrous.

In the middle of the mall, she stopped her two sons, and called for Luke to come over to her. Now four years old, she held him tight and thanked him for being alive and for being her son. Luke didn't know what he did to deserve the affection, but gladly accepted it from the favorite woman in his life. She stood up and kissed his younger brother on the forehead. Brandon sat in his stroller, approving the action.

They visited several stores that afternoon trying on what she thought of as a lot of clothes. She only brought home half of them, and she wouldn't tell Declan they were new, or how she paid for everything. The total bill rang to about five hundred dollars, a small amount compared to what she'd tried on. Grace commended herself for the self-control.

Most of the clothes had long sleeves. The more down she got on herself, the more she continued scratching and cutting her arms. She didn't know why she did it. She only knew that she couldn't feel anything otherwise. Nothing mattered anymore. Her husband didn't care about her. Grace's mother spent all her time with her new church friends, and Grace chose to not share any of what was happening in her life with her own church circle. Besides, Declan wasn't going to allow the imperfections of his family life to be visible.

She and the boys arrived home around eight o'clock. Three hours until Declan returned. She sent Luke and Brandon off to the toy room to play for a few minutes. Recently Grace had told Doctor Subrakash she felt low, that she might be depressed. After running through a list of questions that doctors like to ask, the woman prescribed Prozac. Grace stood in front of the mirror sobbing, wondering where her life was headed and hoping the boys didn't hurt themselves while she napped before she had to work that evening.

Around the same time, Declan's Flat Earth Group dismissed for the day after a lively discussion on how the sun and moon rotated around Earth's tabletop frame. There was disagreement around the track of the celestial titans, but in the end, everyone agreed the Earth was not currently moving through the solar system at 67,000 miles per hour, as scientists suggested.

Afterwards, Declan headed for his favorite study room in the back of the library. Recently he and Amber, after talking a bit more about Flat Earth theories, moved onto more personal topics. He didn't know if they'd be talking tonight, but when he saw her leave, he knew the disappointment he felt was problematic. He pushed away that feeling and got into study mode, but struggled getting her out of his mind.

The feeling of disappointment vanished instantly the moment he saw Amber knock sheepishly on the window of library's back door.

"Come in, come in," Declan said, then repeated the words a few more times under his breath. Old habits die hard, and not constantly taking control of every situation proved to be too difficult for him.

Amber opened the door then flinched, as if expecting an alarm to go off. When it didn't she walked in as if it were her home, that confidence returned. Declan felt breathless as she smiled. For months his mind played through the "what ifs" of their relationship, and now he so badly wanted to find out how she felt about him he worried what he might say.

"I know you're studying, but I had a question. Do you have a minute?"

"Of course. All the time in the world." He chiding himself for his answer. He needed to stay in control.

"We've been talking so much the last few months, and you're such a great guy. I've enjoyed our conversations. I know you're a church guy, though, and wanted to pick your brain about some things I've been going through on a deeper level. Maybe from a different perspective than I usually get from some of my other friends?"

Ok, she brought up the church thing. I have to tread carefully here, Declan thought, then answered, "Yeah, sure. I don't have all the wisdom in the world, but I know a few things and what I don't know, I'll try to find out."

"Ok, good, good." She sat down at the table, not across from him but beside him. Their knees almost touched. "I graduated a few years ago from Worcester State, and have been working and pouring a lot of my time into this group, and you know, our theories? My friends, the few I've kept since school, they want to go out every night so I did that, too. A lot at first, it was fun. I met people and I dated a few guys." Declan couldn't help but hear the slight hesitancy in her voice.

"I guess I thought life would turn out different after I graduated. I don't know how, but it seems like life should be more than this." She looked up at the ceiling and made some non-committal gesture with one hand. "I hope you're not offended, but the highlight of my week has been at the Flat Earth Group and, well, my conversations with you. They seem more real and authentic, you know?"

"I know what you mean," he said, mentally struggling to maintain his breathing, maintain an air of cool. "But my life isn't perfect, either. I've got struggles. I guess, in the end, it's how you deal with them. I choose to give them over to God and see where that takes me." Declan knew in his heart he was a hypocrite. Here he was talking all spiritual to this woman while at the same time wondering what it would be like.... He blinked involuntarily, mentally erasing that image.

"That's what I mean, Declan..." She paused and touched his arm. He liked how she said his name. "You're always so in control. Most men wouldn't 'give all their stuff' to God. But you have, and you're even proud about it. Your wife must be so proud of you."

She looked down when she said this. He couldn't tell if she'd made the statement to hear his response or if she genuinely meant it.

He made no move to pull his arm away. "My wife and I are going through some stuff right now, so I don't know if I'd say she was proud of me." He glanced down, trying to give an appearance of shame. "Since we've had the boys, Grace hasn't been the same, and nothing I do seems to make her happy."

"I'm sorry, Declan. I had no idea," Amber said, though her statement was obvious. He'd never said anything, preferring to keep his two worlds separate. There was no way she could have known, other than any implications from his constant flirtation.

"No, no of course you couldn't have known," he said. "But just you being here and talking with me has been huge in this season of my life. I don't know how to say this but my conversations with you have been the highlight of these last few months. So... thank you."

Amber blushed. She turned to face him directly, sliding her chair a fraction closer. She played with her black hair, not quite knowing what to say, but trying to come up with words.

"Sometimes, I feel so lonely..." She paused to think about her next sentence, then put her hand on the table next to his. Their fingers touched gently without ever crossing. She continued slowly. "...and you. Have helped. Me, I mean. Get through some of that deep, deep loneliness. Thank you."

"You're welcome. I love talking to you, and being with you." Declan's voice had more confidence now.

"Wait. I'm not done. I love talking and being with you, too. Which is why we can't talk anymore." Her eyes glazed over. "It is definitely for the best. and it'll be better for your marriage if we stay away from each other."

Amber stood up and walked out the door, crying from the decision. Declan felt tears down his cheeks, too, though he didn't know if it was because "they" were done before they even started, or simply seeing her heart break like this. He sat a long time in the study room, staring at the surface of the table until ten, then packed his backpack and drove home so Grace could get to work. That night, sleep evaded him.

Introductions

I'll stop here and introduce myself. You know, the teller of the story? I'm Jack. Jack who is nimble and quick. Jack who can leap a candlestick. Jack who in twenty-four hours can keep an atomic bomb from going off in LA, or who crashed on a deserted island and lived to tell about it with all of the other Lost survivors. All of the coolest characters in the world, on television and in the movies, are called Jack. From Sparrow to Bauer to Ryan to Reacher, all Jacks are awesome. Especially me. My mom told me that for years.

My life isn't quite so crazy as those other Jacks, at least not in the physical sense. I don't chase bad guys or commandeer pirate ships. I'm a pastor. Of a church. For the last 15 years I have shared my time with people of all ages, shapes, nationalities, genders, and types. People are why I exist. I love listening to them, talking to them, guiding them, and having them ignore me.

I bring this up now because, as we move along, I will become a part of the narrative and want you to understand that I'm not only telling you a cool story, but I want you to learn from it. I'd like you to soak in the lessons as you read so you won't be doomed to repeat the errors of those who lived this out.

Whatever you do, don't be a jerk and walk away the same person as when you started reading. Seriously, learn to learn from the moments of others. When we are younger, we are expected to make stupid decisions. Everyone walks into eras of their lives believing they are different, but then make the same mistakes. A bad relationship, a betrayed trust or not knowing how to grow our finances can delay any progress we want to make. When we make those mistakes later on in life, however, it makes an even greater impact.

Bad decisions happen anytime, but are usually compounded by a number of other bad decisions that we hadn't thought of as bad. For instance, when I was younger, I made a colossally horrendous decision that altered the course of my life. But it didn't just happen. That decision was the sum of many smaller precarious decisions.

The decisions we make matter, good and bad. A relationship started can lead to a blessing from God or something else. That something else is predicated on the decisions we make leading up to the one colossally bad decision we end up making.

In the telling of this story, it's going to feel like I'm going backwards to get to where I'm going, but in reality, I'm only building a case that the outcome had to happen the way it did, because of the paths

our heroes walked.

So here we go.

When I first met Declan and Grace Dumais, two things were true. First, they seemed very happy. A few years had passed since they had their two boys, and each week when they came into church, they smiled and talked to people and genuinely seemed thrilled to be a family. Second, as I soon found out, they were not happy at all. The young couple struggled every week to keep up the show that everything was great in the Dumais household.

I pastor a church consisting of small house groups that meet each week and at least one other day or night during the week. That could be Sunday or Tuesday morning, depending on the host's schedule. We call it Apex Church. Sounds cool right? When Jack (sorry, I occasionally speak in the third person) goes to church, he simply drives to a friend's house, sings and eats and talks about theology or justice issues.

Before coming to Apex, not long after their second child Brandon was born, Grace had gathered up the nerve to share with Declan she could no longer endure the weekly services at Master's Way Church where they'd been attending. She hated the religious sanctimony, and the other ladies wanted no part of a relationship with her. Depression from her past, the pregnancies and her married life had already brought her lower than she'd ever been.

Declan, on the other hand, had been flourishing. His school loved the work he did each week as a physical ed teacher, and their church gravitated toward his appetite for learning. He struggled at home, but slept fine knowing everything was a balance. Each week brought a new cry for help from Grace, and each week he found creative ways to ignore it or put her down for "poor communication skills." He tried to understand her problem, but Grace had a roof over her head, two beautiful sons that looked like him, and the freedom to do whatever she wanted during the day. What else could she want? he thought to himself.

She begged him to make a change at least in their church life. Her wails when she asked were so much, he responded finally with something about her, "manipulating him but he could be happy anywhere, so whatever...."

Around this time Declan had planned a fishing trip to Canada with a friend. After they'd talked, he gave Grace permission to do some research and even attend a different church if she wanted. The excitement in her lit up in her face. When Friday night rolled around, Declan kissed her goodbye and she headed online to look for new churches. She loved her kids, but it had been years since she looked forward to something like this. Whether or not it was the anticipation of a new church or how much she hated Master's Way, she didn't know.

Somehow, in the abundance of churches in the Central Massachusetts area, she found Apex. She liked that we differed from traditional and prayed we weren't a cult. As she later told me, however, she needed different. On that Sunday, September 6, 2009, she dressed herself and the boys and attended church at my house.

Seventeen others joined her for church that day including nine children playing in the basement or sitting near their parents. We ate brunch, sang songs of worship, took communion together. A few people read passages from the Bible and shared personal thoughts on what they'd just read. The family atmosphere turned electric and Grace felt free and happy whenever she participated.

She talked to the other women, ate with us and apologized several times for not bringing anything to share. She sang when the music leader belted out, "Blessed be your name." A sweet glow surrounded her that morning. We thought she'd always been this way.

After our service, we talked for a few hours more. Many of us had gone to evangelical or traditional churches over the last several years and we hated that the relational piece took a back seat to the academic or production portion of a church service. This usually stifled authentic spirituality and promoted a "faithless, go-to-church-once-a-week" mentality.

My wife Marie chatted on a couch with Grace and they didn't stop for three hours. Over time, they moved to the basement office while everyone else left.

After their conversation, my wife hugged Grace tightly and told her she'd be praying for her and her family. Grace left and Marie shut our big brown door. When it was closed, Marie with her blonde hair and green eyes - all five foot three inches of her - walked over and held me tight. She said, "I am so glad we do this, Jack. People need us, they need the church so bad." I agreed.

The next weekend, Grace brought Declan and her sons. It was the last time I saw him following her lead. Declan gave off an aura of skepticism as soon as he walked in. He barely spoke to anyone, and the only part of the service he connected to was the Bible study conversation, decrying the theological errors of one of the participants. This was a rarity at Apex, because every word spoken was considered fallible in the first place, public criticism was usually not a part of our discourse.

Afterwards as usual we delved into conversation and I had a long but fruitful talk with my new friend. Declan was polite but guarded, talkative but insincere. He attended church that morning knowing he would not enjoy his experience, but our conversation helped us get to know one another. I liked him, but knew from the beginning I would have difficulty trusting him. In the field of professional ministry, you often make quick judgments about people . The longer you do the job, the more accurate these impressions are.

The Dumaises kept returning week after week. Before long they became like family, pouring into our lives as much as we poured into theirs. Everyone loved them and for a while it seemed like they were home, but first impressions mislead like a desert mirage to a hungry man.

Every once in a while, Declan came to me about another problem he had with this or that person and as time went on, Grace's attitude towards herself plummeted. Low self-esteem seeped out of her every time she walked in the room. Declan was obviously a control freak, and Grace was bred to be controlled. She watched for years as her father mercilessly dominated her mother and vowed to never be controlled like that. Without realizing it, she eventually followed her parent's example.

One night after Marie and the kids went to bed, Declan texted me and asked if he could come over and talk. I'm not a saint, so I don't mind saying I was less than enthused with the idea, but answered him affirmatively if he joined me in our living room.

As soon as he arrived, we fell into conversation about what was happening in our lives. We'd become close, but there were still things we didn't know about each other. I told him about a new hobby I was enjoying, making things out of wood. My favorite creations were pens and letter openers. For some reason, people thought pens are were worth more if they were made of wood, and so I loved creating those beautiful writing apparatus to bestow upon my friends and family.

Declan then informed me of his new hobby: the Flat Earth conspiracy. I laughingly asked what the great conspiracy was, and he explained that he believed NASA was nothing but a government conspiracy. I asked him what proof. He had none yet, but would work and study endlessly to unveil the hoax the governments of the world played on their citizens.

Wanting to change the subject, I asked, "Declan, why are we hanging out tonight?" There's nothing so frustrating as a conversation with someone who cares passionately about something which I couldn't care less about but be forced to hear every detail on the subject. Once I had a boss give me an end-times lecture for four hours. By the end of it, I wanted to punch him in the face.

But I digress.

"I'm worried about Grace," Declan said with what appeared to be tears in his eyes. "She's in a bad place right now. She's depressed. I think she's even been cutting herself. The other day I heard Luke ask her why her arm had scratches on it, and she lied and told him she'd walked into a thorn bush."

"How do you know she lied?"

"We don't have a thorn bush outside our house." He said this with too much triumph in his voice.

"Who said anything about your house?" Trying to hide my own responsive jubilant aura. "Why would you want to catch your wife in a lie?"

"Listen, I'm not trying to catch her in a lie. She is lying. And I don't want her to lie to our kids." He started to cry again.

"Declan, she told your son she scratched herself. Not outside of your house. I'm not saying she's not lying, but I do wonder why it seems you might actually want her to be lying."

"Ok, let's not get caught up in that conversation. Let's talk about depression."

"I can do that very well."

"Are you depressed?"

"Nope. My mom's battled depression and bipolar for nearly twenty years, though. As you may know, these things have a nasty habit of being hereditary so I've studied up on the subject."

"Ok," Declan said, thinking through my response. "Since you know a little about this, what do I do with this information? How do I walk with her through this sin or sickness or whatever it is?"

I leaned back in my chair and scratched the back of my head, wishing for a cup of coffee but knowing it would banish me from sleep the rest of the night. "Well, start by never suggesting any of this might be sin-related. Pray for her. Build her up as much as you can. Honestly, I know that you have a personality that can be...uh...critical at times? Keep that in check when you talk to her."

"You want me to change who I am?" He asked like he was offended.

"I want you to acknowledge to yourself that you're not always right and even in the moments you might be, that doesn't mean you have to prove to Grace that you're right and she's wrong. Having to be right all the time means someone else has to be wrong all the time."

"I don't have to be right all the time."

"Ok."

"I don't!" He was beginning to raise his voice.

"Ok." I said again, calmly and knowing he would respond.

"You don't believe me? This is ridiculous. Why are you treating me like this? I thought you were a pastor."

"I am."

"Then why are you accusing me of all of this... stuff towards Grace?"

I paused to allow him calm down. I realized then that I'd responded to an intense person by being quietly intense myself, though I did not want him be able to say whatever he wanted. Eventually I said,

"Declan, I'm not trying to offend you. But you came to me for advice, and I'm giving it to you. If you only came to me to give me information that Grace is depressed or to tell me Grace cuts herself, then you've done that. But you also told me you needed help through this, and the only way I can do that - and I do believe you all are struggling through a difficult time with this - is to offer you some truths about you, and some of the ways you interact with your wife."

Declan was visibly crushed at my words. His usual hard expression had softened, in his face and how his shoulders seemed to lose strength. It was as if no one ever told him how much of a control freak he was or, if they had, he'd simply decided to forget their exhortations. I wondered where the conversation could go from here, but it didn't take long since Declan gladly led the way in a new direction.

"Listen, this church and its leadership are totally unbiblical."

"Ok. Why do you say that? Especially now of all times?"

"You mean besides the church governance, the fact there is no preaching, and there's a ton of heresy being taught in most if not all of the groups?"

At this point, I tried to not be angry, but could feel my face warming as I said my next words. "Declan, we probably need to take a break from our conversation now and process where we want to go in our relationship, where you want to be in your relationship with your wife, and how we can best help her, as a church and as friends. I don't know that I'm in the best state of mind right now to continue having that kind of a talk."

Declan took that last sentence as an admission that he had found his way under my skin and liked it. All of a sudden he was in a much better mood.

"That sounds good, Jack. Thanks for trying, anyways. You are one of my very few friends, and I don't want to lose that friendship. But, I also want to be in a church that loves and is passionate about the Bible."

In my mind I asked him how his mother created such a jerk, but I smiled, stuck out my hand and told him I would be praying for his marriage. I already prayed for Declan and Grace every day, but until then I hadn't realized how bad things were.

* * *

Grace did cut herself on a regular basis and continued to sink deeper in depression. She occasionally attended church, but stopped talking, especially when Declan attended. She often declined dinner invitations or community events with the church family. We never knew if she was depressed or if Declan had created an environment where she felt uncomfortable around him, and us.

Marie and other ladies tried their best to reach out, but every conversation lasted an awkward few minutes too long because she couldn't focus enough to allow any coherent back and forth. She always wore long sleeve shirts, never made eye contact, and apologized incessantly for anything she did. This collapse appeared sudden, yet it was real and Marie and I prayed for her every night. This young lady - once smart, funny, and attractive - had sunk deep into a lonely abyss.

On a Sunday not long after Declan and I talked about her depression, Grace told us she took a job as an overnight Gas station clerk. Declan had texted me that he'd decided to sleep in because of an evening studying "some new stuff."

Marie sat down with Grace after the service and talked about her new job and whether or not it was a wise decision to take it when it could be dangerous, not to mentioned with so much she'd been going through emotionally. Grace thanked her for caring but Declan and she had talked about it and they needed the money.

When Marie told me what Grace was doing, I couldn't believe Declan would allow his wife to work overnights if he was concerned about her depression. I wanted to call and tell him, but I had no currency left to use with Declan. He wasn't going to listen, to anyone.

He was, however, going to stay in his office or the library and study all about Flat Earth theories, right up until the time he had to get home to allow his wife to go to work overnight. He justified it by saying it only happened two days a week.

Theories

The first time I heard 'modern' people discuss the possibility of Earth being flat, I was sitting in a hotel lobby waiting for my ride to a conference. These two guys talked like they'd studied the subject for years. In reality, they saw a few YouTube videos then regurgitated the information to one another, and whoever else listened in on the Atlanta-based hotel's leather couches.

I jumped right in and joined their conversation. They pelted me with tidbits and vague points about the shape of the Earth and the lengths NASA went to hide its lies. It seemed like their beliefs had more to do with them being right as opposed to proving anything with facts. The little bit of information they had which I didn't allowed a smugness in their attitude that lasted the entire conversation. They had an answers for all of my questions.

"Where's the edge?"

"There's no edge. Only a 360 degree ice wall surrounding the Earth."

"What about the sun?"

"In the flat Earth model, the sun circles the Earth in a clock like way and fades off into the vanishing point of the horizons. It's not 93,000 miles away but its closer and smaller. It's the sun circling above us, not the other way around."

"Why can't I see across the oceans?"

"Just because the Earth is flat doesn't mean your eyesight is infinite."

That was the first time since my elementary teacher taught me about Christopher Columbus I discovered people who believed the Earth was flat. I often wonder why people perpetuate this theory. There is nothing that draws us in like the unknown. The more something becomes known, like space exploration, the more we need to create our own "knowns," not willing to trust those who do the work.

YouTube helped. A lot.

Like a middle aged man to a mistress, these guys walked away from what science offered them. They found meaning in the arms of this new chatelaine, but who was she? After all, while only two percent of Americans believe the Earth is flat, only sixty-six percent of young people ages eighteen to twenty-four are firmly convinced the Earth is round.

For years, the ancients debated the way the Earth looked in relationship to the skies. Homer and many other Greeks referred to a flat Earth in their arts, and the Norse and Germanic peoples in Europe taught that all land was encircled by an impenetrable ocean. That ocean was inhabited by a huge snake, stopping anyone daring to travel its waters. Ancient China believed the Earth to be flat, while the heavens were round.

The myth that the Christian church in the Middle Ages fought Chris Columbus's assertion the Earth was round falls flat in the wake of evidence. Christians, like everyone else, debated the shape of the Earth, and the church held opinions on both sides of the issue.

In fact, that's why finding a common "Flat Earth" definition is so difficult. The theory is not based on science, but on vague speculation in pubs or over cups of coffee. The better information always gets generated in pubs.

So when two guys in Marietta, Georgia watch a YouTube video punctuated with mysterious music, giving answers to questions people have about what's beyond the ice, with accusations thrown at the "science," it's not a difficult adjustment to let ourselves walk away from the safe and boring choices everyone expects of us, to the exotic and enticing arms of the beautiful unknown.

September 9, 2010

Now

Grace continued spending money she didn't have by applying for and receiving credit cards she shouldn't have been given. But she was an adult with a job and to this point a decent credit score, so companies gladly gave her the plastic with hopes they would end up with the green.

Her trips to the mall became problematic when she began hiding the clothes, shoes and house products she never used for fear Declan would find out and force her to return them. She lived a huge lie attempting to control her own life, but couldn't let her husband know because if she did, he would take control back.

She finally controlled her finances through the credit cards, her emotional health through prescription pills and her life at home. For now, Declan left her alone, even with he was with her.

She worked hard at the gas station, but it was a temporary fix because she needed a job during those hours. For whatever reason, Declan liked that she worked there. But the hours were slowly squeezing the life out of her.

One afternoon, my wife received a call from her.

"Hi, Marie?" Grace said.

"Yes, Grace, of course this is me. I'm so happy to hear from you."

"Yeah, thanks for answering. I'm feeling a bit, I don't know, down right now. And I just needed to call someone."

"I'm glad you did. What's wrong?"

"Life. My husband. My kids. Some of the things I'm doing. My past. The list could go on and on. Marie, I don't know if I can go on, though." Grace began sobbing. I could hear her through the phone from across the room.

"Oh Grace, you can absolutely go on. You're an amazing woman and I'm better for knowing you. You have two amazing little boys. You might be going through something hard right now, but you have a God who loves you and created you to thrive. You have a fantastic church family who loves you so much. Don't give up, Grace. Let's work through this together. Can I come over and talk for a few minutes?"

"Not right now, Marie. I promise I won't do anything stupid, and I really would like to talk to you more. Very soon. But right now, I've got a few things to work out on my own. Could you email me some Bible verses that I could look up? I could use those right now."

"Sure Grace, whatever you need but please, if you decide you want to do something like hurt yourself, call me. Please?"

"I will. I will call you. Thanks, Marie."

"Promise me, Grace."

"I promise." She paused and a silence hovered between them for the next several seconds.

"Do you think Declan would... Do you think Declan would have an affair?"

Marie didn't know what to say. She certainly didn't know whether or not Declan was actually having an affair and she knew how powerful the mind could be if left unchecked. At the same time, however, she knew that anyone could fall prey to the enticing ways of the forbidden. The first person to know was usually the spouse.

Then Grace hung up without another word. Marie and I spent the next hour praying for her.

Grace believed Declan was having an affair. Her husband was smart, obsessed over details and was as much of a control freak as her father. Declan hadn't noticed the maxed out credit cards, though, nor her cutting or the pills her doctor prescribed.

She realized the reason Declan didn't pay attention to these things wasn't because he was suddenly less smart than he used to be. He simply didn't care. The reason he didn't care was because he was interested in or possibly sleeping with someone else.

Tonight happened to be Thursday. He studied with that that damned Flat Earth group he was always talking about. Maybe not. Maybe he was going somewhere else. She called Marie again, asked her to watch the kids, and headed to downtown Shrewsbury.

* * *

Seven o'clock rolled around and the group met to discuss an experiment the Barnsworth twins produced with a high altitude balloon. Declan rolled in a little tired and anxious as this would be the first time he saw Amber since their conversation last Thursday in the library.

Since then, he felt deeply hurt though he wasn't sure why. Nothing physical had happened in their relationship. He'd arrived early hoping to get a chance to speak to her before the rest of the group showed up, but her prompt arrival at six fifty-nine prevented any such conversation.

Amber looked stunning in a black sweater with a high neck, dark skintight jeans and a simple pair of black loafers. She strolled into the room confidently. Her wire-rimmed glasses helped her look like the smartest person in the room and highlighted her smile that let Declan know that, if she were disappointed by what transpired between them, it would not affect her tonight. Declan made his mind up to be confident as well, for the rest of Flat Earth group. Any hurt he experienced would take a back seat to showing her he was in charge of his own feelings.

That confidence evaded him, however, as the night went on. His eyes repeatedly gravitated toward her. Adam started the evening as usual with some opening comments on what he learned in the past week. Then he introduced Mike and Gary, possibly the two most awkward brothers on Earth, to chat about their experiment. Everyone in the group understood this and expected awkwardness.

Mike started the presentation, looking at the ground almost his entire speech. His voice was low and apologetic and choked as he talked as if it ached for water.

"Ok. Gary. And I...." Every word took several seconds to get out. "Gary and I, as...as...as many of you know, Gary and I b...b...bought a high altitude weather balloon kit, with our own money..." He said as if they were 13 and not in their 30's. Declan enjoyed the group, but he judged the brothers more and more as information about their lives rolled out their mouths. They lived with their mother, worked at a fast food restaurant and spent all their time working on experiments for the group.

"...Cost almost $800. We were excited," that word uttered completely deadpan. "We wanted to install a good multi-directional camera... which we did... and found a 360 degree camera we installed in the... in the balloon. Our goal was to see what the Earth looked like as the balloon rose to around 100,000 feet. We thought maybe it could go a bit high... higher, but 100,000 feet was enough...we...we... believed for our analysis. Gary. You're up." He coughed and sat down.

For whatever reason Gary paused before he stood up, which made everyone think he either forgot what to say or that his brother made a mistake about whose turn it was. Finally Gary stood up. Declan glanced at Amber, raising his eyebrows as if to say, "what in the world is going on here?!," but she did not return the expression in any way. She simply turned back towards the brothers and listened intently.

Gary's voice - high, squeaky, and fast pitched - was the opposite of his twin. His speech was nervous but far more excited than Mike. Unlike his brother, however, he didn't have drawn out pauses. He didn't have any pauses whatsoever. He read it straight from a card.

"So hi guys thanksforlettingmeandmybrothertalktoday. As he mentioned we've been experimenting on our new high altitude weather balloon, but I won't repeat what Mike already said. I want to share our results so far.

"So as you all probably know if the Earth was round, which it isn't, but if it was, the higher the balloon goes up, the less land or ocean you would be able to see because some of it would disappear. Why would it disappear? Obviously because the Earth is round, which it's not, but if it was, there would be less to see from the vantage point of the balloon."

Declan tried to wrap his brain around that logic but decided it wasn't worth the headache.

"Also, if the Earth was round, which it isn't, but if it was, the higher the balloon rises, the lower the horizon would drop.

"Thirdly, the Earth is supposed to be spinning on its axis at one thousand miles per hour, which is about as fast as Mike's crossover when he plays basketball, wait for laughter. Oh wait, sorry. I wasn't supposed to read that part."

The group laughed and Gary looked confused. He shrugged and kept going.

"If the Earth is spinning on its axis, and a camera came completely off the Earth above the clouds eighteen to twenty miles, then the assumption would be that the camera would be able to pick up some of that movement. Does that make sense? I hope so. Thank you. Good night."

Lou looked around like the twins had fourteen heads. "Ok, so are you going to give us the results or what?

"Oh yes," Gary clamored, "sorry. That's another card." He snorted loudly as if what he said was funnier than it was. He grabbed a second card.

"Our results are as follows: First, our balloon flew roughly 105,000 feet in the air, which was awesome. You guys should have been there. It was straight fire and I've never been more proud in my entire life..."

"Let's go, Gary," Mike interrupted. "Stick to our scripts."

"Yes, ok. So it went up to 105,000 feet, which was awesome. But also, when we reviewed the footage, we noticed - and you'll see this shortly - there was no drop in the horizon. It was all flat. Every angle and each position the camera found itself showed us exactly what we would expect if we knew that we had a flat table like Earth. There was no curvature. There was nothing to prove the spherically fake version that NASA repeatedly gives us.

"Next, the Earth never spun from the camera on the balloon. It was perfectly still, aside from what motion we can attribute to the wind. We are not on some huge spinning ball like they told us. Our findings have led us to continue to believe that Earth is not a globe, or a ball, but is totally flat. This is no longer a debate. Thank you."

The group quietly clapped at their friends and thanked them for their research. Adam asked if anyone had any questions. Jenny loudly said that NASA spewed out bull on a regular basis, that the twins were right but stopped short of asking any substantive questions. Amber raised her hand. With a smile she asked, "I'm interested in why NASA would do that. In other words, what would the purpose be to lie all the time? It seems a counterintuitive way to running any kind of a good operation. I know we joke about 'that's what the government is,' but this is pretty excessive."

She posed the question more towards the entire group than to the twins, who were sweating thinking it was directed at them. Thankfully Adam understood their fear, and decided to grab the ball himself. His accent again brought a calming legitimacy to the conversation.

"Great question, Amber. I think this is an important one because it's really the foundation of what we believe about the Earth. As you know, a lot of what we believe comes from faith, just like it takes faith to believe what NASA is peddling. I would state though, that you've begun with the wrong premise. Amber, you asked, 'What would the purpose be for NASA to lie to us all the time,' correct?"

Amber nodded and Adam continued.

"By asking the question that way, you're implying if NASA lies, it would be deviating from its original purpose. But what if its original purpose, the one that feeds you and I headlines after every successful 'launch' is not their purpose at all? What if from the beginning the purpose of NASA was to lie?"

Amber squinted her eyes as if her brain was processing the question. She didn't seem to buy the implication.

"Just so I'm clear," she said. "You are suggesting the purpose of NASA is not 'to pioneer the future in space exploration, scientific discovery and aeronautics research,' but to lie to every person in the world about the way the Earth and by default, everything that might be outside of the Earth, works?"

"Is it really such a leap of faith, my dear Amber, to imagine the government lying about such things? Or that they go to great lengths to perpetuate a lie that, if the world knew the truth, helped them know and better understand how God created the world?"

Amber wasn't backing down quietly. Most of the time she listened and occasionally added an agreeing point, but the idea of government pouring millions and hundreds of millions into an agency whose sole purpose was to lie was too much for her.

"Listen, I'm okay believing the government lies, and I'm even okay with the idea there are people employed at NASA who hold secrets about whatever science they study. Where I'm having a hard time drawing the line is a government agency's 17,000 employees successfully lying every day to constituents about the work they do. It makes no sense. We spend most of our time in here trashing people who just go with the flow without thinking. I'm not about to hypocritically go and do the same because you say that's their purpose, or because we as a group think it. Where's our proof?"

Declan smirked. He wanted to chime in, but also wanted to hear Adam's response. The 'NASA is lying' argument, above all others, struck him as one of the weaker aspects of the Flat Earth theory. Though there were rarely major disagreements within the group, he felt happy Amber brought this up.

"Ok Amber, first of all, I want to walk back an earlier statement I made. The question where I implied the government did this to keep out the idea God created the world. I think we need to think out of our own context a bit more and consider the late 1950's when NASA became an official government agency. Think through what was happening then, please. We fought two major wars in the previous two decades and the USSR was making headway at taking over much of the world. The Cold War was advancing and the United States and Russia were competing to outdo each other in every arena, from espionage to sports to technology. A war for competitive edge fought by the world's two superpowers.

"Now remember by this time there was nowhere left to explore, no land to pursue. The only places remaining were the skies, and so the Soviets and Americans began competing for this as well. There was no place else to go but up, and we had to land somewhere first. So, NASA created the first landing on the moon inside a studio."

He paused for a temperature check. Most everyone nodded as if that statement was the least bit unlikely. Except for Amber, but she said nothing, only leaned back in her chair with a quiet smile and one brow raised.

Adam pushed on. "Maybe NASA's initial purpose wasn't to perpetuate a lie, but when they realized their initial purpose - to get a man on the moon – couldn't happen, well, to spread that lie, for whatever reason you're doing it, one must keep on. Fifty years later, word's going to eventually get out. People are going to question the lies. So, if you're NASA you've become committed to nothing but making lying your sole purpose for existence.

"Also, one doesn't need 17,000 people to spread a lie, only a handful in leadership. The rest get paid to do what they are told. When you get paid for that and speaking truth means you're not getting paid anymore, you will probably keep doing what you're doing. Does all that that make more sense?"

Amber thought for a few seconds. She seemed for a moment to be considering pushing on with her questioning, but eventually relaxed and backed off, perhaps to do more research on the topic herself. The group talked for a few more minutes, then spent the remainder of the meeting looking at the myriad of mostly blurry photographs from the twins camera until it Lou motioned to Adam that it was time to wrap up. He closed out the meeting with a few thankful words and wished everyone a safe night.

Declan longed for Amber to stay later than the others so they could talk. He ached for her to be close to him. Only pure luck gave him his wish. She headed for the ladies room after dismissal and for whatever reason the others in the group all had reason to leave immediately, so Declan sat on a bench outside the ladies room to ensure his chance with her, whether or not she wanted that same opportunity.

When she finally came out, he smiled and asked if they could talk.

"I don't know, Declan. I meant what I said the other night. Not talking is the best thing right now." She looked around as if someone might be watching from the other side of the room.

"Ok," he said, hoping to sound agreeable. "How about until you get to your car, then? Can we talk until then?"

"Fine," she responded, not so agreeably. "What should we talk about? The weather?"

"I want you in my life." He said as bluntly as he ever thought he could, while they walked towards the outside door. "No, I need you in my life."

"You don't need me in your life." She pushed open the door, he followed. "It might be nice. It might even feel good for a while but in the end, it can't work."

"No, it can. My relationship with Grace is basically over. We don't talk. We're only roommates at this point. She's sick, Amber, and won't let me help her." They were getting too close to her car. He wanted to slow down but knew she would not. "We're at a breaking point. And honestly, it's already past broken."

"Then when you sign the divorce papers, maybe we can talk." She struggled to keep her boundaries up. She felt the same way as he did, Declan was sure of it, but had somehow convinced herself this couldn't work.

They stood beside her white Nissan. Amber reached for the door handle. He gently touched her hand. Not to stop her from opening the door, but to let her know his desire. She looked down, but didn't pull away. Their fingers stayed touching for what seemed like minutes but couldn't have been more than twenty 20 seconds. He stepped toward her, closing any space between them and Amber did look up then. They could feel each other's breath. His heart pounded with desire. He knew he needed to walk away, but also since he had chosen not to do so by now he never would. Now the ball lay in her court, and she could do with it as she pleased.

Amber looked briefly down at her driver's seat as if she might hop in, then looked back at him. She lifted her left hand up and over Declan's neck and pulled him toward her. They kissed passionately outside of her car, not caring who else might be coming in or out of the library, nor seeing Grace's car parked two rows behind them.

Having moved into their new home in Shrewsbury, Massachusetts, the Dumais family "faked it till they made it" as the strain of the surprise Christmas gift began to dwindle away. Like many times in their relationship, Grace swept the hurt under an emotional rug and focused on the positive things happening in their new house. There would be countless memories of marital bliss, difficulties, children growing up, family meals enjoyed together and a hundred other moments of people coming in and out of their lives. She considered herself lucky.

Grace insisted they find a church in the area and attend regularly. Declan balked because "you don't have to go to church to be a Christian," but Grace was adamant. If he didn't join her, she'd find one by herself. Secretly, she knew he'd never let her to do that. Sacrificing control in any aspect of their relationship was not in his nature.

They started attending Master's Way Church in West Boylston. Declan suggested it first and loved it. They were "spot on in doctrine and in the way they taught the Bible," and most importantly they believed in the traditional roles of the family. Men were the head and called to lead the household. Women submitted and took charge of their home while the men worked. Everyone dressed appropriately, and Christians who didn't study the Bible verse by verse and interpret it literally were preached against from the pulpit.

Grace didn't fit into this culture, but she wanted her husband to be happy so she compromised. Each Sunday they attended as the early days of Grace's pregnancy went without any problems.

Declan's liked the church's desire to engage the Bible in a literal way. Five hundred years earlier, during the Protestant Reformation, a group of men who read and learned the Bible in an academic way had radically transformed the spiritual landscape of Middle Ages Europe. They broke the Bible down for the common man who, prior to this, had been forbidden by church leadership to engage God's word at all.

Master's Way saw those reformers as heroes. They systematized Scripture so that every man could understand the Bible while at the same time maintaining the Bible's purity. Word for word, in both Greek and Hebrew, the reformers studied Scripture and broke it down to ensure their interpretations fit within these systems and restrictions. Any interpretation of the Bible that didn't fit was labeled "compromise," and compromisers were heretics to be avoided at all cost.

Declan jumped into this approach of studying scripture. Verse by verse he took control of what he believed the Bible's cultural viewpoints were of homosexuality, traditional family values and end times judgment. He studied all the time, and began to take the Bible as literally as he could, grabbing control of his spiritual life more than ever, just after he had given up control of that life to Jesus.

He questioned the way he lived, the friends he had and the words he chose to use in regular conversation with anyone. He asked questions about Grace's wardrobe and who she spent her time with, though most of her time was already given to him. He picked apart spiritual conversations with church friends, asking them if they really meant to say this or that. The more he jumped into this intense and zealous study of God's word, the more people stayed away from him. He often joked about people not liking him, but never made the behavioral changes necessary to do anything about it.

Sleep-deprived from studying, Declan worked non-stop on their new home. He replaced window treatments, painted rooms, and replaced rotten baseboards around the floors of their 'new' old house.

Then in August of 2006, Grace and Declan had their baby boy. Declan was painting the office space in their home while Grace lay on the couch watching the classic movie Tombstone. He'd picked a midnight blue color for the walls and Grace had agreed to it. Declan shouted out quotes from the movie he'd learned by heart, following along with the movie in the other room. Texas Jack asking Doc Holliday why he was fighting, and Doc replying, "Because Wyatt Earp's my friend."

"I've got lots of friends," Declan parroted Texas Jack's response. After a bit of a silence, Doc Holliday said pensively, "I don't."

Grace laughed and then screamed in agony.

Declan was already running towards her, knowing what was happening. Off they went to Memorial Hospital in Worcester.

Luke Gabriel Dumais was born at 10:03 on that Tuesday night, and Declan's entire life changed. Yet, it didn't. He worked even harder to ensure his boy would know the certainties of life through hard work, the Bible and leadership. Knowing and controlling things became the foundation of his life studies. While he admitted that he did not know everything, he worked towards that goal, believing he could achieve it.

This sense of perfection pushed him to be better in every way, and with that came less sleep and more pride. He could know everything, or at least as much as anyone else. He could find the holes that groaned to be filled with truth.

One of Declan's hobbies was going to the local library and researching. He would find a quiet corner, pull out some paper, grab some books and study whatever topic traveled his mind the most that day. Now and again he would look something up on the internet using his phone, but found more satisfaction playing the role of archeologist, pouring through printed books for his answers.

The topic one day was the creation of the world. As a young evangelical, he was learning that the Biblical account of creation in Genesis was literal. God created the world in six days then rested on the seventh. Recently he'd read a book by Francis Collins, Director of the National Institute of Health, called "The Language of God" and he learned how a 'Christian' evolutionist thought.

He could not connect the book to his pre-existing beliefs, however, and so one Tuesday evening after work while Grace stayed home with Luke he drove straight to the library, after calling and saying he'd be home later. Grace cried, so he accused her of manipulating him to get whatever she wanted. He then continued on to the library.

Standing in front of the science section, Declan browsed and grabbed several books on the topics of evolution and creation. He nodded and repeatedly walked around an older gentleman searching in the same area. The white haired man stood taller than Declan, about six feet. He gazed at books with eyes squinted behind gold wire-rimmed glasses. This part of the library was not well lit.

After a few "excuse me's" and exchanges of smiles, the older man gently said to Declan, with a heavy British accent, "So what are you studying tonight?"

"Well," Declan smirked almost ashamedly, "I'm a Christian, and I was looking up differences between Creationism, Evolution, and what some people call 'theistic evolution'. I believe in the literal Creation account in Genesis 1-2, but recently I've read a few things about evolution and thought I'd study some more."

"Aaahhh, sounds like you are a man who loves to learn. And so that's what you're doing. Learning. But there's a problem."

"Problem?"

"Yes," replied the man, smiling. "First of all, my name is Adam. Like from the story you believe in." Declan chuckled and shook his hand.

"Declan."

Adam continued. "I'm a Christian, too. I believe that you are doing the right thing by studying these topics, but you might be starting with the wrong premise." Adam paused for a minute, and Declan assumed it was for dramatic affect.

Adam gestured to the books on the shelf between them. "You're studying these topics based on what you have been told in your science classes. Geography, even Bible classes if you had those, and you learned the Earth looks one way. You may have even seen pictures of that Earth taken from..." He put four fingers up to make air quotes. '...outer space. But what if the world you and I live in isn't really the world we learned about in high school? What if from the outside, it doesn't look how they tell us it looks like? What if the Earth isn't really round at all?"

A long silence fell as Declan ingested Adam's words. He surprised him by not having any inclination to laugh out loud at the statement.

"So... what? Even if that were true, which it's not, I've seen actual photographs of the Earth."

"You have, have you?"

"Yes."

"Any of the two pictures you've seen look the same?"

Declan ran pictures through his head, and mentally processed the question. He walked without speaking to the desk he'd been using and opened one of the books he had gathered, turned the pages towards pictures of the Earth from space. None of them looked alike.

"I... I don't know."

"No." Adam said quickly and confidently. "They are not alike. They're doctored. They are not real pictures. Altered to create an idea or an image in our minds that the Earth is round when indeed, it is not."

"Well, Adam, if it's not round, then what is it?" Declan was baffled by this conversation. He'd never heard the "roundness" of the Earth questioned before. Maybe its age, but never the shape. That discussion had ended with Chris Columbus.

"Before we get into that, let's talk about why. Why does NASA and the world governments give out this information and photoshop fake images? Can you think of any good reason?"

"Nope. I've never even thought about this before and to be honest you're kind of blowing my mind. I also kind of think this is garbage."

"Ok, ok, that's fair." Without being incited, Adam pulled out a chair for himself and sat opposite Declan. "I've had a long time to digest and study this and I see you're a student, so I look forward to you studying this for yourself. But if something is round and constantly moving, and there's a great big world out there that is vast and huge and seemingly forever, then no matter how much you learn, there's always more, right?"

Declan nodded his head. He hated that there was always more.

Adam continued. "But what if the Earth sat on a table? What if it ended? What if all of a sudden it looked a lot more like there was a Creator?"

"Like the movie The Truman Show?" Declan asked.

"Exactly like The Truman Show!" Adam said. "Now you're getting it! They don't want us to know. They do not want us to question the reality they are stuffing down our throats but is not true. Listen... Declan was it? I know this is a lot to take in, but I want to know truth. As a Christian, I don't want to be hoodwinked by the world's systems. I want to study to show myself as being approved by God, like it says in 2 Timothy. I don't want to simply go along with what everyone else believes."

He stopped there to allow Declan a minute to breathe. Declan understood, even empathized with Adam's words. He too, wanted nothing to do with the world's systems. He wanted to study and know more about who God was. He thought about Romans 1 and how Paul said those who "claimed to be wise, but instead became fools." He had no intention of "exchanging the truth about God for a lie."

He would find the truth. He would study this topic.

"Adam, I'm going to study this and I'd love it if you could walk alongside me on the journey. When I study something new, I like to have a guide or mentor to join me. I'm not asking you to join me every day or anything, but could I come to you if I had more questions?"

"Oh absolutely, Declan! I'm excited for this journey and I'm quite the academic myself we can do this together, two strangers in the middle of the Shrewsbury Public Library." He leaned back and laughed lightly. "What a God thing!"

An hour later, Declan checked out a few books and made his way to the parking lot. He sat in his car for a minute, smiling and thinking about the conversation. For the first time in a while he was excited about something he was studying. Though he loved pouring into Scripture and getting into theology, now he felt like he had a piece of information very few people had, and couldn't wait to grow that knowledge, find out what the rest of the world needed to know!

He drove home, got out of the car, and walked into the house. Grace was on the couch watching The Shawshank Redemption.

"Dinner's already put away and in the fridge." She coldly instructed him. "It's in the blue Tupperware on the left next to the sour cream. I would heat it up for about two minutes if I were you."

After two minutes, he carefully grabbed his chili from the microwave, took out a spoon from the drawer, and walked to his computer, opening up a website Adam had given him before they left the library, "Aplanetruth.info."

Confessions

And this is where I must confess something. Although I'm a pastor, I do not believe anyone can change.

I know, I know. We're supposed to believe the opposite. After all, that's the nature of our job, right? In my mind, circumstances, the people we spend time with and our time and food habits can change, but those are external to our nature. What's inside of us, the essence of who we are, stays rock solid through the generations of life we walk.

Before you judge me, I have years of experience to back this up. For decades I've watched as people made choices, felt guilty about those choices, said they'd never make those choices again, made them again, and then came to me seeking advice on how to end the cycle. The skeptical part of me sometimes wants to throw up my hands and say to them, "Just do what you want to do because eventually you're going to anyway."

I'm not sure when this cynical side of me took over, but it may have been the phone call I received a decade ago from Rick Martelli. I've known Rick for years. When I first met him at my old parish, he told me that he'd attended longer than anyone else there. He loved the church and based on the relationships I watched him cultivate, the church loved him, too. A few weeks later, a friend commented to me how we might not be seeing Rick for very long. When I asked him why, he said, "It's just the nature of the addict."

I thought the guy was the biggest jerk I'd ever met, until he was right, over and over again.

It took all of nine months for Rick to first prove my friend's prediction accurate. Around that time, we produced a play and invited the whole community to join us for the "True Tale of a Roman Centurion who Killed Jesus, and then Years Later, Saw Him Again!" We depended on Rick to run the soundboard. He'd attended all the practices, but when the dress rehearsal arrived, Rick disappeared and could not be reached, no matter how many times we called. My friend reminded me of his earlier words and vowed that we would not be hearing from Rick any time soon.

It would be another year before Rick contacted me again.

When he did, it was the first in a series of apologies delivered over the next decade which sound like this: "I'm so sorry, Jack. I took advantage of our friendship, and I'm sick and want to make this right. Do you forgive me?"

And absolutely I forgave him. Again and again I forgave him. And again and again I regretted my decision to let him back in my life. Stolen money, embarrassing situations, even manipulating me to drive him to drug deals had become a part of my life for a time, until I finally said no and put up boundaries between us.

After not seeing him much for the better part of five years, he came roaring back into my life clear-headed and like a new man. I accepted him (again) and we started to hang out and spend time together. Along the way he met a girl with a similar history.

Rick married Lucy and instantly there were problems. I don't have to go into them in detail, but one night I got a call suggesting I go over to their house because Lucy threatened to kill herself and her husband. I immediately called Rick. No answer.

I grabbed my phone and called my friend Stevie B (not the early 90's pop singer) who joined me in driving to their complex in North Grafton, across from the huge Wyman-Gordon plant. We pulled into a parking spot near their apartment door. I told Stevie B I had no clue what we were going to find. He hoped they would be here and answer the door cheerfully.

Stevie B. Is an eternal optimist.

People don't change.

I picked my cell phone and called Rick's apartment again. No answer. I called his cell. Still no answer. We knocked. No answer. Stevie and I both tried to kick the door in. After ten unsuccessful minutes, I called the police. While we waited for them, Rick's car pulled in. He drove slowly into the parking space and exited his car. We met him outside.

"Rick! Where have you been? I've been trying to call you." I said.

"Just out, Jack. Left my cell at the house. Why did you need me?" Rick sounded slow and tired, like the speech of someone on a narcotic.

"When did you leave your house? How is Lucy? Is she okay?"

"Was when I left." He said it a little too matter of fact. People don't change.

As we walked toward his apartment I said, "Karen Robbins called me earlier and said that Lucy told her she was going to hurt herself. Did she tell you anything about that?"

"No, you think I would have gone out if she had?" I didn't answer, though he moved as slowly now as before I mentioned it.

Inside all the lights were on and we heard the bathtub running. Rick walked to the tub, about twenty feet straight past the front door through the kitchen. I heard him yell at his wife, "Lucy, what are you doing?!" She was in the bathtub and only her left leg outside of it. Out of her arms spilled blood from the long cuts she'd made in her wrists. An empty pill bottle sat opened next to her as if it was a plan B.

I had never experienced anything like that before, but when it happened, the world stood still and I hovered above it. Not like I was a superior angel, but as if I stood outside of the actual event. I'm not the type of person who shines during emergencies, and felt useless as Rick held his wife while Stevie B. grabbed paper towels by the rolls.

Soon two police officers arrived and knew precisely what to do. One helped Rick step back and make room for the EMTs who arrived immediately after the police. The other roamed through the apartment, no doubt finding hundreds of empty, half-empty and full pill bottles strung throughout the rooms. People don't change.

I hope this story conveys why I think the way I do. But I point past addicts who have a hard time changing. People struggle to change in many different ways and are addicted many types of vices, fatally destructive or not. The middle aged overweight man who can't shut off his computer before he's tempted to watch some coed show more than she should, or the anxiety-ridden housewife who freaks out and cleans anytime something in her world feels a bit chaotic. People need to be addicted to something. Sometimes, when someone like me comes around and says "give your life to something greater," they do - to a point, but too often get stuck in their own quicksand of crutches that they've always used to get through life, to control it.

Don't get me wrong, I don't know for certain if what I offer truly helps people face the problems in their lives. Perhaps religion like drugs is another tool used to cope with life and its meaning, offering the practical applications we need to use to get through it. Maybe life is a cruel prison whose gates are opened by our parents' conception.

I don't think I'm a very good nihilist.

September 11, 2010

Now

The aftermath of a relational disaster brings a lot of things, but what depends on the attitude of those involved. Are all parties humble? Willing to do what it takes to reconcile? Does one of the parties still want to kill the other? I'm only partly joking.

Even the worst mistakes can be forgiven but, if they are forgiven, there must be steps taken to ensure that the underlying problems that caused the rupture are healing. People are typically not willing to dive into underlying problems. They want to stay on the surface. I want to stay on the surface. I don't want to talk about the fact I make jokes all of the time when someone wants to get "real" in a conversation to avoid having to delve into too much "reality."

Most people are like me but in different ways. Declan and Grace, for instance, had deeper problems than him wanting to kiss another woman. Their issues were soaked in codependency, control issues, self-hate and bitterness, none of which had ever been discussed between them, or anyone else. Until now.

When relational disaster happens, all kinds of mud splashes around through words and facial expressions, but never gets dealt with in appropriate ways. So, usually, a nasty split happens or, worse, they remain together.

Watching her husband kiss someone else was bad enough, then to watch him whisper something in her ear, run around happily to the passenger seat and be driven away in the woman's car, destroyed Grace's heart. The trip home was unbearable as tears waterfalled over her face and heartache wrapped around every organ, muscle, and tissue inside her.

A deep guttural scream strained to come free of her throat.

Back and forth she rocked in her seat, not knowing what to do or who to contact. Should she call him and tell him to come home? Would he answer? The first question she needed to ask was whether or not she should go to work. After she'd finished crying, Grace called her boss and told him she couldn't come in. When he asked why, she told the truth. He understood and said to let him know if she needed any other days. Usually he was a hard ass, but the combination of her normal reliability and the pain she was obviously in helped the man to handle the situation appropriately.

Grace then called Marie's cell phone and asked if both of us could come over. She didn't tell the reason, but clarified she wouldn't ask so last minute unless it was important. We gladly obliged, then called someone to come watch our own kids. It takes a village.

Declan had left a message on the home answering machine. This would have been suspect if she hadn't seen what she did because no one had used the home answering machine since 1999.

In the message, he told Grace to call Marie and ask if she could watch the kids. He was "super focused" on some specific lie he caught NASA in and didn't want to stop. When the library closed, he planned on going to Adam's house and studying with him. Of course he didn't know Marie was at his house now, quietly consoling his disgraced wife while she mourned the death of what she thought was their marriage.

"I can't believe this. I can't believe this!" She wept into Marie's shoulder, trying to keep herself quirt and not wake the boys. My wife held Grace and told her God loved her and that she would be all right. I arrived a half hour later and we prayed and talked some more.

There's something about pain caused by betrayal that weighs heavier than other type. When someone close to you treats you poorly, it is not just an ache that hits you in one spot like a physical stab from a knife, but it is more like torment thrashed upon your soul over and over again, much like how evangelical pastors describe the final destination of those who are lost and without God.

That night we sat with Grace as she wept, blamed, yelled, and tried to reason why, and how this happened. Could she have been a better lover? Was she a failure as a wife, mother and woman? Why would God bring her through this since she'd given her life to Him? Before that had happened, Declan glued himself to her. Now he found any excuse to be anywhere else but with her.

"I need to take control of my life!" She stated boldly during one of her more intense declarations. "I need to get away from him, be my own person. I need to make a life for myself where I make my sons proud of who I am."

"Grace," I responded gently. "Those things aren't wrong. You do need a few of those. But right now, taking control of your life on the eve of this deception is not what you need. That will and should come in whatever form you decide, but right now, instead of taking control, you need to let go."

"I need to let go? I mean, it's a little too early to start talking divorce, isn't it? Maybe a funeral, but not a divorce." Her attempt at humor at least lit up her red eyes for the first time that night.

"I'm not talking about divorce, Grace." I said this quickly with a smirk, letting her know I caught her joke, dark as it might have been. "I'm talking about the difference between control and faith. Faith doesn't mean you don't do anything. Faith means when you do the things you do, you understand that God can take those things, both good and bad, and use them as part of His greater story. When you simply take control, you're trying to engineer your story and how it affects other people. When you 'let go,' it means yes you get some things in order, but you also understand that God's timeline can't be altered. You understand the hard things you go through can lead to other great things you never saw coming."

I then gave the Old Testament example of Joseph, thrown into a hole by his brothers, sold into slavery, put into prison unjustly only to eventually become second in command of the entire empire of Egypt and in the process saved millions of lives including his own family. It didn't help. I realized Grace needed a modern day example."

"Tonight on the way here when Marie told me what was happening, my mind drifted to a time when I was cheated on by someone very special to me. If that hadn't happened, I'd have never moved here and by default, likely never met Marie.

"When you're in the midst of the storm, it's almost impossible to understand where you're going. More than that, though, you forget why you're going there in the first place."

She sniffled, pulled out her fiftieth tissue from the box. "I guess that makes sense. But Declan takes so much control over everything in his life. And I mean everything." She looked up, gaze pleading. "You see that, right?"

"Oh we know what you're saying." Marie squeezed Grace's hand to encouraged her to continue.

Grace said, "And everything he does seems to turn out right for him. He likes his job being a gym teacher. He loves studying for whatever the hell he's studying, then talking about it with his little conspiracy group buddies.... A lot!" She laughed until she cried some more. After a few minutes, she added, "He always seems to come out on top. Everything he does turns to gold."

Prophetically, Marie said, even going to far as to turn the other woman's chin toward her with her fingers, "Grace, you hear me right now. Declan does not feel like his life is gold. He attempts to control things... including you... because there is a void in his heart he can't fill. He lusts for perfection, and keeps finding he can't be perfect. Most people would eventually give up, lift up their hands and say, 'I'm done. Take it, God.' Not him. He craves to take control of everything he can in his endless quest for perfection and domination." She let her fingers drop to her side and sat back against the couch. "And," she added "the reason he controls everything isn't because he thinks one day he'll arrive at perfection, but because he hates himself and desperately wants to be like everyone else. He can't stand that he's different. So he compensates and overcompensates his relationships with others by trying to control them so they'll have no choice but to need him."

"Oh my God, Marie. You just described our entire relationship.. She curled up, and sobbed. "I don't know what to do." Grace dropped her face in her hands in a vain attempt to quiet herself.

Eventually, she fell asleep in Marie's arms. I watched my wife hold her for another hour until I decided to go home and give our babysitter some much deserved time off. I also took the two Dumais boys with me. They were half asleep and only mildly concerned about being woken up and ushered into my car. Earlier in the evening we discussed the inevitable confrontation Grace would have with Declan, and determined that Marie would stay with her and be a calming presence while the kids would be free of the craziness about to embark in their home.

Declan arrived home somewhere short of six that morning. He didn't hide the shock on his face when he opened the door and Marie handed him a cup of coffee she'd made just before his arrival. As he pulled in, Marie had also woken up Grace who promptly walked to the bathroom to wash her face and freshen up before she had to confront Declan.

"What are you doing here? Grace should be home already from work, right?" Declan suddenly looked worried. "Are the boys alright?"

"Oh, they're fine. I came to be with Grace."

"Is she okay? Does she need to go to the hospital? Has she cut herself again?"

Marie was certain Declan added that last question to throw her off and give her pause, throw doubt onto whatever Grace had been telling her up to this point.

"She's fine physically. She's been hurt, but she'll get through it."

"Hurt by what?" Declan asked, not willing to give up any information he didn't have to.

Grace walked in the room with her head held high, red steel eyes and an alert confidence she didn't have five minutes before when Marie first told her of Declan's arrival. She calmly asked Declan to sit down so they could talk.

"Uh, sure. It's late and I'm still pretty tired from studying till this early in the morning. I was kind of hoping for sleep. I called off work today and need to catch up on my rest." He moved warily to the kitchen table, never taking his eyes off his wife.

Marie told me later she wanted to reach out and strangle Declan for being the most ludicrous liar she had ever met. No excuse, no explanation how he could have been studying anywhere considering the library had closed eight hours earlier. She gave mental props to Grace for not physically abusing him in any way, either. It must have taken tremendous restraint.

She sat calmly across from him and said, "Declan, I didn't work last night. I've been thinking a lot the last few weeks, maybe overthinking, about our relationship. Mostly how you haven't been paying much attention to me, specifically in the last three months or so."

"Wait a minute! Marriage is a two way street!" Declan retaliated with a bitterness Marie hadn't heard before.

"I know." Still calm, controlled. "I'm not telling you this to confront you about it, at least not now. Maybe we can talk about all that later." Grace paused with a tightness in her face as if what she was about to say next was the hardest thing she'd ever spoken out loud. "I say all this because I took off tonight because of these crazy thoughts, about you having an affair. I asked myself how in the world, if you were doing such a thing, it could happen. Who could it be with, you know?"

Declan wasn't responding now, but shifted nervously in his seat while his head tilted side to side like a young Stevie Wonder belting out his first recital piece. He knew what was coming.

"Then I realized that the only place I had no clue about was your Flat Earth group. So I drove there last night around seven-thirty or so. I sat and waited in the parking lot. Honestly, I hadn't been to that library before. It's nice." She started to cry, but quickly stopped herself, balling one hand into a fist on the table, and continued.

"Then I saw you, and her, whoever the twenty year old was. You came out of the door and walked over to her car. I watched as you talked and flirted and then eventually put your tongue in her mouth." Grace spoke slowly and deliberately, turning the metaphorical knife around in his heart, over and over as tears filled his eyes, as well. He uttered no words in response. She continued, "You whispered something into her ear, then walked around the car door and drove off with her. The next thing I heard from you was your voice on an answering machine that we never use anymore. I have a cell phone. You know that, but why call me directly when you're about to cheat on me, to essentially walk away from over a decade of being together?"

With a weak, flimsy voice, the only words Declan could get out sounded pitiful. "I'm sorry."

There was a rage behind her eyes as Grace struggled to rid herself of any emotion in her voice. "Thank you, Declan. Now...I want you to pack a bag and leave the house until I invite you to come back again. This is not a negotiation. I am not asking. You need to leave and you need to leave now."

"Where am I supposed to go?" Declan whimpered.

"You can be done with our marriage by going back to your little whore's house. Or if you would like to continue being married to me, and I decide I want to continue being married to you, then maybe you'll figure it out by finding somewhere you can stay that is nowhere near some other woman. How does that sound?"

Declan suddenly began weeping and his next few words could barely be understood. "Please doan may me leave, Gray," it sounded like he was begging her, not for forgiveness, but to let him stay in his home.

Grace's back strengthened as his cries of sorrow intensified. "Declan, I know this is hard. I hear that you are sorry, and came into this conversation knowing you would say that, and that you would beg me to stay. But the best thing right now is for you to leave. With a few months of separation..."

"A few months?!" Declan interrupted like a four year-old being told he couldn't have ice cream before dinner. "What am I supposed to do for a few months? How are we supposed to work on our stuff?"

"One day at a time, I suppose. The same way we screwed up our marriage in the first place, except this time we repair instead of break it down. I love you, but you and I are messed up. We always have been. You are controlling and I am codependent. Let's take some time and work on us."

After a few more minutes of weeping uncontrollably, Declan packed a bag, crawled into his car, and drove to a hotel where he emailed me, telling me he needed to talk. I wrote him back, against my better judgment.

* * *

Rough nights happen, but for Declan they didn't get much rougher than this night. After he and Amber left the library, they drove to her apartment in Marlboro, a half hour drive east from Worcester. They wound through the long, tree lined driveway that led to the third building on the property. The manicured landscaping told Declan rent probably wasn't cheap, and finally they arrived in her carport talking awkwardly about her doubts around her father's view of NASA.

Walking upstairs they held hands and joked about Sweet Lou and his desire to be the big shot in the group. Declan noticed her perfume and moved towards her each time he took in the scent. They both knew the evening's outcome, and a thick sort of energy worked in and out of their interactions.

Amber invited him to sit on the couch as she walked into the kitchen to pour two glasses of wine. Before she returned she made a pit stop to her bedroom to take off her black sweater, revealing a white cotton spaghetti strapped top that curved around her figure perfectly. She smiled at Declan's reaction when she walked into the room. He obviously approved.

Declan's nervousness got the best of him, however, because when she sat down, he began talking and did not stop. She listened for a while, occasionally sipping her wine, until she grew tired of hearing his voice. So she licked her lips, then moved in closely, her hand on his chest.

"I would like you to not talk now." She leaned her face towards his.

Amber tasted like fresh wine as their lips came together.

I'm not sure why Declan insisted on being as descriptive as he was when we eventually met together for a retelling of the previous evening's events, but I'll spare you the post-kiss details here. Perhaps you're confused as to why earlier I'd described his night as "rough." I can assure you it had nothing to do with the liveliness of their physical encounter. Rather, at around five in the morning Declan awoke up lying next to Amber's blanketed body and contemplated what to tell Grace and even how to act after the thing he'd most desired in the world over the last three months was his. He hadn't expected it, but it happened.

As he pondered this, Amber quickly shuffled to her feet and bolted towards the bathroom door. He wondered if maybe she was sick, until he heard her repeatedly say "no" to herself. She walked out of the door, knowing he was awake and moved to her bureau. Amber opened up the top drawer and began getting dressed. Even in the dark, Declan still enjoyed her silhouette as she glided across the room.

The red numbers on her alarm clock read 5:06. The previous night was amazing, but now he found himself in a precarious position. She sat next to him with her knees up and her feet on the bed. He reached over and rubbed her thigh. In response, she spoke quickly, quelling any thoughts he might have been entertaining of continuing last night's adventures.

"Why did we do that?"

"It felt good." Declan answered, then realized it might have sounded cold. "Plus, being with you makes me happy. Our conversations. Our connection. Even the way we made love was magical."

"'It felt good?'" she repeated, as if his other compliments hadn't been spoken. "Declan, you are married. You are married! Are you going to divorce your wife? Are you going to leave her for me?"

"Um, I don't know right now."

"Of course you're not!" She exploded. "You're not going to leave her because you don't really love me. I know I don't really love you. I think you're hot, yes, and it's nice you like my body. You probably liked your wife's at one point too, who knows. But you don't love me.

"And let's not forget you're close with my Dad."

Declan looked up quickly, surprised that he hadn't thought about her being Adam's daughter for some time. Their close relationship and many personal conversations on science and philosophy was one of the reasons Amber had begun attending the Flat Earth Group. She'd never fully bought in to the whole thing, but she enjoyed the back and forth with everyone and seemed especially to enjoy how her father's face lit up when she walked in the room.

Declan looked down silently, knowing this point represented a breach of trust in his friendship with Adam. There was nothing else to say unless he wanted to sound like a schoolboy desperate for sex.

The shame he felt erupted from this and the realization he'd cheated on his wife of more than a decade for a romp in the sack with a young lady whom he knew he would never have a real relationship with. He'd been blinded by lust, but at the same time wanted to reach out, grab her again, and make it worth the sacrifice. He allowed his mind to roam free in that moment with an odd mix of desire, desperation, and misery.

Until Amber spoke again. "Listen, you need to get your clothes on and leave. This is done. We cannot happen anymore. You should have stopped this. I should have stopped this. I'm sorry it happened. I mean, I looked to you for spiritual advice. You're one of the only "church" people I know and certainly the only one I hang out with on a regular basis. Now I know why. Get out!"

And with those piercing words, she laid down and pulled the blanket over her thin small frame. He thought he heard her crying while he sat, wanting to say something profound to help her know this wasn't a waste. Forgiveness was, after all, the "church going" way. But in the end, he stood up and got dressed feeling creepy and miserable, his future in the balance.

* * *

I woke up around 7:00 am. Part of me wanted to call Marie and find out how she fared at the Dumais house and part of me wanted to trust she knew what she was doing and simply go down to the basement and start my workout routine. I hate exercising, but a hundred sit-ups, push-ups, burpees, jumping jacks, and dumbbell lifts later, I climbed back upstairs ready to take on the day.

I opened up one of our kitchen cabinets and brought out a frying pan, grabbed the eggs and bacon from the refrigerator and started making breakfast for me and the kiddos and, hopefully, Marie. Soon the house wafted with the delicious scent of breakfast. My two year old came down from his bedroom, excited to be having his favorite breakfast. "Bacon! The breakfast of champions!" Emmet enjoyed quoting me when he smelled it. He was followed by his smiling older sister and, more solemnly, the Dumais boys.

We all sat for breakfast and talked about the coming day. I tried in the best way I could to describe to my small children why their mother spent the night somewhere else, and to Luke and Brandon why they spent the night here.

"So you know how Daddy is a pastor and sometimes me and Mommy go out of their way to help people? Sometimes that means we go out at odd hours, even if it means overnight. Right now, Luke and Brandon's Mommy and Daddy needs our help so our Mommy went and helped them. They're going through a hard time."

Luke asked, "What's wrong with Mom and Dad?"

"Everyone had a rough time sometimes, Luke. That's why we're trying to help. They're OK, and love you guys very much. You'll see them later. Nothing to worry about right now."

The talk worked well enough as breakfast continued and the conversation transitioned to matters of deeper importance, like playing outside and the Celtics.

After I cleaned up, I moved to the computer and checked my email. Declan had emailed me. So it has all gone down, I thought, clicking on a subject line that read, "Re: I need to talk to you ASAP." The larger email appeared on the screen:

"Jack, I don't know how much you know. I assume you know I lied to Grace and made some stupid decisions last night. But things aren't always what they seem. I need a friend right now. Could we meet up somewhere today and talk? I'm in a really bad place, and could use the support. I know you're busy, so anytime this week would be fine but today would be best. Thanks. Declan."

I stared at my screen for the next minute considering how to answer. Should I scream digitally using all caps about what an idiot he was? Should I feign ignorance? I decided to not do either and just let him know I was available any time after noon. He responded quickly and we made plans to meet at a restaurant on Route 9.

Marie returned home and napped for a few hours before my lunch meeting with Declan. Grace had followed in her own car and scooped up her boys. Very little was said between them, an observation that almost unnerved me more than anything else that had happened so far. Between conversations with Grace and Marie over the last twenty-four hours, I took notes and had a decent grasp of what had happened not only overnight, but in their general relationship.

I arrived five minutes early to find Declan standing outside of the restaurant, looking different than normal as he hadn't shaved. The last seven hours had apparently obliterated his normal self-confidence.

I got out of my car and walked towards him. As we hugged he sobbed deeply into my shoulder, so much that others walking in to eat looked my way a few times to make sure I didn't need any help. I held him tight to let him know I was there for him, but eventually I awkwardly patted his back, hinting it was time to enter the restaurant.

A twenty-something blonde named Tiffany pointed us to our seats and let us know she would be our server that day and if we wanted something to drink. I said a Pepsi, and she asked if Coke was all right. I said that would be fine. I'm not one of those people. Declan ordered water. Tiffany turned around and walked away after informing us she would return with those drinks. For a brief moment I noticed Declan staring at her disappearing into the kitchen. I certainly didn't judge him for this indiscretion. For whatever reason God gave men some need to have something they see as attractive. Many friends in church leadership have fallen prey to believing they should be in a relationship with someone younger or prettier or more in love with them. Certainly it's a drawback to being in what some consider a position of power.

Declan interrupted my thoughts by asking me a weird question, based on his current circumstances. He was trying to control the narrative from the outset - not something a person who "needs a friend" should be doing.

"So," he said, "what do you know about what's happening?"

"I tell you what, why don't you tell me what is happening and we can go from there."

"Ok, first, thanks for meeting me. I know you're busy. I think I've told you that I'm a part of a group where we discuss alternative theories for the nature of the world. This group focuses on Earth being flat."

I smiled. We talked about his love for the theory a few times, but he never told me he attended a group devoted to the topic. I didn't want to make fun of him, so I smiled and motioned with my head that I heard him, inviting him to continue.

"The man who runs the group and who initially invited me into the group has a daughter. In the last year or so, she's been attending."

"What's her name?"

He hesitated for a moment, then, "Amber. She's twenty five and, I don't know, we kind of hit it off. Fast forward to last night..."

"Ok, so wait..." I said, confused. "People don't just go from one relationship to another that fast. Something happens to the first relationship that causes someone over time to want to be with someone else. Otherwise there's plenty of people you can sleep around with, right? You could sleep with our waitress if it was just 'you hit it off.' What happened with Grace and you? What's wrong with your relationship?"

"Huh, that's a great question. Honestly, I think she's depressed and it's been hard to spend any time with her or even talk to her in the last few years. At least, since the kids were born. She's been racking up credit card bills, too, and not taking care of the house or herself while I'm working...."

"Yeah, Declan, but she works a job overnight, right? It's not like she's the only one who has responsibility to 'take care of the house.'"

"I see what you're saying, but you don't know what's happening in my home. I'm holding up my share of the house care and kids care. I'm working my butt off trying to get things done. But if I'm the only one doing it, I'm going to get tired of it eventually, right? At some point, she needs to be held accountable. I'm just tired." He finished the last sentence choked up.

"So what are you doing to get her help?" I tried not to sound curt but his answer still hinted toward defensiveness.

"I mean, she's been to a counselor before. She does what she does." He responded as if that were a good answer, but then threw one more arrow. "And she listens to nothing I have to say. She doesn't. So I guess I kind of acted out. An attractive young lady came on to me and I gave in. I'm sorry. I screwed up, but this is a two way street that she needs to own too. This is not all on me."

Tiffany returned with our drinks and took our order. I noticed this time his eyes never went near her as if he was showing me it wasn't his fault by not looking.

I sat silently for a moment sipping my Coke and processing what I heard. Here on the aftermath of an affair with this young lady, a monstrous betrayal of both his wife and a close friend, Declan shockingly laid most of the blame not on himself, but on the two women with whom he had been involved. I asked another question.

"So what do you think needs to happen now? What do you want to happen in your relationship with Grace? I assume it's to be with her, but I don't know that."

"I want to be with her. I believe in marriage. I believe we can work things out. I'm sorry for my part, and I want to be in my home with her working on things!"

"You know you can both still work on things while you're apart?" I asked.

"How? She's going to be getting bad advice from people who only know her side of the story. Plus it's always easier to talk and work on things when we're together, obviously. That can't be a revelation to you, can it?" Declan was trying unsuccessfully to hide sarcasm as a blanket of matter-of-fact.

Not answering his question, I took another sip of my drink then spoke the logic of my earlier question another way. "Let's say one of you, generally speaking, controls the other and runs the show in your family. Calls the shots, in other words? The other person historically goes with the flow and listens to the other, maybe choosing to be a beat-down puppy. Do you think, if that were the dynamic in the house, that healing could take place, or would manipulation be a possibility?"

"I don't know, Jack. Does having a Biblical household mean having a manipulative one?" He said, upset at my implication.

"Does sleeping with your friends daughter make it a Biblical one?"

I shouldn't have said that, but I couldn't believe I was sitting here listening to Declan give excuses for an affair the day after he had it. He offered little remorse, and what remorse he did show was simply to gift-wrap his feelings as a response to what was done to him.

He stood up, still visibly angry at my words. "I don't know that I can have this conversation right now. You don't understand the extent to which she's at fault. Honestly, I don't even know if you and Marie want us to stay married. You're those people who haphazardly believe whatever they're told about the Earth. NASA this and NASA that. The Earth is round, blah blah blah. You hear things and it sounds right but you don't understand truth."

I stayed seated, keeping my posture as relaxed and non-threatening as possible. "Listen Declan, I'm sorry for what I said, but the truth is, that is what happened. I'm your friend and I want to walk with you through this, but I need to know that you want to walk in truth. Blaming Grace is not going to heal your marriage. That is a fact. Are you willing to do what it takes to heal your home by changing yourself?"

"That's what I'm telling you Jack. I want to come home."

"That's not what I asked."

"Grace and I can change and we can work things out. We need time to get through it and figure each other out. I need to be the person

God wants me to be and that starts with me taking control of our family, of the things I can control. I walked away from helping her to be the person God wants her to be. I was lax in my duties at home, and that allowed sin to get into Grace's life and to my relationships outside of the home. That will not be happening again."

"What sin in Grace's life?" I tried not to sound irritated. He was still standing beside the table, but at least he wasn't shouting. In fact, he leaned towards me and spoke in whispers, harsh as his tone remained.

"Her sin of defiance. Her sin of walking away from being the wife God called her to be. Her sin of not pleasing me or taking care of her family. Jack, these are things the Bible takes very seriously and yes, the brunt of the blame sits on my shoulders for not leading well or taking control of my family situation, but that doesn't absolve her of the part she plays...."

His phone vibrated loudly in his pocket. He pulled it out and glanced at it, shielding the screen from me. I wanted to ask if his friend was calling to reconnect, but held my tongue.

When he looked up, his tone was like that of an old friend again. "Hey Jack, I gotta jet, but thanks so much for talking me through this. Let's do it again sometime." He extended his arms out to hug me goodbye. Confused, I stood up and impressed myself by saying nothing, merely returning the gesture with my own perfunctory hug.

He continued, "Grace and I will get through this and one of the reasons why is because of the love and support of you and Marie. Thanks so much."

He walked out and I silently watched him go, sitting back down as Tiffany laid the sandwiches down (I have always considered a cheeseburger as a sandwich, but that's a discussion for another time). Without an appetite at this point, I asked her for the check.

Experience can be a harsh teacher, but to someone who doesn't learn from its consequences, it will always be a malicious carnivore feasting on the flesh of the human soul. I think this way when I'm angry.

June 30, 2006

Then

Lately Declan always seemed to be in the home office studying or going to the library. Grace desperately needed her husband, but his desire to know everything began to equal his desire to control everything. The latter appetite had been successfully quenched in his relationship with her. She knew it, and felt trapped. Even her present desperation to have him around now signified an unhealthy codependency.

A few nights after conversations that centered around their future hopes and dreams, she got dressed up and, instead of waiting for him to get home from the library, decided to go shopping at the Solomon Pond Mall. As she put on her makeup, she considered texting and telling him where she was going, but in the end decided not to. She needed the time for herself.

Knowing how fabulous she looked in the mirror on the way out the door, she smiled and headed towards the driveway. She jumped in the car (as well as any other five-month-pregnant lady could jump in a car) and drove toward Interstate 290. By the time she arrived at the mall's exit, the sun dimmed over the Worcester hills in her rear view mirror. She drove off the exit and found her way eventually to a huge parking lot at the northeast corner of the mall. The sea of cars draping the lot reminded Grace of Christmas.

She found a spot in a dark corner of the lot far from the building, where the parking spaces gave into the deep woods bordering the property. She got out begrudgingly and found her way eventually to the main entrance. She had little reason to go to Sears at this end of the mall, but figured a quick stop at the Bank of America ATM would be important. She couldn't spend much money so cash might be the wisest way of spending accountability tonight.

Past a group of girls giggling and talking about their favorite band, her thoughts transported her to the previous decade ago when she was the one hanging out at shopping plazas in Keene with her friends.

A messy, bearded man with dirty black pants and a blue Patriots t-shirt that struggled over his belly stood by the entrance smoking and coughing in a rhythmic pattern. As Grace hobbled by, he looked her up and down.

"What sto ya goin' in?" He startled her with his gruff accent.

"Excuse me?" She said.

"Sto? Whe- ya shoppin' at?"

"Oh. I don't know. Just some leisurely shopping I guess." She moved toward the doors, but he wasn't finished with the conversation.

"Gotta any money fo' some cigs? I'm fesh out and will need to get some mo' in a while. Wanna help me out?"

Grace's confidence fell sharply from its earlier perch when she'd set out in this lovely spring evening. She stopped and said, "Ummm... sure," reaching in her purse and grabbing five dollars. "Here you are. Have a good night." She almost ran after he took the money, his fingers touching hers. She didn't wait for the automatic doors, but grabbed the handle on the large side door on the right and threw it open. A jab of pain shot through her shoulder.

She was frazzled by the encounter, but unscathed. After well entrenching herself in the public throng Grace paused, took a couple of long slow breaths. She was free tonight, to do whatever she wanted. Besides church and the grocery store, since Declan and her had been married she didn't really go anywhere else. She often wondered if Declan took too much control of her life. Too often she equated herself with her mom, yet was thankful that at least Declan didn't drink as much as Ed, or treat her the way her father treated her mom.

For two hours she wandered the halls of the mall and enjoyed the sense of freedom, looking for things to buy. She didn't care if she actually bought anything, as long as she could look and breathe in and smell the clothes and food from the food court. She practically danced across the marble floors, looking down over the second floor railing.

At one point, Grace stopped at Aunt Anne's Pretzels and decided to get a big one with white frosting dip. When the cashier handed it to her she walked to a nearby bench and began to eat. In a while she would be moving towards the fancier TGI Fridays but for now she sat and enjoyed this warm, amazing combination of dough and sugar. People came and went past her, while Grace asked herself if her future occupation could be an Auntie Anne's taste tester, traveling from mall to mall eating and watching people. The baby kicked then, agreeing with the idea. As she giggled silently, Grace noticed the messy, bearded man staring at her seven stores away. An instant chill charged over the back of her neck, so she stood and walked the other way, towards the next group of stores she would invade in her dream shopping spree.

After another forty-five minutes of walking through stores and actually buying a pair of shoes and a blouse, she moved to the end of the mall closest to her car and went into TGI Fridays. She sat at the bar, still wanting the feeling of being the girl everyone stared at when she walked into the room. She still was, though now it was her pregnancy that usually caught people's eyes.

"I'm not serving you," the handsome twenty-something said to Grace with a smile and a wink from behind the bar.

"Good. Unless what I really want is a Shirley Temple?" She smiled back and he grabbed a glass, poured ginger ale and grenadine into it, stirred and placed it in front of her with an umbrella.

He said, "Wouldn't it be amazing to be on a beach right now and sitting under this?"

"I don't know that I would fit under this thing even if I wasn't pregnant. But it would be amazing. Summer's coming, and it looks like I'll be spending most of my time trying to stay hydrated for two." She patted her tummy, sipped her drink and sighed.

"Where's the father tonight? Why's he not here with you?"

"Oh he's off studying, having to know every piece of knowledge in the entire world," she said.

He stared at her with deep blue eyes. His face was dark, and handsome. "The only piece of knowledge I would want to know if I were him would be how you got to be so beautiful."

Blushing, she looked away and again saw the sketchy other man smoking a cigarette outside of the restaurant near the name spot he was when she first saw him. When she looked his direction he quickly looked away into the parking lot.

She changed the subject. "Who's that guy there outside of the window? Is he always around here?"

The bartender glanced over and squinted. "I've never seen him before. Why? You want me to make an introduction? Doesn't actually seem like your type. Though your bellies are similar." They both laughed and she gently slapped his arm.

"And what do you think my type is?" She wondered if that had crossed a line. Certainly the fine folks of Master's Way Church wouldn't approve.

"I don't know..." He said slowly, as if were trying to figure it out. "Maybe someone tall? Jet black hair? Dark, dashing features with ravishingly blue eyes!" That last spoken more as a statement.

"Oh really? Like you, I suppose?" She blushed again.

His eyes got big and he smiled. "You think I have ravishingly blue eyes?"

Grace laughed, and then realized she needed to go. She swirled her chair and lifted herself onto her feet. Grabbing her coat, she was surprised when her new friend had walked around the bar, took her coat from her, and helped her put it on.

"Sure you don't want to stay for a bit?" He sounded like a middle schooler asking someone on his first dance. "I think I'm a great conversationalist."

She laughed and flipped her hair. "I know you are, but I'm married and pregnant and need to get home."

"And all of those things are lovely qualities and you will be missed when you leave tonight."

"Thank you. Have a nice night." Grace walked out the door and into the Mall entrance. She zipped her coat up as soon as she was outside as it was a chillier now than it had been a few hours ago. Of course she'd been wearing her coat the entire time, that didn't help matters.

She sighed with relief at the realization the bearded man was not there. Far fewer cars plastered the parking lot, however, and she walked in silence towards darkness beyond the crowded, closer sections. She took the key out of her purse and used the remote opener, beeped the doors open.

As she walked around the car and opened her door a hand aggressively pushed her in. She landed on the seat with her splayed hands, trying to protect the baby. She was bent halfway into the car, trying to turn against the weight on her back but not wanting to expose her belly. The hands continued to press her down, though one moved lower, tried to slide over her right leg. She kicked and screamed, suddenly blind with panic. The broken voice of the bearded man told her to "shut up, bitch." He wreaked of cigarettes and other far worse things as she pushed and fought to get out of the car as best as she could. A sudden, terrifying helplessness filled her.

He let up on her a moment, then tried to turn her around. Once she wasn't forced into a crouch halfway inside the car she pushed away with her left hand and spun around, hitting him as hard as she could with her other, scratching his left eye.

He howled then cursed angrily, spittle spraying across her face. Grace shrieked and begged him to leave her alone, all the while flailing with her arms. He hit her with his own, sweating forearm. She fell back, hit the open doorway. He reached down towards her waist, but another arm and hand between them and grabbed the man, throwing him away from the car. He landed hard against the dark pavement. The bartender from the restaurant stepped quickly towards the other man and kicked him in the face, knocking him out. He walked back to Grace, asked if she was okay.

Tears streamed down both cheeks and she couldn't get control of herself. She didn't know what to do, or say. Why did everything have to turn out like this? Why did she have to come to the mall tonight at all? After five minutes, she began to calm down, the bartender standing beside her the entire time. He said nothing while she composed herself, except once to scream at the dirty man who was slowly waking up and looked like he was going to run. At her rescuers threat, he did not move.

The bartender smiled smirked and said, "If I hadn't come out here to give you my number...." Then paused to let her digest what he said.

"What?" Did he just say that? She replayed what he said in her mind, then tried again to speak. "What - the hell?!! I was almost raped and you're hitting on me?!" She screamed, "Get away from my car, now!" She tried not to cry, but the tears welled up again, blurring everything and everyone around her.

"No, no..." he said, attempting to clarify his words, but she interrupted him.

"That's right no! Get out! Now! Now! Now!" She screamed as loud as she could, hitting her pathetic weak hands against his chest until he took a couple of steps back. Two teenage boys who were getting into their car turned their heads and stood up.

"Ok, ok, I'm leaving. What should I do with him?" Pointing to the bearded man laying in the parking lot.

Grace didn't answer but adjusted herself back down into the driver's seat and turned the car on. She put it in reverse and hit the gas, not caring if her hero had gotten out of the way. Her high beams were pointed at the man on the ground. The teenage boys and the bartender likely were mentally preparing themselves to see a death happen in front of them.

Grace stepped on the accelerator but just before she drove over her attacker (who was definitely awake and curling up in terror) she swerved to the right and drove away. She sobbed during the fifteen minute drive home, blaming herself over and over again. She wondered if she should tell Declan any of what happened. In any normal relationship, it would be the only thing to do. He would blame her for going out in the first place, giving the man five dollars, getting dressed up or any number of decisions she made that evening. Why were those even points anyone would make? He would, though.

Her arm started to itch. She scratched it repeatedly, feeling dirty. She needed to take a bath. Would Declan already be home, wondering what her problem was? No, she would not tell him, and she would get over it.

Declan must have still been at the library since he wasn't home. Grace jumped in the bathtub and lathered herself with soaps and bubbles. She continued to cry and asked God to help her get rid of the feelings, the memory.

She dried off, put on a robe, took out a DVD to watch a 90's movie. Remember the Titans was the movie of the evening. She laid down, turned off her mind watched intently.

Asleep on the couch by the time Declan arrived home, he simply shut the lights off, put a blanket on her, and walked to their bedroom. He thought about waking her up and making love, but he was tired.

So started a slow spiral downward for Grace emotionally. She stayed in their home except for church and grocery shopping. Every evening when Declan worked late or sequestered him in his home office or the library, she put on another 90's movie and watched it alone. If she felt angry, she'd watch a Stephen King thriller. If she felt triumphant, she watched Gladiator or Braveheart. If she felt like she needed something emotional she put in Forrest Gump or Armageddon.

As she watched, she continued to scratch herself to the point of cutting. Feeling worthless, wanting something more. Grace cried most of the day while she prepared for the baby's arrival then made dinner. They ate and talked about whatever Declan did in his day, before he finally left to study whatever he studied and she popped in another movie.

By August, she was as unhappy as she ever remembered being in her life. One night in particular, watching Tombstone, one of her favorites, Grace wondered why she should even bring a baby into this world. She wanted to scratch deeper, tear the hell out of her arms. The world had become such a low place. Maybe she should find a counselor after the baby Luke arrived. Postpartum was such a powerful force, what would happen if she felt worse than this?

Lost in her thoughts, she ignored scene after scene as they rolled by. When Holliday and Earp gunned it out at the OK Corral, grace started to feel pressure. Declan was painting the trim in the baby's room. She thought about calling him, but didn't want to make a big deal if it wasn't time. As a gunfight ensued near the local creek, and she knew without question the baby was arriving. Grace called out for Declan to take her to the hospital.

September 30, 2010

Now

The everyday rut of life can bring lack of excitement, boredom, and a tendency to misbehave as one searches for something of significance. The consequence of a leap into chaos can be even greater, as everyone involved finds the struggle of getting their proverbial feet back on solid ground.

Grace's attempt at getting back on the solid ground of normalcy started with allowing Declan back into the house after three weeks of exile, despite the majority advice coming from her friends and family. Even Marie suggested at least a three month hiatus. When the root of a relationship stems from control and codependency, the only cure is the inability of the controller to control and for the codependent party to beat the withdrawals of not being controlled.

The withdrawals were evidently too great for Grace. Much too quickly, Declan returned home as the king of his castle. The "band" was back together again and they believed things were fine as they moved into a new era in their relationship. Grace acted cold to him for a while, but this didn't work as the tentacles of control wrapped around her like a hungry spider consuming a long awaited fly in its web.

Amber's heart broke after Declan drove away from her apartment that morning, over what she'd done and sympathy with how Grace must have felt. Declan had sent her a message that Grace knew about them, and to steer clear of her over the next few weeks. It was an odd request as Amber had never seen Grace, let alone know where she spent her time.

After a few days, she told her Dad everything. She usually did, but at first, she wanted to keep all of this to herself. After that message from Declan, however, she felt odd with him contacting her. A second text message only reiterated the first, but added a reminder of a funny moment early on in their friendship. When he sent a third message asking how she was doing, Amber decided to go to her dad and tell him what happened.

Like a good father does, he listened intently and held her as she cried with the retelling. He offered advice about how to recover from some of the events she was going through, and reminded her he was always there for her, no matter what she needed or encountered. Amber thought the man was genuinely calm and taking the news in stride.

When she left his house, however, Adam turned from 'protective, nurturing' dad to 'protector, guard dog' dad. Anger grabbed hold of his brain and wouldn't let go. Though he'd recently turned sixty, inside his head was the mind of a trained killer, property of British Special Forces. Retired life suited him well to this point, as Adam enjoyed finding new things to do and study. His former employer often sent their older ops abroad to live and enjoy the rest of their lives free of trouble. As recommended, Adam steered clear of drama, but this betrayal in his personal life stabbed him deeply.

If Declan showed up at Flat Earth group, he would talk to him and scare him with words so he left Amber alone. She no longer wanted to attend the group, and that angered Adam even more than her decision to have an affair in the first place. Over the years he didn't have a lot in common with his daughter, so the fact she joined him in this brought great joy to him as a father, and friend.

The first week rolled around and Declan's disappearing act was a welcome one to Adam, though the rest of the group wondered aloud where they might be. Adam simply reiterated the importance of what they were doing and reminded them that sometimes schedules could be chaotic.

Three weeks after the affair, following a particularly spirited group that focused on the way the horizon looks from the shore, Adam walked out of the library to see Declan standing near his car. That he showed up unannounced angered Adam, but outwardly he remained calm.

"Hi, Adam," Declan said, sticking out his hand.

Adam didn't say anything. Instead he slowly placed his briefcase on the hood of the car, then finally extended his arms out to hug Declan. At first the other man flinched, thinking he was going to get slugged. This gave Adam inward pleasure to know Declan was on the defensive. He stepped back.

"Where've you been?" He wouldn't let on that he knew anything right away. He figured Declan having to guess allowed Adam to find out more information perhaps than Amber told him.

After a stunned pause, Declan answered with a smile, "Oh you know, around."

"Right, I get that. But you know what I'm asking. Why haven't you been coming to group?"

"You don't know?" Declan seemed genuinely shocked.

"Know what?" Adam had an edge to his voice he couldn't mask. Hiding what he knew was no longer possible. He'd hidden things for the last thirty years, but this was personal. Declan had hurt and possibly used his daughter. The anger crept out like a slow rush of lava rolling down a hill toward a doomed village. "That you took advantage of my twenty five year old daughter? All while your wife and kids slept soundly at home? Or maybe not soundly because apparently your wife found out. Then you moved out of your house but after just a few weeks you're now back home, all while continuing to text my daughter, who does not want to hear from you. So... that? Is that what I should know?"

"I didn't take advantage of your daughter," Declan answered defensively.

"That's what you took from all those questions, you pathetic moron?" Adam angrily retorted, the words sounding more gentlemanly than they should, given the British accent.

"Listen Adam, I don't want to get into a fight with you..."

"No, I promise you, you do not."

After another pause, Declan continued, sounding slightly annoyed, "But anyways, I would like to continue attending Flat Earth Group. I don't have a lot in my life right now, but I do have my family who is currently supporting me, and I do have this group. I love this group and all of you. I would like to continue attending."

Adam clenched his fists behind his back, leaning just a little forward to make himself larger. But he didn't move any closer. Not yet. "First of all, what the hell do you know about love, Declan? You do not love me. You do not love your wife. If Amber hadn't broken up with you, or if Grace hadn't caught you both, you'd probably still be trying to get into a relationship with my daughter. We wouldn't be having this conversation. You would be attending FEG and I would have no clue what was going on. You don't love me," he repeated. "You didn't love Amber. You love yourself, Declan. That's who you love."

"It's your right to feel that way, but..."

"No that's not how I feel. The facts tell me that and what they would be telling you if Grace was buffin' with some other bloke. But because you are the one acting on your own impulses here, you can't see the problem. My wife spent five years on her deathbed from a repulsive attack of cancer through her body and with my job plenty of women, both young and old, threw themselves at me. I was faithful and loyal to her. You gave excuses to Amber about your wife's mental illness or the lack of communication or some such nonsense. You are the textbook definition of a narcissist, and so, no, you can no longer attend FEG."

Declan's insides turned hot, and pain flashed through his head. He quickly said, "Look Adam, take some time and think about it. It's clear you're emotional and not thinking straight..."

Slowly, so slowly, Adam reached around, fist clenched as if he was punching Declan in slow motion. Nevertheless, there was obvious power in that arm. At the last minute, his hand opened and rested, palm out, on his chest. No slap, no push, simply there, against his, with an unspoken promise of violence. "I'm not emotional. I don't want you in my group. I don't want you near me. If my daughter decides to come back, she will be welcomed, but you are done. You have no place at FEG. Please do not return, and do not try to talk to anyone in the group or ask them if they can intercede for you. I have told them already and they know what the answer will be. Now, I have to go. Please don't contact me in the future. Good day."

He lingered for a moment longer, then pulled his hand from the other man, and waited.

Declan wanted to reach out and punch 'the old man' in the face, but he chose instead to turn around, walk to his own car, jump in, slam the door and squeal his tires as he drove away.

He tore down Route 9, processing all he would now lose as a result of his friend turning on him. Amber and he no longer talked. His wife could barely look at him when he walked around the house. They stopped attending church so those friends were falling away, though they did still call occasionally. Now Adam had ripped the Flat Earth Group away from him like a Band-Aid from a crusted wound.

Declan tried to create a scenario where he won from all of this. Unfortunately his thoughts flew to proving a Flat Earth instead of healing the emotional injuries of his family. He mused about starting his own group, but he didn't really know anyone else who believed or even wanted to talk about proving the theories behind the truths.

All of those options seemed fruitless, however, as he considered the ways Grace, at least in the short term, would keep him from connecting with the others. Her insecurities would have her looking over his shoulder in every conversation and in every written communication. He liked the fact that his real Mom lived in Burlington, Vermont. He didn't need another one here.

No, the victories he looked for started with actively pursuing truth. How could he prove to himself and the world that Earth was flat, and that calling it a theory was a disservice, not only to science but to truth?

Then it hit him as he passed the bowling alley going 70 mile per hour. He knew the answer and what the focus of his energy should be over the next few years. Declan was tired of talking about issues and never doing anything to help Flat Earthers disprove the lies their science classes taught them. He could do much of it from the comforts of his own home with Grace looking on and maybe even helping.

Declan would devise a plan to show the rest of the world that NASA's sole purpose was to lie to everyone. He would search for and provide proof that the Earth was flat, and all models that said otherwise fell short. It might take months, probably years. Focused time would deliver the proper results. He would convert his large garage into a project headquarters. Soon the world would know the name of Declan Dumais and praise his contributions to the scientific community.

Conspiracies

The thing about change is that when people want it, it becomes an inconvenience, and when they don't, they act out in weird ways to deviate from their normal unfulfilled lives. Take me for instance. In the 15 years I've pastored, when things are "normal" I tend to make things happen to bring about change. That brings a certain amount of chaos, and it is my job to organize that chaos into order until life gets boring again.

The opposite is true, too. Even people who like change don't like to be fired or their loved ones to end up in the hospital. But change happens. (Unless you're talking about human nature - thought you caught me there, didn't you?)

When I was twelve years old, my best friend died in a bicycle accident in front of me. I rode my bike up the road, knocked at the door, and asked his mother if he could come out and play football. She said yes and soon he came running out the door, jumping off his two step porch and onto his own bike. I took the lead on the right side of the road, and he followed close behind. He passed me on my left side. For a short while we raced, turning our pedals hard and pushing our handlebars back and forth. Then in one fateful second, our handlebars slammed into one another, and I fell over into the grass. He fell over the opposite direction, into the windshield of an oncoming car. I never saw my friend again. After three days in a coma, he passed away.

I often wonder what his mother thinks of me. If she mourns not only his death, but also our friendship. I process what she might be thinking, and ask myself if she believes the story I just told you.

Since that time I know that the life of everyone involved in that accident, including the immediate families of me, my friend, and the driver have been changed, and we all probably think through the "what ifs," the "what could have been's" and theories that help us to make sense of the unknown.

I bring this up because life has many mysteries. There are many things about God and the universe, the government and the people living on the other side of the world or our city that we do not know. In order to make sense of these hidden pieces of knowledge, we fill these gaps with answers that help us digest what our minds will not allow us to accept.

Then when things get boring in our lives, we long for change and begin to find holes in knowledge. These are called conspiracy theories.

January 7, 2004

Then

Shrewsbury, Massachusetts connects with Worcester's east side across Lake Quinsigamond. It's a modern, yet somehow quaint community of people not quite ready for Boston, but definitely too good for Worcester. You can find soccer moms trolling around the White City area, formerly an old amusement park in the 50's but a shopping destination in the 2000's. Shrewsbury is also where Declan and Grace chose to move into their first home.

When they married a year after their graduations two years prior, they'd moved into a 2 bed, 1 bath at the Lake Ave. Apartments overlooking the "Long pond." Declan got a job as a high school physical education teacher two towns north in West Boylston and they decided Grace would stay home and care for the details of their living space, eventually preparing for the arrival of their future children.

During those years, Grace began to "lose herself" and transformed into a less confident, nervous, and unfocused version of the young college knockout she'd been five years before. Where at one time the focus of entire rooms landed on her when she entered, now she quietly took care of the home she also hid in, as each day Declan returned and explained, sometimes agreeably and sometimes not, exactly how he wanted his house to be kept.

Declan, on the other hand, grew in confidence. The kids at his school loved him. He worked hard making Gym class one they enjoyed while still getting enough exercise to learn how to build active lifestyle habits.

Time moved on. The first two and a half years of marriage were spent planning, organizing and participating in the growing staleness of a normal, uneventful sex life. Whenever Grace shunned Declan's advances, he reminded her that the more they had sex, the better their chances were of having kids. Grace wanted kids. She realized her college hopes and dreams of working in Public Health had disappeared. Children stood out as the last dream in her life, from a childhood of darkness. She often wondered if having kids was something she should do. Her father had left a mark on her soul that did not seem to be vanishing.

October 1, 2010

Now

While Declan worked out the logistics of the new project, one that would make him a household name, Grace sat at home wondering where he was, and whether or not he'd continued the affair which had supposedly ended. She called his cell several times, but each time the call ended in hearing his voice tell her to leave a message. She grew tired of his commands when he was home, yet wanted him back as soon as possible.

While she waited, she put the boys to bed and tidied up, keeping busy. She noticed how nervous she'd become since finding out about the affair. She'd always been twitchy, but at least she had been able to hide it from herself. Now the problem was laid in front of her like a model posing for a struggling artist.

She washed the dishes by hand and made a mental note to get some detergent the next time she went shopping. She cleared off the counter tops and perused the day's mail, noticing how much had become "junk" since the advent of the internet. She threw away postcards for regarding the local chiropractor and LensCrafters, as currently their backs were strong and their eyes could see.

Grace kept the coupons for Price Chopper. She'd mastered the art of "couponing" over the last few years. There was a shiny yellow postcard asking if she grew tired of her dead-end job. "Why, yes, I am," she quietly responded. The card was from Framingham State College.

The card spurred her to think about going back to school, getting her Master's degree, get a better job than working at a gas station. She needed something to do, to get through the life she found herself. What makes a life worth living? What steps allow someone to feel like they matter to others or themselves?

Answering those questions was not going to happen today, but she decided her next step was to register for classes in Framingham. Soon, she'd quit her job. Worrying each night that she was going to get shot was no longer an option. Disregarding how Declan might feel about the decision, Grace sat down at the computer and registered for classes.

The next stage of life stepped into the limelight in her head. Hopefully it would outshine the last one. Of this she could be certain: her reliance on anyone else, including her husband of seven years, was over.

* * *

"I have some amazing news for you!" Declan exclaimed as he walked through the doors of their house.

"What's that? You're going to start answering your phone?"

Declan looked like a wounded puppy at Grace's words. Immediately his shoulders shrank. "You really know how to encourage someone, don't you? God, Grace, you can be so hurtful." He pouted all the way to the couch, put his head down, and played with his hands.

For the first time in a long time, Grace pieced together how he wanted the conversation to now go. He pouted, and then she felt bad for her words. She always conceded and apologized. Every day his words caused hurt, but with the events of the last month, she realized he'd never apologized for anything. She didn't want to be mean, but she had cowered for the last time to his manipulation. Today she walked away from the living room.

From the kitchen Grace said, "I apologize for my sarcasm, but based on what has happened over the last month I expect you to answer your phone when I call. I don't want to have to wonder where you are." She said it sternly, but not in anger.

"I just drove around for a little bit. I really shouldn't text while I'm driving."

"Which is why I called you."

"I know, I know. Come in here so we can talk."

"We can talk from in here where I was standing and cleaning when you arrived home." Grace said.

Declan, clearly irritated, moped back into the kitchen, crossed his arms, and sighed heavily.

She continued, "Are you going to share with me your exciting news? I'm looking forward to hearing about it, and have some news to share, too."

"I was driving around pondering how I hadn't been going to my Flat Earth Group. I was thinking about how it was kind of my group, you know? Like my community?"

Grace wanted to respond to his rhetorical question by saying, Yeah, I know that community. You slept with one of them and made a mockery of our marriage. She only communicated those thoughts inside her head, but Declan must have picked up on it because he continued in a different way, proving he could think through things with empathy if he tried hard enough.

"But now I have the opportunity to do some of that work from here. From our home. With the people I love, you and the kids."

"Ok?" Grace wondered where this was going. Was he going to start a group at our house? She continued to peel the potato in her hand.

"So of course I have my job, but I also have this passion to see the truth prevail, to see the Flat Earth Theory proven as scientific law. I'm going to be undertaking a project that proves the Earth is flat."

"So you're trying to disprove a negative instead of proving a posit?" Grace asked.

"Something like that, yes, but in disproving the negative, we'll be proving our positive and paving the way for further flat Earth truths and a new wave in scientific exploration. It's not dissimilar from Rocky when he faced the giant Russian guy. He first had to deliver a cut to his face before he could really believe in defeating him. Once he landed a blow, the rest was only nine rounds away," Declan smiled believing his analogy hovered far above Grace's thoughts intellectually.

"Huh, sounds interesting. Who's going to pay for this project? Together we don't even come close to making six digits, and typically, research can be pretty expensive." Grace tried not to sound negative, but Declan rolled his eyes at the question.

"I may have to get creative, but I hate it when you don't believe in me. Though that's typical of our experiences together."

Grace allowed the comment to pass without a response. "What can I do to help?"

"I'll be converting the garage to a full blown workshop. I'll need all the space to be able to work on some of the projects I dream up. Other than that, just your encouragement and love. There will be times I get lonely in there and will need some special kinds of love." Declan gliding his fingers up and down Grace's leg. She flinched and moved away. It was the first time he touched her since the affair, and Grace wasn't prepared for it.

Part of her wanted to grab, kiss, and make love to him like she knew no one else could ever do. Though they struggled to communicate in the last few years, their physical relationship, when it happened, never did. She longed to connect and hold him again, but realized the boundary issues that would incur if she let that happen without really communicating to him, somehow, how much she was hurting because of him.

"I'll support you, Declan. I love you and want you to succeed in this project. I don't always understand why it's so important to you, but I love you. You have my support and encouragement." Grace added a reassuring smile.

"Awesome," Declan said, "Now what did you have to tell me?"

"I'm going back to college. I'm going to get my Master's Degree." Grace's smile was more sincere when she said it. Saying aloud now made her feel even better about the decision.

"Oh," Declan said, while his eyes grew big. He couldn't hide his surprise. "What makes you think that's the right decision?"

Grace thought his response strange, but decided to answer as normally as possible despite his less than grand effort to appear happy in some way. "It's been a while since I've been in school. I kind of feel, and have felt, stuck in a rut recently with my job. I want to do more than I've been doing. I want to do something that matters. Going back to school and educating myself in a field where I want to find a job in is a good plan to move forward, get myself, you know, unstuck."

"How much money is that gonna cost? What about you staying home with the boys? I'm not sure about this plan, Grace."

"Honestly, Declan, I don't care if you're not sure about it. It's something I'm going to do and you're going to pay for it. You'll be spending more time at home working on this project so you can help with some of the things I normally do like cook and clean and laundry. As a team we can make this happen and both of us can be successful."

Declan's head bowed when he sighed heavily again, trying not to appear too agitated. Loss of control was not something he was comfortable with. Somehow, he felt like he was letting down his parents by letting this plan see the light of day. His fidgeting irritated Grace, but she kept calm and continued, answering the concerns she knew he'd have.

"Declan, I understand your desire to have things a certain way, but you screwed up here. For the last few years we've done things your way, and to be honest, I wasn't the wife you needed. I was co...no, I am codependent and needy, depressed and miserable. That's not who I'm called to be. I've allowed things in our marriage and my life to be controlled and frankly, I don't like the person I've become as a result. I want our boys to see their Mom and be proud of the person she's becoming, just like I want them to be proud of you and your projects and the things you're doing. But that won't happen if I'm..." Grace paused before she continued, knowing this truth would hurt him deeply, "...if I'm being controlled by you and by the things that you want instead of the things we need as a family."

"You don't trust me? As a leader?" Declan asked.

"First of all that wasn't the point of anything I said, but since you asked, obviously no. Right now I do not trust you at all. As a leader, a husband, or as a person. Why should I? Three weeks ago you slept with a twenty-five year old daughter of one of your closest friends. So no, you'll excuse me if I don't trust you as a leader!" She didn't realize how much anger was pent up inside of her until she'd over and over tried to be calm during this conversation. But Declan appeared incapable of understanding his own faults, including ones that were so blatant. It would take a narcissist to ignore the obvious.

"Whoa, whoa, whoa, don't get so angry, Grace," Declan hushed defensively. "We're in this together and I'll support you and I know you'll support me. Let's not dig deep into the past. The future is here and I'm looking forward to many more years with you. We're going to get through this. We just need to not accuse each other of past hurts in the process.

"You work on school. I'll work on my projects, and together we'll embrace our home life of cooking, cleaning, and laundry. I know we can do this if we stick together, and our family will thrive if we put one another first and push away the opinions of other people." After he said that, he wrapped his arms slowly around Grace and they embraced. She didn't know what the last sentence meant, but for now, she would forget it. She was tired of second guessing his every word, but typically, every word he spoke was something worth second guessing.

Christmas of 2003 brought an abnormal peace to Declan and Grace that was strange for any season, let alone the adult-stress syndrome known as Yuletide. Because of the transitions of graduation and marriage, they managed to find happiness through the month of December.

They scheduled their family gatherings ahead of time. On Christmas Eve they'd spend the evening with Grace's mother Nancy at her small but comfortable double-wide in Keene, New Hampshire, where they'd have a big dinner and go to Christmas Eve service. They'd stay overnight in Grace's old room, then spend the morning opening gifts between them for the first time as a newly-married couple. Nancy offered to stay in her bedroom for an hour so they could have their own Christmas, too. Around noon, they'd drive two and a half hours north to Burlington, Vermont to have dinner with Declan's family.

They talked openly about the fun they would have over the coming holiday. Grace felt free enough to laugh and joke about how stupid they'd been to introduce their families so soon on that first Christmas six years ago. Declan shared an authentic story of the grief he felt over the sudden death of his college friend, Mark, last fall. Grace grabbed his hand and squeezed as a tear appeared in his eye.

Declan asked what Grace thought her favorite part of their visit with her mother might be. He was surprised when she said that she couldn't wait for church, but didn't dig any deeper on the subject.

They arrived at Nancy's house around 4:15 in the afternoon. Nancy greeted them warmly, looking healthy and delighted to see Declan and her daughter so happy. Over the years she'd felt guilty for being a poor example of how to deal with a relationship, and how that example had affected her daughter in college and even in her early marriage. Today she saw a difference in the way they connected and it made her heart happy.

They decided Christmas Eve dinner would be at Pedraza's Mexican Restaurant in downtown Keene. The main drag was a beautiful, brick-dominated landscape full of shops, restaurants, churches and schools. Keene was a lovely college town sitting in a bowl rimmed with mountains. During the summer, crowds of pedestrians dotted the landscape of the street and customers ate and laughed loudly on the dining patios. Declan was especially impressed that the movie Jumanji had been filmed in downtown Keene.

There would be no eating outdoors tonight, however, as wind chills brought the temperature down to ten degrees. The threesome found a spot in the middle of the restaurant. Orange stucco walls, dark yellow rustic lanterns and rip-offs of famous Frida Kahlo paintings created an environment Declan had seen years before on a missions trip to Monterrey, Mexico.

The conversation hovered on work and friends. Nancy and Grace talked every week on the phone or texted but there were some things distance didn't cover. After they finished their chips and salsa, Nancy started a conversation that brought Declan back to his years in his home town. She took a tortilla shell out of its foil and placed some chicken, peppers, and onions in it. After placing cheese and sour cream inside and rolling it up, she asked, "Have you both thought about the idea of faith? Declan, I know your Dad is a pastor, but I've wondered this for the last few months. Do you talk at all about faith together?"

Silence, as the two took bites of the fajitas they'd made.

Grace responded. "Well, Mom, that's some light conversation you want to get into." The group laughed politely, and she continued, "We haven't talked about it much. I know Declan probably has more to say on the subject but I think we both just believe, to each their own. I did youth group growing up. He grew up in church. But we're just living our lives. I'm sure we both kind of believe there's a God who created the world, but now we're here just trying to get control of life."

Nancy replied, "That's fair. That's very much like the way you were raised. But don't you think, maybe there's more to it than that? I've been attending a new church..."

"New church? We're not going to Saint Bernard's tonight?"

"Calm down, volcanic eruption." Declan jokingly warned, but was secretly happy he didn't have to go to a Catholic mass. "You won't melt if you go somewhere else."

"Thank you Declan. Anyways, this new church has opened my world as far as faith, specifically faith in Jesus. It isn't some out of-this-world magical thing that doesn't have an impact on our daily lives, but affects us every day, in everything we do. Does that sound like what you were taught growing up, Declan?"

"It sounds like you go to a church exactly like the one I grew up in, to be honest. Faith isn't just mystical. It speaks through the Bible."

"Yes, yes, Declan! That's it!" Nancy stopped, and took another bite of a fajita, trying to work out which direction to continue. Her kids did the same. People don't change, but they do change the subject.

After dinner, they drove north on Main St for a few minutes to Harvest Christian Fellowship, a small building that showed neither the tradition nor class of the Catholic Church they passed on the way. Grace was irritated that the place looked "like a dump" compared to St Bernard's. Out of spite, she'd muttered, "It would have been nice if we could have just walked to church," but left it at that when no one replied. The parking lot was packed, however. The car clock read 6:58.

At the entrance, an older gentleman that knew Nancy smiled widely and flung the doors open. His smile showed crooked teeth but also how happy he was to see her family. Nancy smiled back warmly, almost embarrassed by his greeting.

The entrance smelled like Christmas. Red poinsettias, bows and lights decorated the building. As they stepped into the main room of the church, Declan gave a deep sigh, remembering something he'd long forgotten. There's something about the holidays in church that helps even the most intense atheists remember God.

They sat in ugly, purple carpeted chairs somewhere in the middle and left and waited, for only a minute, as the last of the crowd flooded in and took their seats.

Lights shut off and the crowd sat in darkness for a few seconds until a choir holding black folders walked in, illuminated by a group of flood lights from the ceiling. Fog rolled in from a set of black curtains on either side of the stage. Triumphant orchestral music burst from the auditorium speakers like rays of sunlight on a hot summer morning. The scene was set for Christmas at Harvest.

Lights rotated between floods and spotlights turned on and off. The choir and a few actors interacted in what turned out to be a mediocre performance. However, while their initial hesitation still existed, Declan connected to this environment and Grace gravitated to the messages embedded in the production.

The themes of the evening ranged from the birth of Jesus to how his coming and dying allowed for "prisoners to be set free." The choir sang, "Hallelujah, we are free!," and the actors talked of difficult circumstances they found themselves in. Hard relationships, financial struggles, addictions to drugs and food, and poor self-esteem. Declan pondered his walk away from the church. During this time, Declan had felt his freedoms were more restricted than they had been, and that was counter-intuitive to what he thought would happen when he left his family and started living life on his own. He always felt free growing up, but the guilt he held onto pinned him down to feel worthless at best.

Grace suddenly hated herself. Listening to this Christmas event showed her how lost she felt, how burdened. She was missing something. Rather than make her feel bad, however, Grace felt lifted up. She wondered why Declan had walked away from this kind of experience when he was younger.

The program finished and a man stood up and talked about giving one's life to Jesus, or being born again. He asked the audience to consider Christ, and to receive him tonight by standing, walking to the front, and talking to one of their leaders waiting for them.

Declan whispered, "Hell, no," under his breath, attempting to get a laugh out of the ladies. His mother-in-law elbowed his ribs. Grace sat, praying and trying to get the nerve to stand up. She needed to take the step. A piano played softly in the background, noses sniffled around the room, whether by people's tears or colds she didn't know. Then she stood up, startling her family. Grace moved past her husband and mother and walked to the front of the room, where a white-haired lady with bifocals and a long khaki skirt took both her hands in greeting.

Back at the chairs, Declan realized what had happened and quickly stood up and followed her. He was met by someone else, a man who placed his arm around Declan's shoulder and led him gently to a back room.

That night, Nancy received her "Christmas wish" and the "Greatest Christmas present ever" when the pastor announced from stage immediately before dismissal that Declan and Grace Dumais had given their lives to Jesus. The crowd cheered. Nancy and Grace wept. Declan enjoyed the attention.

* * *

The next morning, Nancy, as promised, stayed in her bedroom - the same room where her husband had attacked her years before - and allowed her kids to spend their first Christmas morning as a married couple. In the last couple of months, since she'd become a Christian, Nancy regularly prayed for them and now, her prayers had been realized. She sat on her bed weeping with delight.

Declan and Grace walked into the living room excited to give their presents to each another. Grace poured small glasses of eggnog with whipped cream. Garth Brooks crooned "Go tell it on the mountain" over the stereo's speakers, and they sat on the floor next to the small green and red lighted tree. A few presents waited beneath the tree, but the two they would open now sat in between them.

"You go first, Declan," Grace said. "I'm too excited to wait! You know me, patience is not my virtue."

"Ok, ok, here I go." Declan said, picking up the small box with his name written in typed Calligraphy. "Very fancy, babe." He slowly removed the bow and tag, then unpeeled a piece of tape off the bottom of the gift.

"Would you hurry up?" She said, laughing. "I told you I was impatient and that is not changing!"

"Fine." With one swoop he grabbed the whole of the gift wrap and took it off the box. Now he held a gray, slightly fuzzy jewelry box in his hand. He smiled. Grace smiled as if she knew that he knew what was inside. Actually, he did not. Declan opened it slowly, thinking he would see a ring or a necklace, but instead saw a small silver pendant. He squinted because he didn't understand, even after seeing it. Why did she give him a baby bottle pendant for Christmas? A look of bewilderment crossed his face.

And then he understood. His mouth dropped open, and he looked at Grace's face which was lit up as bright as the star the shepherds saw outside Bethlehem. They were having a baby. They grabbed one another and kissed passionately.

After several minutes of celebrating the new child arriving in a less than eight months, Declan declared it was time for her to open his gift. He smiled as he handed the large box in front of his wife. Grace grabbed the string of the bow and slowly pulled it free. They both laughed but Declan motioned for her to hurry, as pushy as she had been a few minutes earlier.

When she opened the package, she backed up to look at it. A brand new doll house box reflected the overhead ceiling and Christmas tree lights. On the box a little girl played with the doll house. Grace wondered how Declan already knew about her gift to him. He'd acted completely surprised. Unless he was telling her something else. But what? Why would he give her something that to do with dolls if he didn't know about their little doll? Maybe it had to do with the house. He finally took the box with both hands and gently pushed it toward her again, then cupped his hands towards the top if telling her to open it.

So she did, and pulled out the house that was inside. She was somewhat surprised the box actually had an actual dollhouse. Taped to the bottom of the house, however, was a thick Manilla envelope with black writing that read, "27 Fyrbeck Ave, Shrewsbury, Massachusetts."

Grace held the envelope, hoping this Christmas surprise was not what she thought it was. Declan couldn't have done that, could he? Not without her.

"Surprise!" He said, breaking the heavy silence. "It's a new house! Open up the envelope and look at it! We can move in on the 2nd. Isn't this great?"

Silence.

"Well? Are you so excited or what? I can't believe we get to move into our first home so soon!"

"Wait. I don't understand. How did you buy a house without .... No, no no, how could you buy a house without talking to me about it? I mean, we didn't get to go out and search together. We didn't talk about a house at all beforehand. It's like you just made this huge decision, this really, really huge decision for us, and didn't let me to walk with you through the process? I don't even know what to say. I mean, how did you even do this without me?"

Declan was caught off guard at her questions. "One. I had it in my mind to surprise you from the very beginning. I thought it would be sweet, and you could walk into the house, trusting my judgment in making the wise decision. In the end we could live in this house together, with our future children. It just so happens that the timing is impeccable.

"Two. I bought it with my dad co-signing for the mortgage, but I had it written up so that we could change the co-signer to be you, if you qualify. Remember, though, your credit isn't great. You overspent in college. Your parents weren't good go-to people for this stuff. I thought this was the right move."

Grace couldn't believe what she was hearing. Her heart beat heavy and tears now rolled down her face.

"Oh, no, you can't do that. Don't start crying. That's not fair. I wanted to do something nice for you and now you're going to pretend this is something that hurts you? I can't believe it!"

Grace couldn't stay in the room any longer. Her heart hurt so bad that a howl erupted from her lungs and into the room. She stood up and ran into the bedroom where she had grown up, slamming the door and locking it just like she had done so many times in her life.

Nancy came out and asked Declan if everything was alright.

"No," he said angrily, as he too stood up. He headed for the front door, leaving to go somewhere that probably wasn't open on Christmas morning. "She'll never change."

October 5 2010

Now

Declan initiated his plans. The following Saturday morning he woke up around 5:30, and began the painstaking task of cleaning out the garage. Years of memories, tools, holiday decorations and enough photos to wallpaper a large room made it difficult to create a workable space. But the task is a marathon and not a sprint, he told himself. He ordered a dumpster from a local vendor. It would arrive the next morning, so what he didn't keep, he threw behind the garage, not far from where the dumpster would be parked.

Most of the keepsakes transferred easily to the cellar, where he and Grace had previously decided not to move them. The reasoning had been practical. 'Let's keep them in the garage where it will be easier to organize and throw away the junk before we put them back in our home.' Sometimes, however, plans and execution do not align, and the only constant is change. So, the cellar made itself a perfectly acceptable home for the things that should have gone there years before.

After a long morning cleaning, Declan needed a shower, but more work needed to be done. The next step involved planning the work space. Before him were three wooden walls, a rickety old Ikea work desk built into the east wall and a second, smaller free standing desk. Two garage doors bordered the main entrance from the driveway. The walls needed a fresh coat of paint, but painting cost money and time. Declan decided to simply wipe everything down with Clorox wipes and mop the cement floors.

His short visit to Benson's Flea Market two towns over got him a large whiteboard for only a few dollars, along with a small cache of cheap office supplies. Declan hung the whiteboard on the west wall of the garage overlooking the larger desk. It looked out of place with the room's 'Europe meets Little House on the Prairie' feel.

By mid-afternoon Declan stood in the middle of the room and processed what his project looked like. Not bad, he decided. Though he didn't know the outcome, he did want to focus on action. The Flat Earth Group, much as he loved being a part of it, did nothing but talk. Declan wanted proactivity.

He walked to the wooden shelf on the west wall, picked up the Amazon package that arrived yesterday. Yellow and small, Declan felt the bubble packaging and smiled. Yet one more item he could use to change the world. He gently ripped the top of the package, before unfolding the poster and laying it softly on the empty wooden shelf - or "standing desk" as he called it. Declan smoothed out the folds and looked happily at the Flat Earth map. Gleason's New Standard Map of the World encouraged him to move forward and prove to his friends, family, and the world that it really was flat.

Where to start? His mind raced a million different places. He decided to start with the map. This felt like the first day of school. Grabbing a black dry erase marker, and without taking the cap off, Declan perused the map like he was trying to find a black sock in a pile of laundry. He looked for all the obvious ways, or places, to prove the truth. Cape Horn, Tasmania, New Zealand or Cape Alguhas in South Africa seemed to be locations that made the most sense to start.

After hours of viewing the map and looking online for more specific information regarding places and distances, it was almost dinner. He realized how much detail a plan like this involved.

By the end of the day, he was both happy he had the day off and miserable about how much he had to do to make this happen. The amount of work needed done was inconsequential, however, to the truth bombs he would detonate as a result of his research. Moving forward with dedication and action was paramount to seeing the world's view of itself changed.

Infatuations

Infatuation in an unhealthy relationship is like eating fast food. Fast food looks delicious when you see it, and when you dig in and taste the fries or the burger, there's a connection you have with it. The salt and the cheese and the fat in the burger, along with the butter on the bread – all of it is engineered to build a bridge with your senses that you never want to give up, even when you realize that eating those particular foods are not healthy.

Infatuation blinds your senses, preventing you from making a wise decision about whether or not a relationship is healthy or not. Far too many people just enjoy and go along for the ride, until it's too late.

February 12, 2002

Then

Grace was approached by the professor at the end of her Public Health seminar. The woman was tall and gorgeous with a brilliant smile and a bright red business suit that marketed how fit she was. She asked if Grace would stay after so they could talk. Grace obliged while a few of her male classmates snickered as they walked out, one of them muttering, "Can I watch?" The Neanderthals laughed and exited the classroom.

It was no secret that Professor Mariel Gallant was one of the school's first open lesbian professors, but besides that, Grace knew very little about the professor who'd so far taught her in three classes. Grace was drawn to the woman's charisma and wisdom. At the same time, they hadn't spoken more than five words to each other.

"Miss Miller, thanks for staying. I have a few questions for you. Well, one really. You've been exceptional in your work and grades, outside of a few small quizzes. Can I ask what your plans are this summer?"

Grace responded, "I'm not really sure yet, Ms. Gallant. I have some resumes out and I've applied to some internships, but I'm not really sure what I want to do, yet. My boyfriend and I have talked about getting married, but we don't have a date set or anything."

"Ok," Professor Gallant said, "that's not a problem. I'm asking because I've had you now in three classes and to be honest, I like what I see. It's clear you care about the field of Public Health, and I think that's exceptional. My personal goal is to one day be a Public health chair, and am always looking for talented individuals who have a passion for this field." She'd been leaning against the desk, now she stood straighter, hand before her as if giving a lecture to a classroom of one. "So, here's what I'm asking: I'm going on a trip this summer for three months to London. I'll be piggybacking on some research they've done on childhood obesity - specifically in regards to children in schools. I need an assistant for the summer, and I'd love it if that would be you. Grace, if this is the field you want to go in to, it's an incredible opportunity. You'll be paid a small stipend, plus food and housing will be paid for. I'd like you to take some time and think about it. How about you give me your answer in, let's say two weeks? Do you think that's enough time?"

Grace stood in the middle of the room only three feet from Professor Gallant, but her head couldn't wrap around the idea of what she'd asked. Certainly she wasn't good enough to have this honor? What was the catch?

After a silence that hung in the air like a slow moving fog, Grace answered softly, "Yes, ma'am. Two weeks will be enough time. Thank you so much."

"It's not me, Miss Miller. Your hard work and passion for these issues in class are the reasons I've chosen you. I look forward to working with you, should you take the internship." She reached out and Grace took her hand, shaking it and smiling, as happy as a child walking out of a Chuck E. Cheese. She turned and glided across the room as she exited. I am good enough, she thought. I am good enough. For the first time in a long time, she actually felt that way.

* * *

I could paint another scene telling you how Grace arrived back to their room and excitedly told Declan about her new opportunity. Or how Declan responded with venom back at her and her 'selfishness' for not thinking first how a decision to leave would affect those she loves. He lashed out at her going and leaving him and pointed out how it would affect her mother ("she will probably be killed by your dad while you're gone") or him ("I'll probably be tempted by a million other women who want to sleep with me") or their relationship in general ("There is no doubt the 'lesbo-prof' is going to get you under the sheets within days of the start of your journey").

But I'll save all that and just let you know that it was a destructive conversation. The type of conversation that should have finished off their relationship and kept them from ever seeing one another again. By the end of it, Grace left, drove to Maine, and walked York Beach for several hours.

* * *

As Grace met with her professor, Declan attended a political science course to fulfill his minor before he graduated.

He genuinely loved the class. His professor, Dr. Jack Reese, entertained and always shared a good story. Also, every Thursday Dr. Reese waxed eloquent on the topic of conspiracy theories. He was gathering evidence regarding the September 11th attacks. The evidence - even a professor talking about the topic at all - was controversial since everything was still fresh in everyone's minds. Dr. Reese didn't care, and Declan soaked the information in like a paper towel to water.

That Thursday morning, Reese's piece (as the students liked to call it) addressed the towers falling straight to the ground in much the same way that a controlled demolition might, rather than reacting to a plane hitting them from the outside.

Declan gravitated towards conspiracy theories and alternative truths. He didn't know whether or not he believed them, but he enjoyed taming the unknown and finding the truth behind the mystery. The hidden was not okay.

"Mr. Dumais? Are you ok?" Dr Reese interrupted Declan's thoughts with his slightly Canadien accent. "Because daydreaming in my class is not." Declan didn't mind. He liked the man paying attention to him.

"Oh no, sir. I'm simply processing your theory. I love this stuff. I'd take a whole course on this if it was offered, and you were willing to teach it." Declan smiled like he was channeling Eddie Haskel.

Dr. Reese smiled at the obvious suck-up and continued his lecture.

"As I was saying, several of the news stations covering that morning, including the one I was watching, ABC, commented that the falling buildings looked more like a controlled demolition, yet two planes... yes, two very large planes literally flew into two much larger buildings, then there was a pause, and then the buildings came crashing down... straight down... and to me it just looks questionable. It doesn't seem to me that a plane hitting the top half of the building could bring it straight down like that. We're talking 6,000,000 square feet of masonry, 5,000,000 square feet of painted surfaces, 7,000,000 square feet of flooring, 600,000 square feet of windows, two hundred elevators - and one plane brings the entire thing crashing down?

"Maybe it didn't. Maybe there was something else?" He paused for effect, walking behind his desk, head down as if only now thinking through these inconsistencies.

He continued finally, "Several hours later, a bit after 5:00 that afternoon, the World Trade Center's Building 7 came crashing down, as well. Researchers blamed that destruction - also reported as looking like a 'controlled demolition' - on falling debris from the north tower which started mini fires inside the smaller structure. The fires eventually led to its collapse.

"Problem: no one witnessed seeing, or called in any fires in that building prior to its fall. There are no 9-1-1 calls, no one running from its interior - granted some of this was because the building had been evacuated - and no one can verify why this building, home of the Secret Service and the CIA, went straight down...yes, in a controlled-demolition-like way.

"What does all of this tell us? Well, not much. We're still waiting on reports and such to let us know the scientific reasons why this or that happened, but one thing I do know: When it comes to what happened on September 11th last year, there is more than you know about how it happened, who made it happen, and even who it happened to. And why.

"Here is my point. Don't just see what you see on the news or hear what you hear on the radio and believe just because you saw someone or listened to someone talking about it. Question everything! Ask the hard questions. Verify. Talk to as many people as you can regarding the truth. Don't just trust. Don't just believe. Those whom you are trusting might be lying! I might be lying to you right now. Find out the truth. Take control of your own life. Faith is for lazy people who don't want to find out for themselves."

Declan started to get defensive in his mind, while still connecting with what Dr. Reese said. He simultaneously hated this particular 'Reese's Piece' and loved it. Declan wondered whether or not his professor was born into a similar background as himself. Oddly, the man continued with:

"When I was a child what did my parents tell me? What many of your parents told you, of course, that Santa was real, that he was jolly and every Christmas Eve he was coming to our chimney and bringing presents. They also told me that God created me, that there was a man named Jesus who was God, and that he gave his life for me so that I could go to heaven.

"As a boy, I didn't differentiate the stories. They were both real and they were both happening when I put my faith and trust in them. I believed!" The professor said in a preacher voice that caused laughter to erupt in the room. But Declan wasn't laughing. He tuned in and his head spun with the thoughts of his own childhood beliefs.

"Eventually," the professor continued, "They told me the truth. Or at least their version of it. There was no Santa. But there was a Jesus. And if I was a good boy, I would someday die and get some nice stuff from him like a mansion, pearly gates, and streets of gold! I mean, who wouldn't want to believe in that crap?

"But then, if you do believe, it's apparently a free gift. If you don't buy in by serving the church the way the leaders want you to, or giving your ten percent then maybe getting into heaven is still free, but it's possible you'll not be treated like a member of the family. It's all very strange."

As Dr. Reese uttered the last sentence, the class 'bell' rang, and most of the students stood quickly and began to exit the classroom.

"Quiz on the dynamic changes of the U.S. political parties in the early 1900's next Monday. Be ready for it."

Declan sat frozen to his seat with his head down, looking at the notes he took in these last five minutes. Anger and wonder filled his mind, but he had listened to this lecture and believed it. No, he agreed with Dr. Reese and committed to knowing everything there was to know about September 11th, Salvation, and who knew, maybe he'd even figure out political science along the way.

* * *

Following class, Declan walked to his dorm room and fought with Grace about her "opportunity" to spend the summer in London with her professor. The fight left him furious and ready to leave the dorm, but before he could, she stormed out, slamming the door behind her.

Oddly, it was this tension that united his heart to hers. When they passionately riled one another up, that moment when they came back together created an intensity he cherished for days. Her return was certain and when she did, things would be better than before.

Until then, however, he researched theories regarding the September 11th attacks on his desktop computer. For the next hour, Declan focused on this opportunity to research why and how the attacks happened. To him this conquest stood between truth and mystery. His desire to figure what was real drove him to research more, to screw around less, and to stay up till all hours of the night attempting to understand the "why's" that this new world of internet knowledge had to offer.

First of all, he jumped on websites of USA Today, the New York Times and CNN. Plenty of conversation around what everyone "knew," but there wasn't much about fringe theories.

Declan wasn't just going to look for the popular bits of research, but he'd find really smart people with really smart questions. He wanted to uncover the underground conversations everyone wanted to have but no one would because of the controversy around the discussion.

He tried Google, the relatively new search engine which seemed to be the rage lately. He decided to test it out, typing in "Conspiracy Theory 9-1-1" Hundreds of thousands of pages matched his search. Declan didn't have time to go through all of them, but he could click on some sites that clearly matched what he was trying to research.

For another hour, he found himself in research heaven, feverishly perusing through details and facts he hadn't known, and many other didn't want to know. Could any of these 'conspiracies' be true? Or perhaps the better question was 'could any of these things be verified?'

Two more hours passed and his eyes began to close. Declan stood up to get a beer in the fridge when he heard the sound of someone contacting him on Instant Messenger. He minimized his research websites until the only open screen was AIM labeled with his screen name Decdahallz111.

"Shit," he whispered, realizing he forgot to change his status to 'away'.

"Hey Declan!" The typed message read. He didn't recognize the screen name but he laughed when he read it - Sis4shine.

"Ok, I'll play along" Declan whispered, typed simply, "Hi," then ran to the fridge to grab that beer. On the way back, a response waited for him. Apparently this screen name wanted to chat.

"So how have you been?"

He typed, "Not bad. Just doing some studying. How have you been?" Declan hoped the question would help to illuminate the name of the person on the other end.

"A little bored. So tired of classes, and I can't wait for the summer. Can't wait to shed these clothes for something lighter :-/."

This overwhelmed Declan. Was that a suggestive line? He decided to continue the suggesting. "Yeah, I know right? At present I can only take my shirt off here in my room."

The pause in an Instant Messenger conversation in the early 2000's was not unlike the feeling of two people hanging in limbo on a date wondering if they are going to have their first kiss or not, minus being in the same room. Anticipation welled up inside Declan, waiting to see if this girl was hitting on him, and if so, what could it lead to?

Sometimes he grew tired of the fighting and the back and forth with Grace. Recently he pondered being with someone he could have fun with right now, instead of such a serious girlfriend. Maybe that person was right here in front of him. Besides, if Grace decided to go to London, she would leave him anyways. The message sound rung again.

"How are classes going for you?"

He smiled, realizing this was a smart girl. Playing the long game, apparently.

"They're good. I'll be graduating in May. Then I guess I'll go into "real life," lol."

"Oh, you're so lucky! I have two more years after this one. Wish I could be done already. I guess the only sad thing is I won't be able to see you anymore after this year."

She was hitting on him, and Declan liked how it felt.

"What makes you say that? Maybe I'll live around here. And we don't see each other at school that often now, right?" He was walking a fine line between trying to find out who she was and offending her. The latter might end his evening, and he didn't want to do that yet.

"No, we don't," the screen name replied. "You're always hanging around your gf."

Okay, this person knew him and Grace in some way, even if it was from afar. He needed to tread carefully because as far as he knew, this could be Grace, or his mom, or any number of people who were actually not flirting with him. He thought about where to take the conversation. Should he address Grace, and then move on, or just move past that conversation, ignoring her early comment?

"Well, we've both been pretty busy this last semester, so I haven't seen her much, tbh. What bout u? Have a bf?"

"No, not now. I had one last semester, but broke up with him. He wanted to settle down and I wanted to have some fun."

Declan's breath started to get heavy. At the same time, he also felt a little silly getting worked up over a stranger. For all he knew, it could be his friend Mark playing a prank.

He typed, "I could really use some fun in my life, S. Seems like all I'm ever doing is homework, research, or fighting w gf." That felt both honest in one sense and a continuation of what could be in another.

"I'd love to have some fun with you! I'm all alone in my room right now. Why don't you come by and say hello? We can go out and have some fun or stay in and do the same?"

"You have roommates?" Declan asked. This was getting real, and now he jumped deep past any line of common sense. If the person on the other end of this computer was anyone trying to trap him or screw with him, they fully succeeded. It wouldn't be a stretch to show this conversation to Grace and prove he hadn't crossed a line.

"I live alone. Woodside Apartments. You know where that is?"

"Yeah, it's right down the road from me." At first he typed 'us' and then changed it to me. Declan's heavy breathing felt so loud. This was not a wise decision, he knew, but he had a whole life ahead of him to make wise decisions. Tonight, he was going to go over to this girls house, get some of what she had, and feel good about it. Then he'd come back and break it off with Grace. He should do it the other way around, but his desire in this moment told him otherwise.

"My room number is 224. Second floor. We have a gatekeeper at the entrance who checks every person coming in. Ever since 911. I'll tell them I'm expecting you and they'll let you up."

"K. Thx. CUsoon"

Declan stood up and ran to the restroom, stripped off his clothes and jumped in the shower. He sang and mentally prepared for what he was about to do. He grabbed his towel after stopping the water and dried himself off. He put some deodorant on and practically skipped out of the bathroom. As he was putting on his boxers in the bedroom, he heard the front door open, and after a few seconds, Grace walked around the corner.

She looked down and then up at him and smiled with a slightly nervous yet excited look. He felt deflated and turned a slight shade of pink which Grace interpreted as either shower steam or anger.

"I'm sorry," she said. "There was no reason to treat you that way. You've been there for me for the last few years. I think we can have a polite discussion around this without me getting so defensive. You've got every right to ask questions about such an extensive trip." She took a tentative step towards him. "You are the love of my life. If you don't think it's a good idea for me to take the trip..." she paused, getting teary-eyed and silently begging him to change his mind.

He sat down in his boxers on the side of the bed with a towel draped over his shoulder. His thoughts raced like roves of people at Times Square on New Year's Eve. He thought about the night they met at the bar, their first time together, and the girl in room 224, waiting on him even now.

No. If they were going to be together, they were going to be together on his terms. He was the leader in their relationship. There wasn't a lot he agreed with his parents about, but of this he was sure: he loved complementarianism. He was the man, the leader in his home no matter how archaic the idea seemed to others.

"It's London or me." He said coldly. "Your call. Make it now. How much do you want us to be together?"

Dysfunctions

When you truly love someone or something, you will give up everything else to keep it. But what happens when you are giving up everything you've ever dreamed about for someone that manipulates you into doing it in order to keep them in your life? What happens when your whole life is altered by one decision you've made and you alienate anyone else who might help you make a better decision?

The reason this happens is a lack of trust. We respond to our ability to wait and choose and make wise decisions, by refusing to stand against the thick fear of the unknown. When we say "yes" to things, activities, and people in our lives whom we should say "no" to, we allow dysfunction to rule our lives.

March 28, 2011

Now

Apex Church had been bursting with life during the unseasonably warm Palm Sunday. The crowds had continued to grow and we continued to start more house churches. That morning the Dumais family walked into my house for the first time in almost a year.

Their faces glowed with happiness, especially compared to the last time I talked with them. Declan smiled and talked to a few people he knew while Grace ran over to Marie and I, hugging us and thanking us for being "amazing." She explained how she had registered for classes for the fall and that she couldn't be more excited about getting her Master's degree. The boys ran downstairs to the basement to play with the other kids.

Declan and Grace previously scheduled time with Marie and I after the day's gathering. When they first brought it up, I'd hesitated, not wanting our Palm Sunday to be demurred by the intensity of the conversation I was sure we would have.

In the beginning, however, everything seemed fine. Declan spoke highly of his wife, and Grace smiled more confidently than usual lately. After a few minutes of normal chit-chat, I decided to take a step toward deeper conversation.

"So you guys aren't here to talk about degrees and the usual small talk, right?" I leaned back just a bit more in the recliner and hoped Declan didn't notice. I took a sip of my coffee to look less defensive. "Marie and I want to know how you both are holding up, how you're healing through the hurt. What steps are you taking to ensure that what happened before won't happen again."

Declan filled the subsequent bough of silence. "OK, I'll start." He leaned forward from his perch on the couch, intertwining his fingers together and letting them hang between his knees. He looked at Grace a moment before continuing, "We seemed to have found some footing on hobbies and projects. But making those things happen at home will be really important."

"What do you mean?" I said, noticing Grace's old twitch slowly returning.

"For instance, continuing my research on the Flat Earth has been really good for me as a scientist through this mess..."

I did my best to keep from smirking at Declan calling himself a scientist, but Marie and Grace were less successful. Thankfully he took any humor at his expense in stride.

"As I was saying, this research has been very helpful to me personally, but what I've realized is that group I'd been in before had taken me as far as it could. Now I have another step in my research that I believe will change the scientific world forever."

Marie said, Oh really, what's that?" sounding surprised and still smirking a little bit.

"I can't get into that right now, but let me just use this word that will hopefully wet your appetites. Proof."

"Proof?" I said.

"Proof. And the best part is I can work on this at home in our garage. I've set it up so I don't have to leave our property."

"That certainly sounds interesting," I said. "What about you, Grace? How are you healing?"

Before Grace could speak, Declan interjected his opinion. "I think it's going to take time for both of us to heal from what we've been through. It's been a lot, but I know that with God we can do it."

Perhaps knowing how mad I was that Declan answered for Grace, Marie decided to step in. "Declan, I'm not sure why you decided to go ahead and answer when my husband asked Grace the question. This desire of yours for control tells me you have a long way to go when it comes to healing. Not to mention, your wording makes it sound like you both are at fault for your affair."

I took another sip of coffee and watched as she raised her hands before her in what I assumed was a placating gesture (as opposed to a warning for Declan not to interrupt). She continued, "I completely get that a marriage is a two way street. You've both got your issues, but the truth is you stepped outside of your marriage vows. You were unfaithful, so please don't make it appear like you both are complicit in the same amount of unfaithfulness. In the end, maybe you both are the cause of your problems, but seriously, the way you present it makes it seem like you are pushing away any responsibility."

Silence rippled through the room. Declan wanted to say something, but somehow understood the position he found himself in, so said nothing. He bowed his head and looked as uncomfortable as a Baptist preacher in a gay bar.

I nodded my head towards Grace again, and she understood I was asking her to answer the earlier question herself.

"Healing comes hard these days, honestly. Sometimes I love Declan. Most of the time I hate him...and what he did." Tears began falling down her face. I felt for both of them. The pain that night caused shockwaves through every part of their lives, but the worst of it was buried deeply inside Grace's soul. Short term betrayal looks like a small weapon but it can utterly destroy anything in its path. "I'm trying..." her voice trailed off.

I glanced at Marie, but my wife seemed to want to sit this part out. I leaned forward, coffee mug balanced before me in both hands. "So you've talked about your degree, Grace, and your science project, Declan. What about your time together? How much are you spending dating each other, trying to fall in love again?" I asked this knowing the answer, but really wanting to challenge them into thinking about it more.

After a minute of silence and obvious discomfort, Declan spoke. "We haven't spent a lot of time together. It's kind of a weird time, you know? I don't want to pressure her into it. And she's still healing through her thoughts. But I have a few ideas on that."

"Ideas?" I asked, interested in what Declan might say next.

"Yeah, I figured Grace and I could spend our first date night together going over a plan to schedule more date nights. Time together, time separate, time with the kids, you know? All those sorts of things."

"Are you kidding?" Marie said in a way that I almost thought she was joking.

"No, why do you ask that?"

"Your idea of healing is to plan more? To take control more?" She was clearly not enthused about his plan. There was even a touch of sarcasm she couldn't help but communicate in her tone.

"Yes." Declan answered. "Part of Grace's problem hinges on her inability to plan and organize things so she can be fruitful in her endeavors. Our family flourishes when she walks that line of organization with me. Then she..."

"So your affair with Amber happened because Grace wasn't organized?"

"Well, no...."

Grace wept softly into a tissue conveniently lodged in a box on the end table beside her.

"You kissed Amber outside of your car, while your wife watched. What part of her lack of organization could she improve so that won't happen again?"

Declan was clearly irritated when he began, "Marie..." but she interrupted a third time.

"Then you took her to her house, left your wife at home all night with your sons, and slept with some twenty-five year old who somehow believes your ridiculous theories? What does that have to do with Grace's organization? I guess that is what I'd like to know. Please help me understand."

"It is NOT A RIDICULOUS THEORY!!! YOU HAVE A SMALL MIND, AND DON'T UNDERSTAND THE THINGS OF GOD! That's what I know about you!" He stood up and walked to the side of the couch, turned back, took a step forward as if not sure if he should leave or spew more venom. He chose the latter. "I'm trying to save my marriage. I am trying to help my wife! And all you do is bring up the past! What are you? Perfect? Go ahead and cast the first stone, I don't care. I will organize my home. I will organize my Bible study! I will organize my wife, who yes, does struggle in this area. I have already said I'm sorry countless times to Grace, and here you are, trying to tear us apart!"

My wife hadn't blinked, nor moved in the slightest since Declan stood up. She was good that way. For my part, I pressed myself deeper into the back of the recliner, trying to look as calm as Marie.

"You said you're sorry," she said, "but are you actually sorry? Do you feel what you've done? Do you feel how much you've hurt her? Because if you did, organizing her life would be the least of your concerns." She seethed as she spoke. Declan's face turned red with rage, but he did not storm out. That would happen in a moment, of course, but for now, Marie wasn't done. She continued, though calmer. "I don't know how to tell you this Declan, but someone needs to. You have such enormous emotional issues. You try to fix your wife and come up with ideas for healing but really, those ideas are just ways she can fit into whatever outlandish version of life you want her to fit into. She's not your puppet. She is an amazing, gifted, smart, funny woman who loves you and her family and her God. But she is not you. So go ahead and organize. But you need to also understand her for who she is, appreciate her gifts. But, but but.... I don't know. You're so busy getting mad at people who call your Flat Earth theories "ridiculous" you can't see how hurt your wife is. It's why she can't touch you. It's why she can barely look at you, Declan. You both are going to need help, and you better lead the way in getting that help or your relationship is over. There will be no one else to blame but you. Grace seems to want healing, and I'll assume you do, too, but plans and organization so soon after the hurt and betrayal is not the way to make it happen. Unless it's the plans of someone with an outside perspective."

She looked at me only with her eyes but I merely shrugged. I had nothing to add. She was speaking truth. At this point Marie had calmed down enough to communicate some more points about love and sacrifice and healing and I could only hope Declan received them from his standing perch beside the couch in the way they were intended: A teaching moment. Unfortunately, it didn't take long to understand that, while Grace may have appreciated what Marie vocalized, the words hit Declan's ears and heart much differently. The red on his face only brightened. Finally, he looked down at his wife and mouthed the words "Let's go." Then he grabbed his coat and walked to the basement door where he yelled to the kids that it was time to leave.

"Thank you both for your time," he muttered, half turned towards us. "Grace and I will continue to work hard and fight for our marriage. Have a good day." He walked out the door with the boys.

Grace's eyes were still wet from the earlier tears. "I'm sorry, guys," she barely got out before the tears began again. We both stood up and hugged her, telling her we were always there for her. She walked out with her head down, scratching up and down her arms.

* * *

A cool breeze turned into rain a few hours later so Declan hunkered down in the garage and accomplished plans to prove "Flat Earth."

He sat in the middle of his newly designed garage office, staring at the two whiteboards and the large map he had placed on the walls. Walking over to the laptop that sat in front of the map, he Googled "Airports in Chile," then clicked on images.

Pictures of the country of Chile appeared with twenty airports in the results. He assumed most of them were not major, so a good deal of planning needed to be done in order to ensure the best possible outcome.

Declan asked himself whether or not to fly solo with all this or build a team of people, starting with a pilot. He didn't know how to fly any kind of plane, let alone one that might hold enough fuel to cross where NASA's fictitious ocean laid between Antarctica and Australia and New Zealand. He needed to fly there, to that point, to prove there was only land and not ocean. Then he could turn around, drop the plane off at a nearby, smaller airport and hide in whatever jungle might be around there. Of course he needed to also plan for parachuting out before the Chilean Air Force shot him down. Unfortunately they shared runways with the specific airport he'd decided to begin his quest.

He thought through this dynamic, staring at the work he'd accomplished a few nights earlier, planning and organizing the life of his family. Maybe Marie didn't appreciate the hard work he put in to help Grace get better at life, but he didn't care. He loved Grace. Sure she had issues and things to work on, but after all they'd gone through, he loved her and loved their marriage. So, he organized and planned for her. It wasn't about control, as Marie assumed. Declan's planning always centered around helping her thrive in their household. He used his strengths for her benefit.

After he processed this for a while, he searched online for a pilot to help him accomplish the tasks ahead. It needed to be someone who believed in the mission because he wouldn't be able to himself. It also had to be someone he trusted.

Until recently Declan had avoided joining that website, Facebook, though most of his friends and family had been on it for some time. Against his own judgement he'd finally created an account. Now that he had 1100 of his "friends," both old and new, he wondered if any of them dabbled in the flight industry. He searched the list using the word "Pilot." Several faces came up, but most were not actual friends. Probably spambots.

He repeated the search in the general population. Many more this time but one, near the top, looked familiar. He clicked on the profile of a man named Ronnie Cable. He and Ronnie happened to have several mutual friends, so Declan took a chance and requested a friendship. He searched the man's profile. Ronnie had attended the same elementary school growing up, and though Declan didn't think they ever met in person, this could be a good connecting point between the two men.

He continued reading. Apparently Ronnie plastered his page with anti-establishment posters and self-quotes shared with the world how much he hated authority. Ronnie also flew as a pilot in the Air Force for several years. Declan thought maybe his disdain for superiors was the reason he no longer hung with the armed forces. He wrote Ronnie a message via Facebook asking about his experience in the armed forces, and over the next few weeks they carried on a back and forth about various conspiracy theories which Declan had studied in the past. All of these were hooks with which Declan slowly reeled the guy into his circle. They finally decided to grab some dinner and talk in person soon.

Meanwhile, Declan continued to think through the How. Any meeting with Ronnie or anyone else would involve sharing his plans. He needed definite answers to their questions, and the more organized and thought out those answers were, the more likely people would be to join him.

So the first how was, How and where would he travel? Currently the plan was to fly from Boston to Punta Arenas, Chile, in the region of Magadellas, hijack a plane and fly south towards Australia. The team would have to fly due south over Antarctica which, according to Google Earth, lay directly between Chile and Australia. If the Earth looked like what Google Earth and the other NASA propagandists said it looked like, then they should be able to fly roughly 4500 miles across the Drake Passage and Antarctica before they saw the ocean again. If the ocean appeared after 4500 miles, and it really was an ocean and not some large lake in the Antarctic, then Declan would be proven wrong and all of this research and theorizing would be for naught. The team would continue on to Australia, dump the plane somewhere while they parachuted out of it, and make their way back home. Somehow. That was a question for another time.

However, if they flew 5000 miles and were still looking at land, then they would have definitive proof there was no way to fly "across" Antarctica, because Antarctica was literally the end of the world. Of course, they might also reach the end, see the Earth simply stop. What would happen then, neither Declan nor anyone else knew. His arms filled with goose bumps. If this was indeed the outcome, then all kinds of problems needed to be solved. Chief among them was a way to communicate the research findings to the world at large. And defying -or accepting - the consequences that came with their actions.

This dream kept him up at night. He envisioned reporters knocking on his door, begging him for interviews, politicians calling on him with the possibility of changing the name of the continent. A lot would shift when word got out that the seventh continent was not a mid sized piece of island, but actually wrapped around the entire circumference of the tabled Earth. "Antarcdeclan" struggled to have the smoothness of the originals name, but someone, somewhere could craft a beautiful bumper sticker (or Tweet, whatever that was) name for the colossal ring that circled Earth. He smiled to himself, then shook his head a few times, attempting to refocus on the goal. He must buckle down and work harder than ever to accomplish his mission. After all, as Robert Burns wrote, "The best laid plans of mice and men often go awry."

* * *

Grace knocked at the garage door a few hours later. She didn't know why she knocked, but each time she brought Declan's food to him while he persevered in the garage, she voluntarily warned him of her presence. He seemed to appreciate it.

Tonight's meal showcased grilled salmon marinated with a balsamic vinegar base, a cup of cooked rice and lightly oiled asparagus, also grilled. Grace proudly served Declan using a large round tray, two plates, and two glasses of Oak Aged Chardonnay, a white wine she bought just for this evening. Touching Declan was going to be difficult the first time after his affair, but she wanted to do it soon. Time ticked by and she didn't want to be held in bondage by feelings of bitterness to the one person in her life she promised to love forever.

"Hey babe," she smiled walking in with dinner. She hoped that made him happy. "Dinner is served, and oh my, it is going to be so good. The kids are playing happily in the basement. I told them not to bother us, either."

"Cool," Declan responded without paying attention. Then he looked up. "What's up? Are we eating here?"

Trying not to be offended at his ignoring her, she answered him slowly. "Um, yes. We are, like I just told you. "

He didn't respond but went back to studying Google Earth on his laptop. She perused the flat Earth map on the wall Declan faced, then turned her attention to the two whiteboards. On the wall opposite of the garage door hung what he'd titled, via a dry erase marker, "Flat Earth Plans." She didn't want to look at it in depth. As smart as she knew her husband to be, she couldn't fathom what possessed him to believe in such a silly idea.

Then she closed her eyes and tried harder to understand his desire to do the things he did, to believe any of the things he believed about himself or the world around him. Certainly he had potential to be a good guy who loved others and wanted to do the right thing, but something always stood in the way - a deeper desire to control everything, including her. And she was constantly willing to let him, but now it had to stop. She had to be her own person.

That was her exact thought when she moved her head left to the other whiteboard marked, "Grace." She wondered why she hadn't seen her name before, but the letters looked smaller than the other title. This board lit up with bright red tables filled with schedules and time plans. After scanning its entirety for the next few minutes, she realized Declan had created its contents specifically for her. The items within the spreadsheets were not for the family or the boys, but a tool Declan made for her.

"What the hell is this?" Grace bluntly asked. Declan looked up from his laptop and smiled.

"Oh, that's just some plans I drew up so you can be better organized in school, and as a mother and such."

"And where are your plans? The ones you drew up for you?"

Declan knew Grace would be upset about the board, and was prepared to answer, calmly. "There's no reason to be pissed. I'm more organized so I built some plans to help you in that area. I'm sure you could probably fill up that board telling me all the things I need to get better in my interpersonal relationships." He smiled in a way that actually gave Grace a reason to be pissed off. She grabbed the whiteboard eraser and began making the bright red letters invisible. After the board was white again, she picked up the red marker and wrote:

The Earth is effing round. I love you!

She didn't write effing.

Then she walked out with the wine, leaving the food to get cold in the garage office.

Addictions

Even so, Grace pressed into their relationship even more than before. She started saying things like, "I would die without you" or "Please don't ever leave me," and when she would, it would make Declan feel much closer to her.

The thing about unhealthy living, addiction, or codependency is that these things feel just as good for a time as being free or living a healthy lifestyle, except they are much more difficult to sustain.

Take me for instance. I have two problems (that I'm willing to share with you at the moment). First, I have a soda addiction. I love it so much! People ask me all the time what kind of soda is my favorite, and I tell them "whatever kind has bubbles." Morning, Midday, or evening, I will drink soda, and do so without hesitation.

A second problem I have is an addiction to socializing. As a pastor, I'm around people all the time. Even then, it's just not enough. I want to be with people non-stop, but the problem is, my wife does not. This tends to be a source of conflict in our marriage.

Anyway, these addictions to soda and socializing ultimately connect in this way: I believe that by partaking in these potentially destructive habits, I am closer to a happy life. I fundamentally understand that this is not true in the long term, but in the short term, I "need" to drink the drink or talk to people about weather and sports not because they are good for me, but because my brain communicates to me that they fulfill me. The same lie perpetuates all of our brains to some degree. Depending on the 'what,' it can be quite destructive.

Ted Bundy claimed in interviews while on death row that his pornography addiction started out simply as, "soft core pornography." Then his cravings demanded more for himself, and more became increasingly violent forms of porn. "Like an addiction," Bundy said, "you keep craving something harder, which gives you a greater sense of excitement, until you reach a point where the pornography doesn't go far enough."

I have little interest in comparing Declan and Grace to Ted Bundy, but certainly all of our addictions have a tendency to make us murderers of some sort, whether it be the killing of our healthy state of mind, relationships, or physical bodies.

Here's the way I look at it: Deciding not to engage in an addiction and not letting anything or anyone make you its slave, is a form of trust. Another word for trust is faith. Having faith that freedom is found in not letting anything enslave you is called self-discipline or self-control. As you exercise self-control, you grow closer to the freedom you were created to live in by your Creator.

February 1, 2001

Then

Declan and Grace sat quietly on the couch watching a new show called 24. Declan started watching it two weeks ago and begged Grace to join him at his place for the third "hour" of the show. She obliged, if he made love to her first. He happily succumbed to her demands.

As the episode began, the phone rang. Grace answered and her mother, hysterical on the other end of the line, was screaming.

"Mom!" Grace pulled the phone back from her ear because of the volume of Nancy's wailing. "Calm down. What's wrong?"

"It's... It's... It's your father. He's trying to kill me. He's completely drunk. I already hit him on the head once with a pan, and he keeps trying to come at me. I'm locked in the bedroom! Help me, Grace!"

Declan paused the TiVo.

"Mom, call 9-1-1. Now! I'll be there in an hour." She felt helpless even as she said it.

Having heard part of the conversation Declan had already jumped up, grabbed his keys and to the car. He turned the dusty Ford Probe engine over. Grace followed close behind and jumped in the passenger seat. She breathed heavy, her heart feeling like it was exploding out of her chest.

As he drove, Declan reached out and grabbed her hand. He reassured her everything would be fine. Not wanting to say anything stressful, both of them drove to Keene without saying another word.

Though she didn't intentionally ignore her daughter, Nancy never called 9-1-1. Instead she continued to move pieces of furniture in front of Grace's bedroom door. First she locked the door, and every time Ed hit it in anger, she expected it to come crashing down. Nancy scooted Grace's bureau a few feet sideways to also cover the door.

In his intoxicated state, her husband heard the movement and screamed that he would, "get in there and beat the life out of you!"

A few hours earlier, she'd sat alone in their rundown mobile home and watched Wheel of Fortune, a weekday ritual. Pat Sajak introduced the show and Vanna White looked like Vanna White had every weeknight since September of 1983.

As the actual competition began, a car pulled up the driveway. The walls of the home were thin enough she often cringed at the sound of animals walking outside. Nancy knew the car was Ed's. She was particularly nervous about tonight since John had decided to stay at a friend's house. When she and Ed were alone in the house, he took liberties he normally did not. Not that he didn't do damage when the kids were home, too.

She sat glued to the television as he walked loudly down the sidewalk, talking and swearing to himself about the patches of ice that crunched as his feet stepped on them. The door opened, and he walked in without acknowledging her presence on the couch. Ed dropped his coat on a chair in the corner of the living room, turned around, put his hands on his hips, and sighed as if he were thinking how long of a day it had been. He walked over to the television and shut it off without fanfare.

"Why the hell do you have that on so loud?" He grunted once as he walked by where she sat and moved into the bathroom, shutting the door loudly.

Nancy knew better than to turn the television back on. This exact scene had happened once before a few years prior. Then, after she'd turned it back on he'd come out and slapped her across the face to "show her lazy ass a lesson she deserved." Now she sat quietly and didn't move.

He exited the bathroom and stared at her, daring her to make a sound or look at him funny. The silence felt like an eternity. Nancy assumed Ed was drinking that afternoon. He took a right out of the bathroom and made his way to the kitchen. If he hadn't had a drink tonight, he was certainly opening up a beer now.

She spoke from one room to the next. "Dinner is in the stove. It's ready. Just warming now."

"Well, get it ready, and I'll eat! I'm tired. Had a long day. Haven't had the opportunity to sit on my butt and watch game shows and soaps like you."

Nancy learned a long time ago to not respond to Ed's accusations. Any past retorts about doing the laundry and cleaning the home and picking up after their kids usually resulted in physical damage. Instead she stood, walked slowly into the kitchen and around her husband, reached for the oven handle and opened the door to grab the food.

But there was no food in the oven.

Nancy pulled out a satin-stained Smith and Wesson 629, .44 Special. When Ed turned around from opening up his Coors, he came face to face with Nancy's new self-defense machine.

She spoke slowly, yet with a tremor that showed her struggle with confrontation. "I want you. Out of this house. Now. And if you lay a hand on me in the process. I. Will. kill you. You have tortured, insulted, abused, crushed, embarrassed, and turned me into nothing. We are done. Get out."

Ed smiled as if this was a game and he was about to win.

He turned around and picked up his beer again, took a long sip. Then he gulped and smacked his mouth and let out a long drawn out sigh that made Nancy nervous. "I suggest you get that gun away from me. If I get my hands on it, Grace and John will be attending your funeral by the end of the week, and then what? What for? Is this worth them not having a momma?"

Quickly and without thinking much about what she was doing Nancy picked up a huge black and rusty frying pan from the stove and, with all her one handed might, swung it towards Ed's head. It connected like Rocky hit to Ivan Drago in round twelve of the fourth installment.

Ed fell immediately to the floor, hitting a wooden chair with the other side of his face on the way down. His stunned body sprawled across the floor. Blood from the initial wound poured out, trickling along the floor toward his red-faced wife. Nancy stood shocked, not knowing what to do next but not wanting to wait around for her husband to wake up - if he was going to wake up.

He was not going to leave the house now, so Nancy quickly moved towards her bedroom to pack a bag and leave. Her hands shook wildly as she picked up each piece of clothing – enough for one night away, she could come back later to get the rest of her stuff and leave Ed for good, their marriage was finished long before today and like a butterfly out of its cocoon, she was stepping out of what was already dead - and placed everything inside of her small flowered print suitcase. She often laughed thinking of how ugly the suitcase was, but how handy it was when a thousand black suitcases came strolling out of the conveyor belt at the airport. Hers was always so recognizable. Movement from the other room. She moved quietly out through her living room and towards the kitchen. Did his finger just move? Time seemed to circle the clock like Edwin Moses at the Olympics while she pondered what to do next.

After grabbing a couple of plastic tubs of leftovers, for no reason she could rationally explain, she returned to the bedroom to grab a few more things. Nancy looked at the gun sitting on her bureau. To her, it was scarier than it was beautiful. She'd bought it from Malooly Gun Dealers, a gun store on the other side of Keene. She'd passed the background check, though Tim, the store's owner, wondered out loud why she wanted one. "Self-defense," she sputtered, nervous about why he'd ask. "I'm outside a lot at night after work," then she stopped talking about it, for fear that she already said too much.

Lost in her thoughts, Nancy suddenly heard a roar of anger coming from the kitchen. If he'd been standing, it would have taken him six seconds to get to this bedroom from where she left him. She shuffled to the door quickly and slammed it shut seconds before the other side boomed with Ed's hand slapping it with such incredible force.

By the time Declan and Grace drove into the gravel driveway of the Miller-Mobile, as her brother John called it growing up, Ed had vaulted himself into the door one final time, crashing the bureau and everything on top of it to the ground. His shoulder broke with the last heave, but his anger pulled him off the floor and over to a cowering Nancy, who wept in the corner.

He yelled, "You bitch! You're dead!"

Blood still poured from his head. He could barely move his right side. He looked briefly in that direction and saw the gun resting on the desk in the opposite corner from his wife.

He took two steps to the desk, picked up the shiny steel revolver, pointed it, pulled the trigger once. Nothing. Then again. Still nothing.

Nancy yelled out. "I didn't load it!" Tears poured down her face.

"Of course not," he slurred. "That's why you hit me. But you should have loaded it and you should have killed me, because now... Now you'll die."

He flipped the gun around in his left hand, which was still strong enough to do damage to her face. As he moved toward her, he whispered, "You're dead." He lifted the gun and began to bring it down when Declan leaped across the room and unknowingly destroyed the rest of his right arm, catapulting Ed into the wall next to Nancy. Grace rushed to her mother and gently pulled her up.

Untouched, Nancy stood quickly and scooted across the room with her daughter leading her from the house and into the car idling down the walk.

Declan tried to keep Ed down, but the pain and anger of the man kept him from being calm. As Ed stood up, Declan begged him to stay down until the police arrived. Hearing the police were called only agitated Ed more and he charged at Declan, who then delivered a blow his future father-in-law's jaw that sent him backwards as powerfully as he'd vaulted himself forward. Lost in a sudden fury, Declan leaped towards him and hit him a second time in the chest, and then a third time in the face.

When Grace returned from the car, she found Declan beating the life out of her father. Blow by blow Declan's fists crashed down as Grace rushed over to stop him. Her father no longer struggled or fought back.

She finally succeeded in stopping Declan, but it was clear the job was done. Grace bawled at her father's mangled face on top of everything else that had gone wrong that evening.

When the police arrived, they called an ambulance to transport Ed to the hospital. They believed the coinciding stories of the remaining three people involved, mainly because it wasn't the first spousal abuse call they'd responded to at this address.

April 4, 2011

Now

Ronnie Cable was interested in talking further about the Flat Earth theory.

Declan excitedly called him and they talked for an hour, promising to get

together in the Garage office over the next weekend.

Declan immediately liked Ronnie, whose potty mouth, poor

hygiene and dry humor made him laugh whenever he so much as made a

sound. From their first conversation at the office when Ronnie walked in,

made a b-line to an empty bucket in the corner, and acted like he was

going to urinate inside of it, each move and sound created laughter.

Ronnie arrived at Declan's house each afternoon after he got off-

shift and they studied the various "hows" of the project. They freakishly

planned every detail without actually being at their target site, and divided

up areas of research they needed to do. One of the early self-given

assignments they accepted was the need for a third team member.

Declan felt they were going to need more fire power as well, since

they were hijacking a plane at an international airport, and one shared by

the Chilean Air Force. Ronnie, of course, would be the pilot, ensuring that

the plane could get off the ground. Declan's job was to smuggle guns and

run interference for Ronnie as he snuck himself into the pilot entrance of one of the hangers. But as they talked through the plans, Declan wanted one more person proficient in firearms. Initially, Ronnie disagreed, citing a third member added additional opportunities for the plan to go south. After more conversation on the topic, Declan gave himself a new task.

Ronnie's job was to scout and study the airport from its web site, google Earth, Google Maps, YouTube and any other technologies necessary to get an overall picture of what accomplishing their goal might look like. Though from an outside perspective he didn't look like someone who championed technology, his pilot's license and high powered computer, which he moved into the Garage office, confirmed otherwise.

Now the team had Declan's leadership, Ronnie's brains, and needed to find a skilled weapons specialist to pack some major heat.

* * *

Declan thought through old school friends and co-workers, but no one came to mind when finding a third member of his team. Ronnie was the perfect guy for his role, but this next acquisition was going to need to be better than perfect. He took an inventory of just about everyone he knew, but he already understood who the best man for the job was - and fully expected him to refuse.

Declan clicked on his email and wrote out a message similar to the one he wrote Ronnie a few weeks before. If he responded, Adam, his old "FEG" friend, could carry out their plans. Of course he might also kill Declan for reaching out in the first place, but sacrifices needed to be made.

To his surprise, Adam responded to the email shortly after Declan sent it, and agreed to meet at Osaka's restaurant in White City, Shrewsbury the following Thursday at 9:00 pm. Declan immediately told Ronnie, and they discussed what it might take to convince Adam to accept the mission.

In Declan's mind, it wouldn't take much to convince him of its importance because of his desire to see Flat Earth Theory proven. The harder part would be to convince Adam to work with him, for he'd made it quite clear he didn't want to see Declan anymore.

On Thursday evening, Declan drove to the restaurant and arrived early to mentally prepare for the meeting. He knew Adam wouldn't be early because of FEG, so he walked in and was seated by a hostess. He asked for a two person table instead of the hibachi grill where the chef squirts oil at an onion tower to make it flame.

Exactly at 9:00 pm, Adam walked in, saw Declan, and moved toward the table. As usual, Declan couldn't read Adam's face so he just smiled, stood up, and shook the man's hand. Adam reciprocated the handshake, then started the conversation as he sat at the table.

"Ok Dec, your email grabbed my attention, and as luck or time would have it, I am not so spiteful of you right now as I had been. So here I am. Shoot straight with me about what you want. If you lie to me, or if I think you're playing me, I'll either stand up, walk out and go home, or I'll do those things, then wait for you to do the same and kill you." He didn't smile when he said it, so Declan couldn't tell if he was joking. With Adam, he found it best to not assume a joke.

"Ok, Adam. Thanks for coming. I've been creating a plan to prove the Flat Earth Theory. I'm building a team of three people - for obvious reasons we have to keep it small - that will fly to the tip of South America, get on a plane in Punta Arenas, Chile..."

"It won't work," Adam interrupted. "That airport shares runways with the Chilean Air Force."

Declan continued, holding his hands out to Adam as if asking to hear him out. "...then commandeer a plane – safely, with much planning ahead of time, of course - in Punta Arenas, Chile, where we fly south at least 5000 miles over Antarctica and towards Australia, at least according to the popular view of the world. If we fly the 5000 miles and Antarctica is still underneath us, we will return home, probably as fugitives if our plan is successful, imprisoned if we get caught. Either way though, we will send our information back to someone here who can then share our findings as soon as they are received."

"Unless you're shot down."

"If I'm not shot down first, yes," Declan retorted. Honesty was the only way he could hope to deal with this man. And optimism. "But I don't see that happening. Not if we can get over Antarctica quick enough."

"Faster than 2 or more F-16's?" Adam's tone remained matter-of-fact.

"Proper planning will help some of those details, but I'm not looking at doing this tomorrow. I want a successful mission that brings down the machine of lies we have been fed for decades. At the other end of this, our names will be in the science and history books, and what we know as a society will look so much different. I think that's worth the risk. Of course we've talked about this in the past, but this puts actions to our words. Wouldn't you want to be a part of changing the face of what truth looks like to millions and millions of people?"

Adam stared out the window towards the White City parking lot in silence. Declan knew he didn't trust him, but he would connect with him on their common belief. Adam's younger self would likely have jumped at this opportunity to do so much good for the world, but now, at the age of fifty-eight, it likely seemed like a crazy endeavor. Yet his age could prove to be a tremendous advantage. Not even the Chilean Air Force could foresee a fifty-eight year old man coming to break down their systems.

"What would I be doing?" He finally said. "Why do you need me?"

"Because of your background, you would be the 'gunsmith' of the group. Your focus would be figuring out a way to get the necessary weapons where we need them at the airport. Also, as we plan, we need your intel experience to make sure we don't walk into something dangerous with our eyes closed."

More silence. More staring. More questioning in Adam's mind. At least Declan assumed this. Again, Adam was not an easy read. Ninety seconds later, Adam stood up. A quick shot of disappointment ran through Declan's chest until Adam said, "I'll call you in two days and let you know. Have dinner on me."

He threw a $50 bill on the table. Declan smiled, knowing this man wouldn't be able to resist the mission. The gang would be complete. This time next week, planning would begin.

He caught the eye of the waitress after Adam has left the restaurant. "Miss, could I get my dinner to go?"

Struggles

In life, those who wrestle with something or someone generally grow as a result of their match, whether actual or metaphorical. In the Hebrew Scriptures, Jacob, one of the patriarchal Jewish fathers, wrestles with a stranger who turns out to be God. Jacob and the stranger wrestle (Scripture doesn't give a specific reason for their bout), and after a long night of Wrestlemania, the stranger blesses Jacob, changes his name to Israel, and leaves him with a hip injury.

I don't tell this story because I am a pastor, but because I like the idea of wrestling with something. Some crazy stuff has happened to me. But wrestling with life and with relationships can be some of the hardest yet rewarding experiences of growth anyone can have.

In the 80's I always loved the World Wrestling Federation, commonly known as WWF. The WWF is as much about acting as it is about wrestling, but sometimes in our everyday wrestling matches, we rely on our acting skills to get us through how we really feel on the inside. We can be amazing wrestlers on the outside, but in our minds, we struggle to get through each excruciating three minute round.

The problem with spiritual people today is they don't want to wrestle with anything. They want everything to be easy. Consequently, they struggle with their faith as much as any atheist.

December 12, 1999

Then

Declan and Grace continued their struggling relationship through their sophomore year of college. Unbeknownst to their families, they requested to be roommates. Declan's wrestling career launched in the fall of his freshman year, and did so quite successfully. Win after win pushed him to become a better wrestler, to work harder for the next victory. As he did, Grace worked that much harder at getting his attention. His presence became more elusive, except when she spent time with anyone else.

One night in early December, Steph and Stephie, who hadn't spent much time with Grace that semester, called to invite her for some Christmas shopping. At first she declined, citing an abundance of studying before finals, but after some insistence on the part of her best friends, she gave in, and made plans to go while Declan was at practice.

"Who was that?" Declan said, putting on his sweats.

"It was the girlies. Steph and Stephie. I'm going shopping with them tonight. I hope you have a great practice." She leaned over and kissed him on the cheek. "Knock 'em dead, baby."

Declan didn't hide his frustration. "Why do you do this to me?"

"I'm sorry, baby," Grace said quickly, reflexively rubbing her arms. "What did I do?"

"My practice isn't going to go all night. You're studying all the time, and I have practice, and we don't see each other anymore. I thought you wanted to be with me."

"Declan, come on, that's not fair," Grace said. "I just... I haven't seen my friends in a long time. And I love how they have such a good relationship with you. Don't forget they were part of the reason we met, right? They practically dragged me to the Thirsty Moose that night." Silence filled the air as Grace rocked anxiously back and forth waiting for Declan to answer.

He stood up, grabbed his duffel bag, and stormed out of the room without saying another word.

* * *

If Steph and Stephie were angry about their inability to see Grace for the last six months, their eyes and arms never let on as they beamed when they saw her and embraced her like a father to a long lost prodigal son.

As they talked, it became clear that Grace's leadership the year before gave them more excitement in life than they seemed to have at present. Walking in and out of stores, they talked about classes and boyfriends and the newest makeup products available. No stories of reckless adventures or embarrassing mistakes. Eventually they moved to a Chili's in the mall, all of them talking non-stop as they took their seats.

Grace basked in the moments her best friends talked about their lives. They left little opportunity for her to interject something about her life, but this offered a reprieve to how she had felt over the last few months. She knew something was wrong with her relationship with Declan, but as if he intuited how she felt, he inevitably would change his tone for a time and do something sweet to help her remember why she couldn't be away from him.

But tonight she sat with her two best friends in the world and felt calm and loved, yet also like a stranger. She found herself so lost in her thoughts, Grace didn't hear the question that came at her suddenly.

"What are all those scratches on your arm, Grace?" repeated Stephie.

Seconds felt like minutes as Grace thought about how to answer this question. It made the air feel as heavy as the weight Declan claimed to lift each morning.

"It's nothing." She said slowly, not wanting to sound guilty. She pulled the sleeves of her shirt down so the object of attention disappeared.

"You can talk to us, you know." Steph said, reaching out to hold Grace's hand. The moment was awkward. Grace would never be able to confront anyone like that, and being on this side of it felt no better.

Of her two friends, Stephie usually had the most to say but in terms of content, usually played in the shallow end. "Did Declan do that to y...?"

Steph quickly interrupted her. "No he didn't. Not directly anyway. How long has it been going on, Grace?"

"I'm sorry, guys. I don't want this night to be about me and my problems. I'm having a great time. I need it to be fun. I need it to be normal. Let's not ruin it."

"If you're hurting yourself, Grace, then we need to confront it. We're your friends. We're here for you. Through shopping..." she paused, trying to navigate her words carefully, "and through dysfunctional relationship problems. We don't see you anymore. And you know, I get it, relationships take time and you have to spend time with that person. But I also know that they don't or they shouldn't cause you to do that to yourself." She pointed to Grace's sleeve. "You're too important. Not just to us, but everyone in your life."

"It's not my dysfunctional relationship causing it. It's me. I'm so stupid. I can't do anything right, and I'm trying. I'm really trying." Her voice trailed off as she thought about her earlier conversation with Declan.

Steph persisted with this line of questioning, trying to be as grace-filled as possible. "Grace, you're not stupid. You do plenty of things right. And you should never be made to feel like you're some sort of failure. Especially to the point of..." She paused and looked again at Grace's arms. She continued softly, "...of you doing that."

Stephie, who had been texting throughout the evening and listening half-heartedly to the latest part of the evening's conversation, chimed in. "I think it's time for some nachos. I'm dying for some chips and queso."

Steph and Grace stared at one another, not really knowing where to go next in the conversation when the waiter stepped forward.

"What can I start you beautiful girls off with?" He said. His muscles ripped out of his Chili's t-shirt as he pulled a pen out of his back pocket and placed it naturally onto the pad of paper in his other hand.

Stephie quickly quipped, "I have a few thoughts on that, but you're working so we can always get to it later." The other girls laughed, though they were not surprised, as things like this tended to come out of her mouth.

The waiter, clearly flattered, wasn't about to let the opportunity slip by when he responded, "Good thing I don't work a late shift then. I'm off at nine," he smirked while acting as if he was writing some earlier order down on his pad.

"Good thing I'm available at nine then," Stephie answered back. The rest of the table roared with laughter. Everyone knew no one was kidding. The waiter looked straight into her eyes and said, "Nine it is, then. Here's my number." He ripped off the piece of paper and continued, "Now, what would you like to eat tonight?"

The girls laughed again, then ordered appetizers and drinks. At that moment, Declan walked up to their table and sat next to Grace, nearly pushing the waiter aside.

A heavy air rolled over the table and Steph noticed Grace rubbing her arms. The waiter, having finished the order strolled away confidently.

"What are you doing here, Dec?" Grace said, and then lowering her voice, said softly, "How did you know I was here?"

Steph and Stephie glared at the intruder.

"You told me you'd be here, remember?" He said it so confidently, she believed him at once, though it was Stephie who'd suggested coming to dinner here after they'd shopped.

He said, "After practice I made this amazing dinner. I just noticed you were only ordering apps, so why don't you come home and we can have dinner together? You guys have been hanging out for a few hours now, right?"

No one spoke. After the initial shock wore off, however, Steph said, "What the hell, Declan? Get out of here! We're hanging out right now, and Grace isn't your property. She'll come home when she's good and ready!"

"Wow." Declan countered. "I didn't know she was your property either, Steph. Can't a guy invite his girl to dinner without getting accosted?"

The waiter, having heard the commotion, stepped in and stared straight at Stephie. "Everything okay here?"

Knowing this was getting out of hand, Grace whispered to the group, but mostly to Declan with her head down, "It's ok. I'm tired anyways. Let's go Declan. Let's go home." She scooted out of the booth behind him and he helped put on her coat.

Steph stood up and grabbed Grace away from Declan for a deep embrace. She whispered to her, "You don't have to go, Grace. Stay with us. Come stay with us tonight, too. Please," she begged in a hushed tone and squeezing her shoulders a little too hard.

"I love you, Steph," Grace responded and looked back at her friend with empty eyes. "Love you, Stephie. Thanks for a great night." She walked away, holding the arm of her boyfriend.

***

Declan's wrestling season kicked off a few month later, and Grace filled her time with more of the things she wanted to do like working on school projects and applying for internships which focused on her major. After initially deciding to go into the nursing program, she's changed to the field of Public Health. She loved the idea of making a change for the greater good, especially in families where there was a breakdown in "normal" family values.

Heading into March, Declan obsessed about end of the year tournaments and, hopefully, getting an NCAA championship ring. He didn't eat anything that might raise his weight class, obsessively running and lifting weights. He ignored virtually everything Grace said, whether she wanted a serious conversation or simply asked how his day was going. Steph and Stephie called a few times, but Grace felt so awkward about their last exchange that she never responded.

The weekend of the NCAA Wrestling Tournament, Declan's expectations soared. His single goal was to win in the one hundred twenty-five pound weight class, but his emotions were out of whack. He talked to himself constantly, made himself throw up everything he ate, and wore a trash bag every time he stepped foot into the apartment to shed any weight he might have put on in the weight room.

This year the championships were held at Worcester Polytechnic Institute in Worcester, Massachusetts. The bus parked next to the gymnasium. A huge banner read "NCAA I-AA Wrestling Championship Here This Weekend". The motto for the event ran in smaller letters along the bottom: "Tap out or pass out. The choice is yours."

Declan walked slowly toward the sign with his headphones, his head filled with Jay Z's "Where I'm from," imagining himself dominating his first opponent, feeling the air across his raised arms as the ref pronounced him champion, the crowd screaming with excitement as he became the fan favorite over subsequent matches. There was no doubt, this weekend was going to be his weekend. His dream of being a champion clearly on the horizon.

Declan opened the door and walked into the gymnasium lobby. Historically, he hated walking into gym lobbies. They smelled like popcorn - and he loved popcorn - yet he never ate popcorn on tournament days. He learned to ignore the smell, except for the first thirty seconds walking into the gym.

His teammates walked with him, although most of them listened to their favorite hype music. This weekend there would be only six champions. The UNH team alone carried twenty wrestlers, and forty colleges were represented here. Time, training, and tenacity would show which athletes would meet their goal.

They walked into the locker room and ignored the team manager yelling instructions about where to put their stuff, so he looked at them individually and pointed, then followed along. One by one they placed their duffel bags into the lockers and headed for a designated room they were to meet as a team.

Declan hated team meetings before he wrestled. To him, wrestling was an individual sport, not like basketball or football. He got no awards (that he cared about) if his teammates did well or not; didn't care if they wrestled poorly or not. He only received an award if he won. That's what he cared about, whether or not he won, then kept winning. Losing to an opponent was losing the award waiting for him on the other side.

His agitation carried over to how he reacted to any instruction given to him by the coach. He finally reached a point where he ignored any instructions given, which of course agitated his coach further.

"Hey, Declan, what's your deal man?" Coach Bowen said immediately after the team meeting. "Where's your head and why are you treating everyone who talks to you like crap?"

They didn't always get along, Declan and Coach Bowen, but Declan respected the man's experience and excellent track record. Coach Bowen was one of the reasons Declan chose UNH. Bowen confronted Declan, Declan straightened up and responded quickly.

"Uh, nothing coach. I'm just focused, you know? I've been thinking about winning this tournament and I'm really not that interested in team meetings. I'd rather just focus on winning."

"Is that so?"

"Yes, sir."

"Ok," Coach said with a smirk that only reached the right side of his face. "Here's what I, your coach, want you to do right now to prepare yourself to win. There's a running track on the second floor of this gym. Go up to the second floor and run a mile right now."

A few guys on the team were standing around and heard the conversation. Declan felt self-conscious, and immediately got defensive.

"In my dress clothes?"

"Did I stutter?" Coach Bowen said louder this time.

"No, sir." He turned to find the second floor stairs, following a sign that read, "2nd floor balcony and running track". He walked towards it, turning right around the corner, and collided into another athlete turning left.

"Watch where you're going!" demanded Declan, his emotions spinning out of control. The young man graciously stepped aside, choosing not to counter.

When Declan arrived on the second floor he paced himself around the track. A few spectators watched and wondered why a young man probably wrestling in an hour or two was jogging around a track above the six giant mats below.

Declan's thoughts now focused less on winning a championship and more how much he hated Coach Bowen and his "loser" team. He shook the thoughts away, would think only about his win. When it happened, he'd give no credit to the coach who tried to hurt him on meet day. He'd let everyone know it, too. Maybe the school paper would interview him after he received his trophy. The picture would be of him, smiling, holding the giant award under the headline, "Sophmore Phenom Wins Championship Despite Having a Screwed Up Coach Who Hated Him". Declan's battle against impossible odds would be lauded as monumental. Sports Illustrated and ESPN would probably do some sort of documentary on his season, and the lack of help he received from the coaching staff.

These bitter thoughts accompanied him all of the six and a half minutes before he finished his mile. By the time he walked downstairs, his teammates were back in the locker room preparing for their meets.

Anger controlled his mind as he pulled off his warm up clothes, letting anyone who stood nearby know he was pissed. He didn't care. He placed his skin tight shirt and black jeans into his locker, stuffed his socks into his black and white Vans. Reaching into his blue duffel bag, he pulled out his singlet and the rest of his gear. He stopped, and breathed, realizing if he didn't get control of himself he would lose this tournament.

He had no intention of losing.

Declan calmed himself down then finished decorating his body to be wrestling-friendly. Above the locker room exit, an inspirational sign read, "The pain of preparation is nothing like the pain of losing." His eyes focused on the quote as he slowly moved towards it. In an almost over dramatic gesture, he hit it with the open face of his hand and walked out of the room, turning right and moving down the hallway to the huge gym waiting for to enter and win the biggest wrestling match of his life.

***

There's something about walking into a gymnasium full of spectators excited to watch one perform that either makes a person anxious or like they are walking into the front door of their home. The latter people belong there, in that place at that time. Those who feel anxious and excited may have the talent to do well, once they calm down, but ultimately they will be at the mercy of the second group, as nerves tend to call the shots in the head of the aforementioned athletes.

That day Declan couldn't get control of his own head. Though he heard the cheers of his fans, Grace and his family chief among them, his coach's slight still hovered in his mind. In his head, all great victors fought and defeated great enemies, and his coach had become Declan's version of King David's lion or bear. Now he faced some unsuspecting Goliath in a wrestling singlet with the name of another college written on the threads.

Declan stretched. Huge blue mats with circles on them had been laid neatly across what normally was a basketball court. The backboards and rims that normally hung ten feet above the floor had been mechanically raised towards the ceiling rafters of the monstrous college gymnasium, like the George Washington Bridge over the Hudson River. Loud pop music beat across the loudspeakers with Will Smith admonishing anyone who heard his words that they needed to "get jiggy wit it."

He stood up from the butterfly position, responsible for stretching his groin, and partnered with Sawyer, a young freshman who, Declan assumed, looked up to him like a child to a full moon on a warm summer night, in order to "clear ties" for a few minutes. Escaping the hold of an opponent was a major part of Declan's successes, and he loved to practice it. This part of his warm up routine went a little longer than it was supposed to.

Then, when he jumped down to do 20-20-20's, he looked up to see his parents, gleaming at him proudly from the bleachers. He also saw Grace cheering like a fan of the Backstreet Boys, and his sister, Darcy who looked around as if hunting her next conquest. Declan half expected Grace's brother John to show up because of Darcy, but rumor had it that their brief fling was merely her using him during a lonely period in her life after last Christmas, and he probably didn't want to face her.

With fierce tenacity, Declan laid on the ground and pounded out twenty pushups, then turned his lean and rock-like body towards the rafters and squeezed out twenty sit-ups before finally jumping to his feet to squat twenty times until his thighs and buttocks felt the burn. His heart raced now, something good was happening to his body.

After some escapes and quick sprints, he rocked another 20-20-20, and then returned to hand-fighting with Sawyer. He noticed how quick the kid was with how he reacted to everything Declan brought at him. Secretly he delighted that Sawyer's weight ranged bigger than him, so they would never have to compete. In a few years, Sawyer would dominate any college athlete he faced.

Declan felt in control and no one could stop this train from rolling. He stretched for another minute, then walked slowly back to the bench, where Coach Bowen handed out instructions from tournament officials as to who was fighting whom, and when.

"Dumais!" The coach yelled out looking through the ten or so wrestlers who stood in between them. "You're up first. 10:00. You'll be at Mat 1." He pointed at the southeast corner of the gymnasium.

Declan took one of the day's schedules and looked at the name of his opponent. Scott Michel from Brown University. Declan said the name again in his mind after he read it. He thought to himself, "No damned Ivy leaguer is going to beat me today," then crumbled the schedule in his hand and threw it on the ground in front of the bench. Six minutes until the match. He moved his neck back and forth like an athletic Stevie Wonder. Moving slowly towards Mat 1, he watched as another wrestler with a crimson singlet moved confidently to the same circle.

Jet black hair, a smooth face, and wiry thin - Scott Michel. This was the second time they'd faced one another. The first was when Michel had turned a corner earlier in the morning at the same moment as Declan. Then, out of anger Declan had screamed insults. Michel hadn't responded to the verbal beatdown but chose to stand back quietly and allow the angry stranger to pass. Now here they stood, across the wrestling mat and in three minutes would wrestle for a continuing spot in the tournament.

Unfortunately for Declan, this second meeting messed with his head. He stared angrily at Scott Michel to let him know telepathically the domination that laid in his future. Michel, for his part, acknowledged their previous meeting with only a slight nod, before he continued to stretch and prepare for their upcoming match.

Sensing something wrong, Coach Bowen walked over to Declan and whispered into his ear, "Get everything out of your mind. You know the moves. You know how to win. You can be the champion. The only thing in your way of winning this tournament..." He paused, wondering whether or not he should continue, "...is you."

* * *

Four minutes later, Declan laid wrapped up in a nasty cross-face cradle, both shoulders pinned to the ground in an unbreakable hold. He tapped out. From the very beginning, his opponent dominated the match, was in control mentally. Declan's physical advantages did not matter. He could hear the roar of the Brown University fans, and could barely see his parents frowning with disappointment as the official called the match after a three second count. His line of sight while pinned did not offer a view of Grace. When Michel jumped up in victory, Declan laid on the mat and stared up at her. She stared back, letting him know how much she loved him. He stared blankly back, only thinking about how to never lose - at anything - again.

Friends

As a pastor, I love building communities of people who eventually become friends – not just on the surface but deep committed friendships that grow over time and produce the value of love.

The seeds of those relationships are planted by bonds or shared experiences that connect them, such as school or travel. In college, for instance, I traveled from Florida to Arizona in a beat up Caprice Classic with three people I didn't know and ended up making lifelong friends. We traveled through intense heat in Louisiana, gang fights in Houston, thunderstorms in the middle of a Texas desert, running out of gas on the New Mexico border, violent vomiting from one of our four cast members, and getting run off the road by a lovely elderly couple driving a white Buick who decided to switch lanes and not check their rear view mirror. Twenty minutes outside of Tucson, our destination, the car completely shut down and we had to call a tow truck to take it away.

Twenty five years later, that story still sticks in my mind, along with my fellow passengers. There's something about long road trips, school, combat or any traumatic or dramatic event that connects people, and bonds them together into a relationship that carries for decades.

Church communities thrive when the community itself flourishes, but tends to dissolve once the parts become more important than the whole. The quality of the parts, however, can remain strong and dependable within the whole.

A hilarious movie came out around the time the Dumais family began attending Apex Church called The Hangover. In the movie, a group of guys travel to Las Vegas for a bachelor party. One of their own accidentally gives then "rufees" early one evening, and the rest of the time, they create unforgettable experiences which they can't remember afterwards. One of the funnier actors in the film refers to their brotherhood as "the Wolfpack...."

April 20, 2011

Now

Declan wanted to create his own Wolfpack. He wanted Ronnie and Adam to be his best friends, not only in this endeavor, but in life. Unfortunately his natural likability skimmed the bottom of a ten point scale, and he had huge obstacles to climb in his relationship with Adam. Ronnie liked Declan well enough, but in his world, he needed friends, too. Declan liked these guys and wanted them to know he was in this for the long haul. They were going to change the world.

Adam eventually called Declan and gave him an affirmative answer. Declan couldn't help but smile when he listened to the man's voicemail telling him he would be a part of the Wolfpack. He literally jumped up and down in the garage office, envisioning the three of them hard at work, going over their plans to change the world. He daydreamed about their friendship and nights together hanging out and challenging each other.

In fact, the excitement built up so much in his head that he sat down at his laptop and typed what he thought was a visionary statement about the future to his new comrades in scientific exploration. His brain buzzed as he communicated through his fingers:

My dear brothers,

Tomorrow represents a day which will change the world for the better, for it is the day we officially begin our work to prove, as a team, that the Earth is indeed flat - not just talk about it theoretically. I am honored to participate in this endeavor with you fine men, and look forward to planning and executing the greatest and most shocking discovery in half a millennia.

As we embark on this journey, let us remember there will be many difficult circumstances ahead. The path before us is stricken with hardship, haters, forceful tyrants, and a world that does not want the information we have, but needs it. Let us not allow these enemies to wedge their way between our friendship as we forge towards the finish line.

There will be nothing like the feeling we will soak in when we finally prove what should have been told years before. It is both unfortunate and wonderful that the time is now for truth to prevail, for generation upon generation could have profited from it, if it had been unveiled by earlier explorations.

So when we meet tomorrow night, know that it is an important time, but it is only the beginning. Thank you for being a part of it, and thank you for being my friends.

For the sake of truth,
Declan Dumais

"Get the fudge out of here with that dumb Shasta email of yours!" Ronnie joked, walking into the garage office with Adam following close behind.

I should interject here a moment and explain that Ronnie, upon entering the garage, never actually said the words 'fudge' or 'Shasta.' He is a man gifted with a rather colorful, some might say vulgar sense of the English language. For the sake of those with whom I am sharing this story, I have decided to replace some of his more euphemistic choices for words with those more palatable to the human ear (even if admittedly the original words might actually make more sense).

"Yes, seriously, Declan," Adam followed along in his golden British accent. "I'm not sure what that was all about, but it was a bit much, bloke."

Declan's earlier feelings of exhilaration over tonight's gathering disappeared into an abyss of self-doubt. His face turned red, and he turned towards his laptop, laughing politely in an attempt to hide his embarrassment.

Adam realized what happened and quieted down, but Ronnie, never one to grasp social cues, kept talking. "I mean, 'For the sake of fishing truth?' What the fish! I almost peed myself. In fact, I had to close my porn site, I was laughing so hard."

"It's a wonder you're still single, Ronnie," Declan sneered, trying to make a joke but was now clearly not in a laughing mood.

Any levity in Adam's face disappeared with Ronnie's joke. Worried it had possibly reminded the man about why he hated Declan so much, he immediately changed the subject.

"Ok guys, let's get started. I thought we'd begin by having a baseline conversation. What are our common denominators, and what we're all thinking. If we start off on the same page, then it'll at least be easier to keep us all on task. So, Adam, why don't we start with you? What have you been thinking about our mission?" As he said this, he remembered the new mini fridge he'd installed in the corner of the room yesterday, stocked it full of beer. He grabbed three bottles and handed them out to the others. Everyone took a few moments to open and enjoy them.

Eventually Adam answered, "I am intrigued by your theories of proving Flat Earth, Declan. I also believe it will be very difficult. We need to be very careful with what we do and how we do it. I'm talking about everything from how we search on our laptops to the kinds of questions we ask people, especially at airports and libraries. These are the kind of people who are trained to talk, to take suspicious activity and to turn that information over to the appropriate law enforcement. It's possible you've already tipped them off by the research you've already done."

He took a long pull of his beer and sat at one of the spare, plastic chairs near the map before continuing. "Our current advantage is surprise. I mean, right now, we don't even know everything we're planning on doing. If we can keep to ourselves, get our act together and accomplish what we set out to accomplish, then Dec's right. We will change the world."

Declan smirked when he heard Adam's last words. He sounded much more natural giving inspiration than Declan. When he said the last sentence in his "King George" accent, even he was more pumped to make it happen.

"Very cool, Adam, and thanks so much for joining this team. I don't know if we could do this without you. Your expertise will be valuable."

"And what of my friendship, Dec? Is that valuable too?" Adam spoke jokingly, and Ronnie heaved with laughter again. Declan answered only with an authentic smile, then motioned his head to Ronnie, as if to tell him it was his turn.

"Ok," Ronnie said loudly, like he was Chris Farley's twin. "I like you guys. I must because, honestly, I don't give a Shiite about any flat Earth. I just want to stick it to the Monday flagging man! You know what I mean?" Both men laughed in response. Pleased with this, Ronnie continued.

"I'm a bad-to-the-bone pilot, and since I am not always an 'obey orders' kind of guy, I got kicked out on my butt by Uncle Sam. So, here I am, hanging with my homies, and ready to change some spit and take some names." He raised his beer in salute. "I'm not always the most respectful, most ordinary guy in the room, but I can fly an F-5 through the St Louis Arch while eating a popsicle and a hot pocket. I guess I say all that, to say, Whatever it takes."

Adam held up his own bottle and echoed the sentiment. "Whatever it takes."

When Declan repeated the salutation, he added, "Whatever it takes, Wolfpack."

The three men bellowed with laughter, and then spent the next four hours talking through what they decided to call, "Operation: Frisbee."

* * *

The next morning Declan woke up tired after a long night of talking with the Wolfpack. Grace placed breakfast in front of him when he came into the kitchen. It smelled good and tasted even better as the entire family ate together. Afterwards he stood up, grabbed his briefcase and coat and headed for the door, saying 'goodbye' to everyone as he did.

Before he got to the door, Grace ran to her husband, turned him around, and kissed him on the lips for the first time since the affair. He kissed back. The boys both groaned, "Yuck!" Everyone laughed.

"Have a good day, Declan." Grace said, holding her hand to his chest. "I love you."

"You, too." Declan replied, opening up the door and walking down the porch steps. He wondered what changed. Whatever it was, he liked it and would wait till tonight to let her know that even though she erased the plans on the whiteboard, he'd taken a picture of them and could reproduce everything for her at a few minutes notice. She needed them, if she wanted to get more organized in her life. He hoped it would make her happier.

He also made a mental note, as he jumped in the car and saw the garage office door in front of him, to talk to Ronnie about cursing so much before nine o'clock. Controlling that guy was going to be no small feat, but he didn't want his kids learning those words from his own house, and especially from someone they knew as 'Dad's friend'.

He drove to school and spent the day teaching and thinking about the Wolfpack. His mental energy typically funneled towards Flat Earth any time he had a break from class, and this gave him extra time to refine some of his more outlandish ideas. Lunch came and he ate alone, making to-do lists for each of the Pack. His theories would only stay theories if he didn't plan to succeed.

Declan now referred to anything they talked about as "his theories." He took ownership of everything he dealt with in life, and this was no exception. His flat Earth theories were his theories and he would address them that way. If people didn't like his confidence that was their problem.

After school, Declan drove to one of several Starbucks in Worcester to meet with me. He'd emailed me a few days before asking if I wanted to grab a coffee after school, sometime. I didn't ask him if he wanted me to bring Marie along.

When he arrived, I was already sitting at a table as far in the corner as I could manage, drinking an iced chai tea latte. He grabbed some sort of dark roasted coffee and sat beside me. He looked tired but chipper at the same time.

"Hey, Jack! How have things been? Man, I've missed you." Admittedly I was not prepared for his having missed me over the past few weeks since what happened the last time we'd seen each other.

"Yeah, Dec, it's a been a little bit. How've things been? I haven't seen or heard from you, or Grace. You guys doing ok?"

"Oh, yes, we're great! I'm so excited about the future. In fact, let me tell you, I've got some new friends, and they're helping me with some of the Flat Earth proofs I told you about. Do you remember?"

"Oh, I remember," I replied.

"What's up with you these days, Jack?"

I didn't want to let him in to my world, but I hoped that the more authentic I could be, the more he would repay the favor and be more forthcoming himself.

"I'm doing okay right now. We're having some growing pains at church. In the past year we've launched sixty-four house churches across New England and stories keep rolling in about what God's doing through the community. As we grow, though, things get more chaotic. It gets more tempting to try to control as much as I can. But," I raised my cup and hesitated, as if I hadn't actually rehearsed this part of the conversation a few times since getting his invitation, "this is God's church and it's for Him to do His thing. Currently we're talking about spreading our network outside of New England, but something doesn't quite feel right about that, so we're praying through it and will probably land on the side of allowing things to go where they will naturally, through organic spread as opposed to being intentional about expanding. I have no real interest in a five year goal. I'll let God handle that."

Declan had been listening intently, leaning slightly on the table and ignoring his coffee. "What's your plan to help people know the Bible better. You know, in a way where they can understand it but at the same time, not be spreading heretical theology?" He said this in such a matter of fact way I had to pause, using my tea as a crutch, and work out a response. I rarely trust Declan, so walking on egg shells when I talk to him has become something of a favorite pastime for me.

I finally continued, "Basically, as we always have, we work to ensure those who are a part of Apex get to know the Bible by always being in it, daily if possible, and allowing the Holy Spirit to grow them up as believers. I don't want to train great Bible teachers unless that's their gift. I don't want to train great servants of the poor unless that's their gift. I don't want to train people to speak in tongues unless that is their gifting, but what I do want to do is train people to love Jesus and to love each another. Once they begin to do that, they'll begin serving Jesus using the gifts He's given them.

"Let me ask you this, Declan, what gifts are you using right now?"

"I think I'm using gifts in the area of research. I used to use those gifts solely for Biblical research, but currently I'm pretty focused on scientific study. Good things are happening as a result, too. I'm headed towards a collision course with destiny," he said with a smile and a dramatic flourish of his hands.

"Ok, and that's good, Declan. That's what you should be doing. I'm proud of you for using your gifts that way. Are you working with a team, or flying solo with this endeavor?" I was just trying to build some rapport back into our relationship.

"I'm working with a team. Two guys jumped on board when they heard what I was doing. They're as excited as I am, so, yea, things are going pretty well."

"Who are the guys? How do they fit in with what you're doing?"

He hesitated in answering, then quickly seemed to come to some decision and volunteered the information. "Well...uh...the first guy is a former classmate of mine from elementary school. His name is Ronnie Cable. He lives down here in this area. Like us, he moved this way after college.

"The other guy used to lead the flat Earth group I was in. He also used to be into some shady military stuff, which made him the perfect candidate for his part in the mission. His name is Adam Starr."

"As in Amber's dad?" I said, my eyebrows raised higher than a flag during times of celebration.

"Yes. He came to me when he heard what we were doing. He's the perfect guy for the job."

"Have you told Grace who he is?"

"Not yet. I'm not keeping it from her, but I haven't found it to be relevant at the moment. Currently I'm making plans to change the world so petty squabbles among individuals is not at the forefront of my mind." Declan said this with a bit too much confidence.

"Let me ask you this, Declan, and shoot straight with me. I really have no reason to think you won't. Do you consider why your wife might be upset when she finds that out? It seems to me that most people might feel some sort of anger towards you once they learn that information. Me, too, considering you invited him into your project without mentioning it to Grace. You're both still healing from a pretty tragic turn of events that turned your marriage into a battleground. You're both wounded in some ways. Grace certainly is. Your kids might be young enough still that they might not have realized the full extent of what happened. But, because of the healing you both are doing, over time, the boys most certainly will feel the effects of what's gone on in these last few months.

"So, revisiting my question, do you really feel like inviting Amber's dad into your life without mentioning it to Grace, in some way giving in to her 'pettiness' as you called it?"

Thankfully Declan took some time to consider my question and didn't leave like he'd done in our last conversation. However, he answered much I suspected he would.

"I hear what you're saying, Jack. I even sympathize with my wife who might be hurt when she hears this news. But the things we're dealing with in that garage office –" he looked sideways a moment, "I have to give that a cooler name - those things are bigger than one person's feelings. Though she'll be hurt, I know her resilience. She'll come back after some initial anger, apologetic and ready to continue to work on our marriage."

I could only stare for the a few seconds, but still, I wasn't ready to give up this fight. It sounded like he was trying to pin his indiscretions on her emotions.

"So is that what you are doing right now? Are you working on your marriage? Are you investing into your wife?"

"Jack, not everything is this perfect little Biblical world you have in your head and at church. What I'm doing is important. The project is going to change the way the world looks at science and, honestly, the way the world looks at itself. For thousands of years, men have sacrificed their families and friendships to do great things. Now I know you're just looking out for me but honestly, Grace is going to be there at the end of this. While I'm busy having my picture taken in some of the world's most prestigious science magazines, she'll be right there with me, happy to be along for the ride. She has been for this long."

"While all that may be true, Declan, have you ever wondered why? Have you ever wondered why she sticks around through some of this.

Right now, only months after your affair, would she not want to keep you accountable to some of your actions? Why would a beautiful young lady, and she is still young and beautiful, stick around for the ride when frankly, the ride is no longer with you?"

Declan thought deeply about my question, and though he was obviously offended by it, he decided to play along and answer. I had to give him that much.

"I would say, Jack, that it's because she loves me. She loves me so she knows what I'm doing is important."

"And what about her things? Are they important, too?"

"Of course they are! She'll have plenty of time to do them, especially with me working on my stuff."

"And will you be as supportive with her schooling as you want her to be for what you are doing?"

"I won't have as much time to support her, but I'll do what I can."

I'd been trying to help him see the problem in as roundabout way as possible, but now I had be straight with him.

"Declan, have you ever considered that the world doesn't revolve around you?"

"No, Jack, the world doesn't revolve at all. There is only us, and our creator. He created a flat table-like Earth for us to live on and as far as I know, has no interest in anyone exploring outside of that table. So, I believe that the sun and the moon and anything we see does actually revolve around us."

Stay on target, a small voice whispered in my head. "Not referring to your project in any way now, ok? You're asking everyone around you to take a back seat in their lives because you believe that what you're doing is the most important thing you could be doing, would you say that is correct?"

"Yes. It is the most important thing anyone could be doing."

"Ok, and what things has Grace done that have been so important to her, that you supported her through them with all of your time and actions, that you put away everything you were doing yourself to support her?"

Declan shut down and became less coherent with his words from that point forward. He knew I was on to something, and could no longer participate in a conversation where me being right and he being wrong was central to the back and forth.

We parted ways amicably, and I realized we'd made some headway and welled up with excitement of my own. Maybe Declan would take my questions and consider ways to improve his marriage. Grace needed to be poured into in healthy ways. Maybe Declan could change enough to help facilitate that. As I left Starbucks that day, I prayed silently for a change in the wind, and that the Dumais family could start a new era of health.

I really believed it was possible, too, until I woke up the next morning to three emails in my inbox, beginning at 11:28 pm, much later than my bedtime.

Jack,

Thanks for the conversation and the coffee. I have been thinking a lot this evening about some of the things you asked and implied as we talked. Essentially you said I neglect my wife and I only do my own thing. So you put the problems in my marriage on me. The problem, though, is Grace. I don't know if you know this, but she's had a lot of trauma in her life. I hate bringing it up, because it's no one's business, but you're a pastor so I figured it was important for you to know.

Grace had a rough home life and her dad regularly beat the snot out of her mom and, though she doesn't really talk about this, probably abused her physically, as well. This trauma doesn't take a lot to see once you get to know her better. She's constantly scratching herself and never looks anyone in the eye. She struggles with a lot, but at the same time doesn't hold herself accountable to becoming the person God wants her to be. I need Marie and you to help me keep her healthy and on track during this time of health and rebuilding.

I'm sorry that I haven't been to church in a while, but you guys are like family to me, and I appreciate the time you have spent with us.

Declan

And then at 2:08 am...

Jack,

Sorry, I was just thinking of a few things tonight and I can't seem to put myself to sleep. I also need to make you aware that Grace could really seriously hurt herself during this time as she struggles with depression and anxiety, and I'm trying to help her, but she's going to need more support as well. Please help. Thanks so much.

Declan

And then again at 4:41 am...

Jack,

I need you to stop blaming me for this relationship. Your implications that I'm not pouring into Grace and her healing are so far from the truth that it's clear she's gotten to you regarding my relationship with her and what she needs from me. She needs to be the mother and the wife God calls her to be, and needs to stop playing the victim. In truth, I am the victim here. I am trapped in a relationship where someone needs me so bad that they can't live without me, and I didn't ask for that. I just loved on her like any husband would.

Please stop asking me questions like I'm the culprit and she's the victim because that's not the truth. I need you to be my friend during this time, and enabling Grace to continue blaming me for everything wrong in our marriage will not help things. She is getting all these ideas and clearly going against God's ways by thinking of leaving me. Thanks.

Declan

Then

Declan and Grace began dating after their first encounter at the Thirsty Moose. To their friends and his family, they hadn't known each another long enough to start "officially" dating. Their relationship began with a bunch of little dates and constant phone calls and pages, then morphed into spending most of their first college semester together.

Steph and Stephie worried that Grace was losing her identity inside of this sudden relationship, which was a surprisingly deep thought from the collective mind of Steph and Stephie. They weren't seeing her as much and when they did, Grace seemed rushed and... different. When she asked them to point out how, they fell silent, unable to articulate what they were feeling.

When two people become dysfunctional, they're typically the last to know. This is due to their individual dysfunctions. You might never know it if they were young and single and attractive and spending most of their time in college settings like the classroom or athletic fields. Generally people are only looking at their external circumstances , not who they're becoming as individuals and as a couple.

If you've heard the phrase "I can't get enough of you" spoken from one lover to another, you have heard the very foundation of a codependent relationship. So it was with Declan and Grace in their first year of dating. Every night Grace came over and stayed with Declan, and they did all of the things their bodies craved.

Every day she walked him to his 8:00 am class, then went home (his dorm room) and slept until his class was over at ten, where she met him and together they returned to his room for what usually ended up as a romantic interlude before walking to their respective 11:00 am classes. Lunch followed at 11:50 am. After that, they returned to his room and Declan prepared for his dreaded class/wrestling practice combo and race studied for a full afternoon of classes.

This schedule repeated itself for a month, until one day Grace forgot about a quiz in her 11:00 am class. She rushed nervously to meet Declan and told him about the issue. He came out of his class with his head down, moping like he just watched a small puppy get run over by a John Deere.

"What's wrong?" Grace asked, immediately stroking his hair, as if that alone would nurse him back to proper emotional health.

"I think I failed my instructional method quiz," he lamented. "It sucks because I really needed a good grade in that."

"I'm sorry, baby. Oh speaking of which," Grace remembered, "I forgot about a quiz I have at 11:00! No fooling around today, I have to study." She smiled and began to walk in the direction they walked every day for the last month, leaving Declan to mope in the middle of the empty sidewalk.

"Come on," she pleaded, teasingly.

She was stunned at his sudden response. "How come everything is all about you? All. The. Time!" He walked ahead, and pulled his arm away as she reached for it.

"Baby, what are you talking about? "

He quickened his pace and lowered his head, mumbling obscenities under his breath so she could, but still couldn't quite hear at the same time.

She followed along, starting to cry, and tried to make some sort of conversation out of a situation that was quickly getting out of hand. They walked the rest of the way in silence.

When she crossed the door's threshold, she broke down in a flood of tears. He said, "You cannot do this to me. This is not my fault."

"Fault? " she replied, angry now. "All I said was that I had to study for a quiz I forgot about and you went off on me and said... I quote... 'How come everything is all about you? All the time!' That's what you said. We've been so happy for the last month. I'm happy, but now... now... I don't know."

"It's ok, Grace," he reached out with a changed affect yet a more somber, whiny tone. "I forgive you and I know you can change. You can get better." He wrapped his arms around her and began to slowly and softly kiss her neck. She continued to cry softly.

"Your tears make your face too salty," Declan joked. "How about we take a shower?"

She laughed and grabbed his face, bringing it close to hers. "I am so sorry. I will be a better girlfriend." She began unbuttoning his shirt.

The rest of the morning went as Declan had hoped it would and Grace, true to her earlier thoughts, failed her quiz.

April 21, 2011

Now

Since his affair, Grace slept in the guest bedroom, but tonight her body craved his, and she thought about going in and quenching her desires. The withdrawals intensified as the night wore on and kept her awake. Late into the evening she could hear Declan getting in and out of his bed several times. She assumed he was using the restroom, but then eventually heard the click of his keyboard.

She wondered why he hadn't attempted to reach out and connect with her. If she confronted him on it, she was certain he'd wax eloquently about giving her time to heal, but in truth it didn't feel that way. Days passed since they'd talked. He immersed himself in everything Flat Earth, and virtually ignored everything Grace Dumais. Worries filled her head that Declan would leave her. She needed him. Since their first night together, there had been plenty of opportunities for her to walk away, or them to break up, but she could never do it. Her attraction to him pulled her like water constantly finding the lowest point. Even though she knew how stuck she was, she couldn't wield the power to walk away from the most toxic thing in her life.

Her own conspiracy theory was believing they could have a healthy relationship. She would always need him to be her savior, partly because he needed to be everyone's savior and partly because she didn't possess the strength to walk on her own. So, while the entire world looked at the two of them and saw a messy, distorted codependent relationship, Grace believed in its beauty and kept trying to prove its allure was real, despite instance after instance of living out an existence that looked exactly how everyone else viewed it.

She decided to take a walk. If he could constantly get up and send emails or look at porn or whatever he was busy doing all night, she could put on some clothes and take a walk down Route 9. The clock read 2:06 am. Declan typed away in the office.

She climbed out of bed, put on a pair of shorts and a tank top, and walked toward the front door. She didn't bother announcing to Declan where she was going and he didn't bother to ask. At the front door, she simply put on her shoes and left.

The walk to Route 9 was less than ten minutes. Grace turned right, heading toward Worcester. She had no destination, only knew she needed to walk away from Declan right now. Despite her deepest longings, she had to move past her own need to be with him, at least within the context of their current relationship. The air outside was moist and cool, yet warm enough where she felt comfortable without a coat. She walked slowly past CVS and eventually past a closed-down Spag's.

She missed Spag's. It was one of those early pioneer merchandise discount sellers, like a Wal-Mart that never became a franchise. It opened in the 1930's and closed down six years ago. Here it's sat since, empty and dead in an otherwise healthy and vibrant commercial area.

Passing Trader Joe's and Moe's and Burger King, Grace eventually came to the Kenneth F. Burns Memorial Bridge which reached over a narrow inlet to Lake Quinsigamond. She stood on the bridge as a few cars passed by. Because of the time of night, they seemed to slow down as they moved past the young lady standing alone, staring out at the water.

Leaning on the rails, she looked down and watched the water rush faster than normal tonight. She heard the sounds of the night birds in the distance, water below her and vehicles passing behind her. The loudest sound was the voice in her head telling her she couldn't live without him. Of course, that was what the voice said. She had told herself this every day for fifteen years. How could she leave Declan now?

But, she must walk away. The sounds of running water covered her thoughts as she considered the possibility of simply jumping and letting go of everything, letting the water carry her, or her body, away. Despite living only an hour from ocean, she couldn't swim. The distance to the water below her was not far, but she'd likely not be able to get herself to shore.

That wasn't the way to walk away from all of this, and she knew it. Grace needed to let go, but not to death. She needed to let go of Declan and walk toward a free life, void of guilt and manipulation, of withdrawals and pain. She'd lived her life as an addict, and Declan was her drug of choice. Could she do it, she wondered? Could she really be free on her own. or would the cravings be too strong for him again?

She answered her own questions, deciding at that moment to walk back to their house and tell Declan that the next morning she'd be leaving him with their two boys. Grace would call Marie, find a place to live short term, and make longer term plans on how to live life with a horrific job, two kids and a very small support system. She asked God to clear her head enough to see a brighter future.

Walking back, her footsteps felt light and she surprised herself by smiling. She loudly sang Tom Petty's "Free Falling" all the way back to her doorstep, where she walked into the house around 4:30. Declan was at the office computer. She pushed open the door, which was mostly ajar and looked at him, hoping to view some sort of compassion and love as their eyes met.

"It's late," she said, "and I have no idea why we're up right now, yet here we are. Tomorrow I'll be packing up my things and walking away from you. I don't know if it's long term and I don't know if you even care, but I'll be finding a place, taking the boys, and we'll be going away for a while."

He stared at her saying nothing. Grace briefly wondered if he'd even heard her. Nevertheless, the continued, "For years I've been codependent, needy, and at times manipulated by you to be your little wife doing whatever you needed me to do. Honestly, Declan, I won't be living that way anymore. I've been like you. I have lived my life trying to control whatever I can, and what that's meant for me is I have forced myself to be in a relationship that reeks of an unhealthy stench. You've lived happily trying to control everything, and I do mean everything in your life, and I can't let you control me anymore. I can't be that person.

"So, tomorrow morning, don't try to stop me. I have no idea where we'll be going, but we will be going. I hope, maybe, that we can work this out. But we can't do it with me in this house. I have to go away. I have to walk away."

Still, Declan only stared at her without saying anything, then slowly turned to his computer and started typing. Grace reached for the door, closed it, walked to the guest room, and cried herself to sleep, asking God to give her strength.

* * *

In my life, I hadn't met too many people like Declan. People who were 'never wrong,' super insecure, yet felt superior to others when confronted with a challenging viewpoint didn't come along often, even in my line of work. Regardless, wherever there's someone who needs to be in control, there's another who needs to be controlled. If you haven't figured it out yet, this is the story of what happens to the former when the latter no longer needs to be controlled. The ripped Band-aid gets messy, and the bleeding, previous inhibited by the bandage, flows without proper attention.

Declan's mental incapacities, however, led him to believe there was no flowing blood and, therefore, he didn't need a bandage. Because of this, as Grace confronted him with her plans, he decided to let her "burn to the ground" if she wanted to. He would pour his energy into finishing what he started. Now, nothing would come between him and the notoriety he deserved.

Dark clouds can make the morning feel like night when you wake up to them, especially when it comes so fast. After a long and punishing evening of little sleep and excessive thinking, Declan forced himself to roll out of bed. He could sleep later. Things needed to get done; the world needed to be changed.

For a brief moment he panicked that he might have overslept for school, then remembered he'd called in before he went to bed a few hours ago. Having settled that issue, he walked to the bathroom and washed his face. Declan thought about how silent the house was. He usually left around this time, and the boys were almost always up laughing and playing or crying and fighting. But today he heard nothing but the water splashing.

He walked towards the kids' bedroom, glancing into the guest bedroom on the way. Grace wasn't there. Fear gripped him as he moved faster down the hall and opened the kids' door. The room was empty.

She warned him she was leaving, but he had no idea she'd be gone already. He didn't get a chance to say goodbye or try to change her decision. Declan's mind raced. She would pay for this gaffe. She struggled with thinking for herself, anyway, and she obviously hadn't thought through the consequences of what she was doing.

The positive side to her actions, however, was now he could go head-first into Project: Frisbee. Declan believed it would take between four to seven weeks before they launched the initiative and he could use all his time now to ensure it was a success. He'd accrued plenty of sick time. He'd use it over the next several weeks, and he didn't have to worry about Grace or the kids at all. She had given him a gift.

While Declan thought this, something deep inside of him hated what she'd done and hated her all the more for not needing him.

Raindrops tapped against the window. Declan's thoughts were interrupted by the quiet sound of thunder from a distance. A miserable day would not hinder his work. Adam and Ronnie would arrive by 9:00. Grace needed to be dealt with, but there was plenty of time for that. For now, he would get ready and head to the garage office.

* * *

A few hours later, the Wolfpack stood around discussing the most difficult part of Project: Frisbee - the airplane. Ronnie could fly anything, but the type of aircraft was at the mercy of the specific airport they used. They assumed that countless numbers of travelers were not traveling in and out of Punta Arenas, so they studied whether or not the location housed aircraft with the fuel capacity they needed. They needed a plane that could fly 16,000 kilometers, so a primary order of research was to find out if they could access that type of plane from that airport.

Also important to their immediate future was planning for the heist. Chile's Air Force wasn't the size of the United States, nevertheless it was a branch of that country's military. Not to mention one of the reasons they shared those runways with the international airport might be to squelch the very thing these three men were planning. They considered the possibility that they might not receive any mercy from the Fuerza Aerea de Chile who may use any means possible to keep them from proving Earth is flat. How did these people live with themselves knowing what the Wolfpack knew, that it was not just a theory, but full on science?

Truth can be funny sometimes. The news media attempts to find truth and share it. Their audience have their own versions of truth, yet still try to sort out all the different versions from all the different storytellers they hear it from. There are those who see things in black and white and others who see those same things in shades of gray, still more who see things in vibrant colors. One person's chameleon might be another person's leaf.

The men working in the garage office on that wet, dark day were all men who saw things in black and white, knowing what they know and adamant they were correct in their knowledge. They left little room in their minds that what they believed may actually be wrong. Men who believed in something would change the course of the world. Or, who end up in disaster. The difference between the two walks a fine line, and usually separated by the actual truth and the lengths people will sometimes go to hide it.

After some conversation, the three started working on their separate roles. Declan pushed them hard, and they made headway regarding planes, fuel, and communications. Once they'd finished their joint mission and proved the Earth flat, communicating their findings to as many people as possible as quickly as possible was vital. For if they proved what they knew, but no one else yet knew, they wouldn't be granted leniency from a Chilean (or Argentinian) prison or, worse, the bottom of Drake's passage, or on top of some huge ice wall mountain. If nothing else, even in death, people had to know the truth.

They worked for hours on their roles, telling stories and Ronnie making the occasional dirty joke.

At noon, they stopped and ate chicken and vegetables for lunch. Declan said they needed to eat well to ensure there wasn't an afternoon lull. Around 12:45, his phone rang. The screen read, "Grace".

"Excuse me guys. I'm gonna get some fresh air." He stood up and stretched. When Declan opened the door to the garage office, he was surprised to find a ray of light hit him in the face. The sun was fighting to show up in the midst of the clouds still spread throughout the sky. He answered the phone.

"Yes?" he said, sounding irritated.

"Hi, how are you?"

"You know, I'm in the biggest project of my life, working on something that is literally going to change the world, and I wake up to my wife leaving me...oh yeah, and she took the kids. So I'm not great. You?"

"I'm okay. I'm sorry I did that, but I needed... I need to take a break. It doesn't have to be bad or hurtful. We have some things to work out, that's all. If we can do that, then things can change. If not, then they won't and I won't be back, and we can work through that, too."

"Listen to me, Grace," Declan snarled. "You will bring my kids back to me right now. Whether or not you stay is of no concern to me. You have no right to take them from here. Who do you think you are?"

"So you want me to bring the kids back? I can do that, but I'm pretty sure you just told me you are in the 'biggest project in your life.' I know you have to be in control, Dec, but this time, we're doing it my way. If you can't handle that, then I guess we'll have a problem. But you'll be handling that problem while working on the 'biggest project of your life.'

"Or, here's another solution for you. How about you drop the Flat Earth project, stop trying to control me and everything around you, and I'll come home and we can work through our marriage problems, even our own mental problems?" Grace calmly stopped and allowed Declan to think through his choices. Apparently he didn't need much time.

"I need to go. I will deal with you later, but I want you to know that I will not forgive you for this slight. You've disrespected me, my family, my friends, and you will pay. You had no right to leave this house and you certainly had no right to do so with our children. I've invested years into my relationship with you and you go ruining everything in a matter of a few hours. I can't imagine the insolence it takes for you to make that decision. Who do you think you are? Is there some royalty integrated in your blood? What am I supposed to tell my family? I'll tell you what I'll tell your family. I'll tell them you went off the deep end and need to be in a mental hospital! That's what I'm going to tell them! What do you think about that?"

Grace thought nothing about that, for she'd hung up the phone as soon as Declan told her he needed to go. He hadn't heard her leave, but upon realizing it later, he stormed into the garage.

"You okay, chap? You seem a little tense," Adam said, with a slight smirk on his lips.

"I'll be fine. I have to write an email. Give me a few minutes."

Jack,

I don't know what to say right now. It feels like my world is falling apart. I have no doubt this is one of those times when I am trying to do something extraordinary to change the world, and Satan comes around and feverishly attempts to thwart my plans by throwing darts of idiocy and using me as the target. Grace left me last night. She took the kids and walked away like a filthy whore. I feel like Hosea. God called him to love his wife, too, and despite his constant love and devotion, she would keep walking away into the arms of other men.

In truth, I'm wondering if that's what this is all about. Could she have been cheating on me already? Could she have someone she's sleeping with? At first I wouldn't have thought so, but mental illness can have a strange effect on people.

Jack, I think Grace needs help. I mean serious help. She may need to be hospitalized. I'm afraid she's going to take steps to hurt herself because of the way she gets when she's away from me. You've seen her scratch herself, and what happens to her when she gets nervous, right? It's like she becomes a different person, and that person could do a lot of damage to herself, and to our kids. Would you talk to her and convince her to go to the hospital?

I need your help here, man. Grace is struggling down a difficult path, and she needs true friends to help her do the right things and take the right path, instead of the places she finds herself in in the midst of her episodes. Thanks so much, Jack! Talk soon.

Declan

I read the email and responded accordingly.

Declan

I know you started your email telling me you didn't know what to say, but unfortunately you said a lot in the four paragraphs that I completely disagreed with, and need to tell you immediately. I should say these things in person, but I'm afraid you'll send someone else a similar email or let everything simmer in your head, and I'm out of town for the next few days.

First, Grace is not having an affair. Of course I cannot say that absolutely as I am not God, but there is nothing in our conversations or her behavior that leads me in any way to believe she's participating in another relationship outside of your marriage. Even that you would insinuate this to me or anyone else without a single shred of evidence makes me very nervous about you, Dec. You seem to be acting out against Grace in ways that are inappropriate and honestly, quite frightening.

Finally, as it pertains to Grace's mental illness, I find it appalling you're choosing this moment to bring your worries up to me. If you've felt this way, how come you wouldn't share them with me before Grace chose to leave the house? Please ask yourself, is there a part of me that wrote some of the things I wrote to Jack because I want to gain back an advantage I'd lost when Grace left the house with the kids?

Declan, I'm trying not to come down too hard on you in this email, but as your friend and as your pastor, you are walking down a *path that is not only unsettling, but is also dangerous, both for Grace's mental health, and for yours.*

The truth is Grace needs some time away. Her MO has been to overly depend on you since you started dating. I don't necessarily condone a divorce, but would time away to get perspective be so bad? What about you? Could you use some time to get perspective on your relationship? You have an MO, as well. You need others to depend on you so you can control them. You need to hear this Declan. I'm not speaking out of an absence of knowledge regarding your relationship. How this ends depends on you. You can have a thriving, healthy relationship, or you can leave things as they are and Grace will walk away.

Let's talk about this further when I return. Maybe next Monday? Thanks for hearing me out. I know hearing stuff like this can be hard but if you decide to make some changes, I believe God will do great things in you and your marriage!

Jack

In my mind, and I'm not sure why, I felt like that email was going to make some changes for the better. My optimism can be a weakness, sometimes.

Jack

I need a friend and you send me that email? You have no evidence she's not having an affair, yet you claim boldly she's not? Ok, that doesn't seem wise. Then when I asked you to help me with her mental illness, you turned it around and focused on my issues. I don't know who you think you are, but whatever it is, you're way off-track. Why in the world would you believe that time away would be good for us? Time away will destroy us! Is that what you want, Jack? That's odd. I'm trying to figure out why you would want our marriage destroyed. Hmmmm.

Anyways, apparently you won't be the friend I thought you would be. And as far as a pastor, you're absolutely horrible, unbiblical, and worse, you betrayed me. There is such a feeling of loss I have in my soul right now. I'm fairly certain it will be a while before I recover from this.

As such, I am discontinuing our friendship, and will no longer be associating myself with you. I'm sorry it's come to this, Jack, but I can no longer trust you.

Declan

With the exception of three additional emails he wrote me later that night, he did discontinue our relationship.

This story begins in a college bar in Dover, New Hampshire. The University of New Hampshire hosted about 8,000 undergraduate students, and one of them, a freshman wrestler from Vermont, stood with his friends playing darts and talking about the midterm he'd just passed "by unethical means." Declan Dumais hailed from Burlington, four hours northwest of Boston. His father was an ultra-conservative Baptist preacher and his mother played the part of the good pastor's wife, cooking and cleaning and making sure the ladies of the church didn't gossip too much or stray from their husbands.

Declan loved his family, but by the time college rolled around he couldn't wait to "live a little," as he told his friends in high school. On this night, he stood with his new college friends, bragging about cheating "with 100% certainty for an A."

"I slept with the TA," he shouted, or the Guinness shouted for him.

"No way! The red-haired goddess?" This from his newest friend, Mark.

"You know it!" Declan said with a smile. "That's the one! And let me tell you, she was worth it, as was the A."

Mark had listened to stories like these before from Declan and didn't usually believe them, but he didn't care. Declan was fun, girls liked him and, as such, he enjoyed plenty of attention himself. The females of UNH frequently traveled in packs.

"Holy Hell, Declan! That's your third bullseye this game! You should drink more."

"I'm pacing myself. Don't worry," he said, making sure the bartender heard him, hinting that he needed his services again soon.

The Thirsty Moose was their favorite bar in Dover. They loved playing darts, eating pizza, and scouting their next pick up attempt. The lighting in the taproom shone just brightly enough to see everyone, but also dark enough to urge you to behave badly. Nearly a hundred coeds spent their late evenings at the Moose, especially on weekends.

Declan asked, just prior to Mark letting a red-feathered dart fly out of his hand, "I've heard this song before, but I can't think of who the group is. Can you?"

"Come on, Declan! That thirty points lost because of your big mouth!"

"That is correct, but this big mouth occasionally gets you beers for free, right?"

"Truth." Mark resigned himself to take the defeat gracefully. "And they play this song all the time on the radio, so that's how you heard it. It's called - oh my...."

"Yeah, no, that's not it," Declan said as he moved in front of the dart board.

"No, you idiot," Mark hushed him. "Look at that beautiful creature."

Then Declan froze and could not throw another dart. This tall, light-skinned, brunette entered the room with her "pack" and sabotaged his record-winning dart game. He didn't care. He was smitten at first glance.

"No way, man," Mark said, stepping in front of Declan's future conquest, "she's mine. I saw her first."

Declan responded quick and smooth, "You know that's not how this is going to go, Marky Mark. I'm going to go over there, walk up to that dream and introduce myself. Then I'm going to point out to her and her friends that you and I have been ... lonely. Then I'm going to invite them to join us. And they will, and you will enjoy yourself for the rest of the evening; Maybe even a double portion's worth." Declan smiled at the line he'd heard once at his parents' church.

Mark stepped aside and with a wink and a smile. Declan picked up his beer and walked over to the trio.

An hour before the women had entered the Thirsty Moose, they'd chilled in the brunette's dorm room. The two blondes, Steph and Stephie, performed surgery on each other's fingernails while the brunette waited by the phone for a call from her Mom. The last time they talked her mother warned her she was going to leave her father; was going to tell him she was tired of the verbal, emotional, and physical abuse; was going to tell him if he didn't leave the house, she would go to the police and get a restraining order.

All of this didn't sadden the brunette. On the contrary it filled her with overwhelming joy. For years she wanted and even cheered for this to happen, but her mother couldn't build the courage to have the intense conversation needed for it to happen.

She worried there would be no one else with them when her parents talked. She'd suggested two or three of her mother's friends join her. Mom excused the idea, saying that her husband was "not worth bringing someone else into the drama."

So her daughter waited. Then the phone rang.

"Hey, Mom!"

"Hi, honey," her mother replied, sheepishly. Instantly, she knew the woman didn't walk away.

"Mom?" Her disappointment was evident in that single word.

"Oh, don't worry about me, baby. I'll be fine. Your father means well, and I'm too old to do anything other than be with him."

"Mom, he's going to kill you someday, and I'm not being dramatic. You know I'm not. He will kill you!" she yelled, startling her two friend. "Mom, I have to go. I hope you know what you're doing." She hung up.

The brunette walked to the bathroom sink and washed her face. The last thing she wanted were puffy eyes tonight. She straightened and walked to the fingernail princesses. "I need a drink."

In the late nineties, in a college town in New Hampshire, it wasn't difficult to get your hands on alcohol, even when underage, especially if you looked like the brunette and especially if you looked like her on this particular night.

At five feet eight inches she towered above the two blondes. That night, she wore a tight pair of denim jeans that showed the lines of her legs. Her white T-shirt was form fitting quipped appropriately in black lettering, "My best friends hate the same people." She donned a pair of black string sandals.

The minute she walked into the Thirsty Moose that night she felt his eyes on her. She looked away immediately, but knew she would see him again soon. The guy stood across the room at the dart board with his friend. He stared, but she would not. Instead she glided across the floor towards the bar. Her two friends followed.

Declan was the same height as the newcomer, but didn't seem like he towered over anyone. He kept his hair military short, and was skinny, though his athletic build attracted the opposite sex on a regular basis. As a college athlete, he worked out all the time and had the energy of that bunny in the commercials who kept going and going. In fact, his nickname turned out to be "Rabbit" because of this.

Holding his beer, he crossed the bar floor to introduce himself to the trio, especially the brunette.

"Declan is my name, and my friend and I - uh, his name is Mark, and he's over there, that good looking chap - would love to buy you three lovely ladies drinks and maybe have the privilege of a few minutes of conversation. Would that be all right?"

"Are you always that smooth and intentional?" She asked in her own, sultry response. The two blondes glanced at each other and smirked. The game was afoot.

"I'm not always as smitten as I am tonight standing here looking into your eyes. But I'd also like to be smitten by our conversation. You see, the one thing I love more than exceptional beauty is exceptional intellect."

The woman couldn't resist and quickly replied, "I know a really smart and hot sociology teacher who would probably have a really intellectual conversation with you if you'd like."

"Feel free to invite her along. I'd love her to teach us both. We have so much to learn together."

And with that bizarre (to the others) back and forth the group laughed, interrupted suddenly by a cleared throat. "Uh, hello, Declan? When are you going to introduce me to our new friends?" Mark stood behind him. The two blondes responded by carving a spot for him to sit between them.

The evening flew by as Mark captivated the two blondes with his wit, at least they made him think they were, leaving Declan and the brunette to have some alone time.

"Ok" Declan said excitedly. "I can't believe I forgot, but I haven't even asked your name yet."

"What if I haven't given it to you on purpose?" She retorted. "Maybe I'm some sort of super spy and if I told you, I'd have to kill you. It Could be extremely dangerous for you to know my actual name."

She flirted well, Declan had to admit. He had no intention of neglecting this opportunity. More importantly, he actually liked her. Not like some of the others, but someone he saw himself with long term. First impressions could be wrong, of course, but he felt a connection with this tall stranger.

"In that case, I would rather not know your name. We should just skip over names and go right to what we want to do with the rest of our lives."

"I have a question for you," she said, losing her smile and appearing playfully serious. "What do you think of God?"

"God! Wow! You're going deep for a first date huh?"

"Oh, so this has become a date now?"

"Sure, why not?"

"Because you never asked me out like a gentleman does, that's why."

"Great point. So back to God. I am a fan of God. My parents are big fans. My dad is a pastor and before college I practically lived at church. Now that I'm in college, I'm pondering his validity or if he exists at all. If he does, what might that God look like. What about you?"

"Yeah, I think there's a God. I think I like him, but I don't know about the whole 'God the Father' thing. I assume you know more about that since your dad is a pastor. My father is a monster and I'd like nothing more than for him to not be my father. So when I hear God called a father, it irks me."

"Then where'd you learn about God? I'm assuming not from him."

"My Mom took me to church sometimes when my Dad was, let's just say in a bad mood. There was a church down the street from our house. I think it was Catholic. Walking in it was like looking at everything I didn't have that I wanted, so it was kind of rough. It felt like every family had a dad who was nice and had money. My dad was mean, put my mom down all the time, and had a job that paid nothing. But he never let my mom work."

"Seriously? Is that a thing in the 1990's? I mean, my mom didn't work, but that was her decision."

"She really never made decisions. I'm trying to get her to leave him, but to this point she hasn't built up the courage."

At that moment, the music volume turned up. They both said, "It's 10:00." At The Thirsty Moose, dancing started at ten, and conversation became too difficult.

"Do you want to get out of here?" Declan shouted, leaning closer.

"Where do you live? I want to go there." She said this with a seductive tone that made Declan excited yet nervous. She sounded very much in control and he usually liked to drive when it came to relationships.

"What's your name, and I'll make that happen." He said, attempting to grab control back.

"My name is Grace."

"Let's go, Grace."

Part 2

To Hell and Back

Don't be misled - You cannot mock the justice of God.
You will always harvest what you plant.
Galatians 6:7

Week 7 and Counting

Any energy Declan could have exerted saving his marriage, he instead chose to divert into his mission to prove a flat Earth. This included finances. It was also apparent to the Wolfpack that whatever was going on with his personal life was frustrating him. Finally, Adam spoke up during a period of silence.

"So, we're doing all this planning, Declan, and you've taken all this sick time off. Of course I'm retired, and Ronnie, well, perhaps he'll have a job someday. We have all this time, right? Which is good, but no one's bringing up the elephant in the room. Where the hell will we get the funds to make this project a reality? It's going to cost a lot of money, and though I'm excited about our mission, I am retired as I've said, and excitement isn't going to get me to Chile or the appropriate amount of firepower we'll need for the job."

"How much do you think it'll cost in total?" Declan asked. "I've been thinking about this, too, but give me an estimate, of course with a bare bones budget."

"Hmmm, bare bones? I would think we could get it done with, I don't know, 50,000 US."

"Great, I have $39,000 in a hidden account. All my bills are paid up, and I have $4,000 in my checking account I can clear out. What about you guys? Could you throw in the rest?"

"Shoot, Declan, I don't even have a pot to piss in." Ronnie declared.

Adam added, "And as I said earlier, I'm retired on a government pension, which means I have nothing."

"Ok, ok, I'll find the rest of the money we need. No worries. I'll invest my life into this thing. It's going to happen, I'll make sure it does. Currently I've got nothing on a few of our credit cards, so our travel can go on that as well.

"Speaking of which, to stay on our timeline, next week we need to fly to Puntas Arenas to plan for the final initiative. Everyone in?" Declan smiled with excitement that tangible steps were about to be taken.

"I can't next week, Dec," Adam confessed. "I'm having lunch with my daughter whom I haven't seen in a while." He didn't mention why, though they both knew the implication. "But I'll abide by your plans. You're detailed enough for me to be able to follow and execute them."

"What about you, Ronnie?" Declan asked.

"Can't, Dec! The VA has some flooping tests they're running on me all week. I'm even getting a flippin' colonoscopy!"

The guys laughed, but Declan was nervous that he'd end be doing all of the on-site work for Project: Frisbee. What if it wasn't good enough? What if every detail wasn't spelled out, if they missed something?

Adam sensed his nervousness and spoke to it. "Declan, you have the passion, the drive, and the smarts to make this happen. I hate what you did and I know it stunted our relationship, but when it comes to planning and following your lead on this mission, I'd gladly follow you. We can prove real science to the entire world, but it starts with you. You go, plan, and we'll follow those plans literally to the end of the world. The best is ahead for us."

Adams words alleviated Declan's worries, and to hear him speak out loud about Amber was a relief, too. For the last several weeks they worked well together, but he knew the past always laid in Adam's mind, but he didn't know how deep. For some reason hearing him mention it made Declan feel better.

They worked for a couple hours more, then Ronnie and Adam left. Declan bought his ticket to Punta Arenas for the following Monday. He would fly a combination of Jet Blue and Latam Airlines. A week from today he'd be standing near the tip of South America.

* * *

Grace spent the rest of the day with Marie, talking and figuring out how to live without her incessant need to fulfill Declan's wants. Chatting with her friend, she realized and understood the hurt she caused in her relationship by enabling Declan to control so much around him. But it was still difficult to imagine life without his direction. Every so often, in the middle of the conversation, she checked her phone. After a while she admitted what she was doing, not because she didn't know whether or not he'd called or texted, but because she'd wanted him to.

The hardest thing in the world to do, when you should do nothing, is to dismantle the training in your head that you must do the thing you're trying to not do anymore.

Marie arranged a place for Grace and the boys to stay while she looked for an apartment. Grace was never a genius when it came to details, so she'd overlooked this important detail before leaving her house. Marie told her about a place they could stay for a while, yet could see Grace was already considering the possibility of returning home.

"I'm not telling you to leave home, Grace, but I will remind you of the feelings you felt and the quality of your emotional health when you were there. Until you know things will change, definitely change, do you really want to go back?" her words were clear, and brought Grace back to reality. This time things had to be different. Change could happen, but not while she lived in the same environment where her codependent behavior had thrived for so long.

Marie would watch the kids while she worked overnight. Grace was thankful for her constant support in the last few months. She hugged and kissed her kids goodnight and drove to the home they'd be staying. She promised herself that she would rework her resume and find a new job by the end of the week.

The house Marie connected her with was a lovely McMansion east of Shrewsbury in a town called Westborough. Marie hadn't told her how nice it was, and all of a sudden she felt insecure about leaving Declan for a such a spacious, wonderful home, temporary as it was. She knocked at the front door, and a lovely sixty-something woman answered. Her name was Pauline, and she radiated joy the moment she saw Grace. Pauline told her she was thrilled to have her and her boys stay in their home, which she declared much too big for her and her husband, anyways. Thankfully Marie had explained the plan with the boys ahead of time, sparing Grace the embarrassment.

Pauline's husband, Virgil, owned a software company, which he was in the process of selling with the promise to retire. Pauline shared jokingly that she didn't really believe her husband would retire, but she hoped at least for more travels in the warmer parts of Europe. She showed Grace to the place she would be staying. It was a monstrous finished basement with a bathroom, two bedrooms, large furnished general living space and a walk-out porch leading to the pool area. Pauline had decorated the space to look like a "man cave" for her husband. Large, framed posters of the Patriots, Celtics, Bruins, and Red Sox hung on the wall, while a curved leather couch seemed to expand nearly thirty feet and faced at a hundred-inch television. A small but useful kitchenette sat in the back corner of the room.

Pauline told Grace to make herself at home and to call if she needed anything. Grace smiled, thanked her then walked around the apartment, in awe of the space she would call home for the next few weeks. In the silence, with the faint footsteps of her new proprietor trodding upstairs, she sat on the couch and let herself cry. She didn't want to admit it would be easier to be away from Declan in a space like this, nevertheless that would be the case. Am I so shallow? she thought to herself. Still, they would be safe, clean, and taken care of in their new temporary home.

Despite all this, her stomach turned with the idea that she'd walked away from Declan. It was the right thing to do, but she wondered if she would ever rid herself of the feeling that she couldn't do life without him. Withdrawals always ravage the addicted when the addict craves what it has chosen to leave.

Grace checked her phone. She'd a missed call from her boss. Quickly she dialed his number and listened to the phone ring. He answered, sounding rigid and cold.

"Hi Jim," Grace said, "I saw you called."

"Yeah, yeah, hey, Grace. So...don't bother coming in tonight. The last time you worked, we were short quite a bit in the cash drawer. I know it was the first time thing for you, but honestly, the last several months you've been kind of hit and miss in terms of your attendance, and I just can't have that, ya know?"

Grace felt her stomach tie in ways that were even more intense than before. "Jim, I know I've been gone a lot, but I've had a lot going on. I recently left my husband and I'm living in a nice place with the boys so I know things are going to calm down. I know they are. Please let me come in tonight!"

"I get it. I really do. But I'm sticking to my guns here. When you work, you do a decent job, but really in the last several months you haven't been trustworthy. I can't have that on my team. I wish you the best, and I know you'll come out on top, But right now it just can't be here, ok?"

Grace told herself not to cry while she was on the phone. She did not want to be that person, but she felt herself losing it as he spoke. Her own voice might quiver should she choose to use it. Jim needed to hear her reply, however, so he repeated himself.

"Ok, Grace? I don't want you to come in tonight."

"Ok. You won't see me there." She said it as if she never intended on being there in the first place. Immediately after, she hung up. If Grace had cried before, it was nothing compared to the tears that now flowed from her eyes. If she felt a turning in her stomach before, her stomach erupted now. She ran to her new bathroom and lifted the toilet seat, barely in time to discharge the contents of the mornings breakfast.

She laid down on the floor and wept until she fell asleep.

* * *

Declan told the Wolfpack he had $43,000 in the bank, and he believed that he did. Not once did he consider that his wife and kids might need some of that money. He did consider that Grace might take part of the $4000 in checking so the next morning he rushed to the bank and transferred $3900 to his hidden personal account. He figured leaving $100 in there showed how charitable he was to his 'runaway' Grace.

He also took $10,000 out of his 401K. There would be a heavy penalty for the action, but Declan figured the IRS eventually got theirs anyways.

The rest of the week he organized plans for an autumn garage sale. He sold a lot of stuff to make a little more spending money, even though he had the amount Adam thought they needed. You can never have too much, Declan thought.

When the week was finished, Declan had $53,400 for Project: Frisbee, and he celebrated by getting online and purchasing his ticket to Punta Arenas for next week. One passenger, from Wednesday, November 10 to Saturday, November 13. He looked forward to the trip and seeing the lay of the land before the final phase of the project began, not to mention getting some time to be alone. Planning the project was going to take over his head space for the next several weeks so he'd utilize that time to mentally prepare himself for the craziness his life was going to become.

Normally he would have flown economy class, but since he had more money than he needed, and he was going to fly this trip solo, he purchased a first class ticket. This set him back $5000 more than economy and added a fifth leg to his trip, but it also saved him eleven hours of travel time according to the website.

He purchased the ticket and received the corresponding emails that came with it. He prayed silently at his desk, God help me show the world the true power of creation they want to repeatedly ignore. He noticed Grace's email tabs were left open, and spent the next several hours looking through her correspondence over the last year.

Sometimes when you go through something traumatic, you run into strangers who will change your life forever. Those strangers might not have had a starring role in your life, but they changed you, either in the things they said to you, the places they took you, other people around you they affected or the things they've done.

Maybe it was an abusive parent or a mistress or your best friend's worst enemy, those people affected and changed your life in ways you never even noticed. In the midst of hardships, most outside of those closest to you become a type of strangers. You keep them at a distance and build a wall made of surface relationships so thick, their natural response is to step away for fear of offending you.

In one of my most difficult seasons of life, I replaced the extroverted Jack for someone who wanted very little communication with anyone. I didn't tell myself this, but it was more of a protective measure to make sure I wasn't hurt again. Over the next few weeks, Marie kept in contact with Grace more than I, though we'd both become strangers to Declan. But the interactions both of them had with strangers, changed the course of their lives forever.

Week 6 and Counting

Grace spent the rest of the week and into the next preparing her resume and cover letters to send out. She decided not to settle for a "gas station" style job any longer. She wanted her kids to live in a healthy and comfortable circumstance. Grace knew this would require hard work and grit, but in the end, meeting her goal was worth the sacrifice, and risk.

By the time Tuesday rolled around she'd sent out thirteen resumes and wondered if she would hear back from any of the companies. This past week with the boys had been healing in many ways. Marie had cautioned her, however, not to transfer her dependencies from Declan to her kids.

"You're good enough on your own," she'd said the first morning when Grace had come to pick the boys up. "You were created by God to accomplish his beautiful purposes. You need others around you, but you don't need them in order to live. That's an important difference," She spoke with the skill of a professional counselor, but with the love of a wise friend.

Playing with the boys was so freeing. The last year she knew she'd been a horrible parent. Her desires had flared up for her husband only, God and others be damned. Now the tension dissipated as Marie and Pauline tag-teamed to love and care for Brandon and Luke, and her. There was still the matter of not having a job, but for now she was being taken care of in amazing ways by these God-given ladies.

On Wednesday, Marie told Grace to go do whatever she wanted. She would watch the boys for a few hours. So Grace drove down Route 9, eventually turning into Shrewsbury center and found herself near the Main Street library. She drove past, cursing its existence and her past experience there. Instead she rode towards Dean Park for a walk around the pond.

A gorgeous Fall day meant that the sky was blue with a slight chill in the air, leaves spread across the ground. A few stubbornly clung to their original homes, which in Dean Park primarily meant Maple trees.

She parked near the tennis courts then walked towards the pond, passing the playgrounds on the way. Children ran and climbed between the two huge wood and steel contraptions. Mothers looked on, talking to one another and occasionally calling out to their children to behave or warning them not to climb too high, anything to help them feel in control of the fate of their kids.

Grace realized now more than ever that control was not something to grasp or aspire to, but to run from. For the better part of her adult life she watched a master controller attempt to organize and manipulate everything in his world. The more he tried, the less control he had. Of course the same proved to be true in her own soap opera of a life. She'd made plans and thought her life would look a certain way by this point, but it looked vastly different. Her marriage lay in shambles, and her job situation sat in a coffin of her own making.

She decided to pray for Declan and the boys every day. She laughed when she thought about praying for what she didn't have, but she knew it was important. For the moment she would pray and wait. The time would come when she would take more than the small steps she'd already taken towards a new job or finding more support. For now, she felt her heart telling her to do nothing. This created a feeling of vulnerability she didn't like, but believed she needed.

Grace looped around the pond a few times, then turned back towards her car, stopping for a few minutes at the playgrounds again. She again watched the kids and the moms interact as lunch time grew closer. She must have looked sullen staring at the scene by the fence because suddenly one of the mothers was standing next to her holding a baby.

"Are you okay?" A young woman's voice said, startling her out of her thoughts. Jumping slightly, Grace smiled and moved back a half-step, apologizing for no reason at all.

"Yes, I'm okay, thank you. I'm sorry."

"There's nothing to be sorry about; I was just checking on you. I thought you might have recognized me."

Why would I recognize you? Grace thought, then looked closer and she knew she did recognize her. Where do I know you from?

As if hearing her thoughts, the young woman answered the question.

"I'm Amber."

***

Declan arrived at Boston's Logan airport just after 6:30 am on Wednesday the 10th of November. He wouldn't land in Punta Arenas until the 11th. His mindset, however, was fixed on accomplishing this first part of the mission: To build reconnaissance at the airport and surrounding areas, and create a game plan for the Wolfpack to fully realize Project: Frisbee. Details would be important, as with everything he did. Details, and focus.

Ronnie had driven him in that crisp morning. They gave each other a bro-hug and Declan walked to the terminal door, anxious and excited for what he would experience over the next several days. At the ticket line, he stood and waited for several minutes until the lovely Hispanic agent asked to take the next customer. He could have taken the first class line, but didn't want to stand out this early in the trip.

She looked at his passport and ticket, then looked at it a second time.

"You're not a Flat Earther, are you?" She said, smiling as if making a joke.

He didn't know what to say, so he lied. "No, I'm not. Just going to do some sight-seeing. I do it for a living, in fact."

"Oh wonderful. Well, have a fantastic trip. Here's your boarding pass. Do you have a bag to check?"

"No, ma'am. Just this one. I'll keep it with me."

"Sounds good. Just walk this way to the security gates, and you'll be flying out of Gate 8, okay?"

"Thank you so much." Declan nodded then walked the direction she'd pointed.

Because of her question, however, he felt more nervous than before. Was anyone watching him? Was he monitored more carefully because of his destination?

He strolled through the security gates in twenty-five minutes, making it to Gate 8 with an hour and fifteen minutes to spare before the flight. Declan sat down and took out a book. Terra Firma: The Earth Not a Planet, Proved from Scripture, Reason, and Fact had been on his reading list for some time, and now with this trip he had plenty of time. Opening the book, he smiled at the opening remarks of the author, David Wardlaw Scott. The author went after the 'long-known' notion that the earth is round. For the next forty-five minutes he read until the agent called for all first class passengers to make their way to the gate.

Declan jumped up and grabbed his bag and book, practically skipping to the gate. The agent took his ticket and welcomed him to enter the plane. He thanked her and made his way into the transport which would carry him to Mexico City, then Santiago and finally Punta Arenas.

* * *

Grace stood awkward, and confused. Awkward, for her poor luck running into the woman who'd slept with her husband. Confused, because of that woman's courage to tell her who she was. The tiny infant in Amber's arms was also confusing. So confusing; in fact, Amber obviously needed to defined her relationship with the baby.

"This is kind of my job now, I'm a nanny."

"Okay," Grace replied, still dizzy from this surprise conversation. "I guess I don't know what to say right now. Why did you say hello?"

"I wanted to know if you were okay. I thought you recognized me. And also, I wanted to, and I know this is weird, but you're here so... I wanted to say I'm sorry."

Grace fought to keep her tears back, fearing that the emotions that might come out in this public place if she didn't leave right now. But she didn't, nor could she talk because of some nervous ball appearing in her throat.

"What I did was horrible," Amber continued, slowly rocking the baby in her arms. "It was hurtful for you and to your family. It wasn't something that should ever have happened. I don't want to embarrass you here, but I needed to say it because I have no idea when I'll ever see you again. So, well, I'm sorry. I really am. I needed to be the better person and I wasn't and I hold myself personally responsible for that. I was wrong. I found a group of friends recently who invited me to church, and I feel like I'm changed somehow. That probably doesn't matter to you... and that's ok. But I had to reach out when I saw you and let you know. Again, I am so sorry."

Rubbing her arms as the wind suddenly felt much cooler, Grace turned her head towards the car. She couldn't respond. If God wanted her to forgive her husband's mistress, it would happen serendipitously again on another day.

"Thank you." Grace mouthed, turning and walking from the other woman. This was better, wasn't it? She wanted to scream at her, and tell all the woman in the park not to let their husbands anywhere near this tramp. But she didn't. Instead she stopped the rage before it could take over, choosing instead to walk away. She unlocked her car, opened the door, and sat in the driver's seat. By this time Grace was heaving tears of sorrow loud enough to get the attention of a guy getting out of his car next to her.

He mouthed the words, "Are you okay?" She nodded yes and drove away, deeply sorrowful for every event in her life that led to this moment, today. Minutes later she passed by the library again. Continuing to cry, she slammed her palm on the steering wheel and screamed, "God!!! Why are you doing this to me?! Why do you hate me?! I'm trying to do right. You just keep kicking me over and over!"

She starting shaking, still hitting the steering wheel. Grace forced herself to pull into the nearby CVS parking lot.

"Don't hurt yourself. Don't hurt yourself," she pleaded quietly, scratching her arms over and over.

***

Declan walked out of the plane and into the only terminal of the Presidente Carlos Ibanez del Campo International Airport. The airport was named after a two-time president of Chile in the early 20th century. His politics had vacillated like a fan on a hot Ecuadorian day, but he was well-liked enough to gain a good deal of notoriety.

Politics wasn't Declan's mission, however. He gazed around the airport. Huge rafters overlooked a crowd of senior citizens reading together at tables, backpackers gawking at their maps on the overcast day. Monstrous flying whales hung from several of these rafters. Because of his focus, Declan forgot that this airport would be have been close to the water. An important detail to remember for later.

He took mental notes with every step, his eyes darting around the room to soak in as much detail as possible. The official strategy wouldn't be finalized until he arrived home, but everything hinged on what he remembered from these moments. Declan stood at a wall for a few minutes, writing down details, doors that might be important, concession booths, and the general layout of the airport. All around him glass walls displayed the incredible beauty of Punta Arenas.

Declan eventually grabbed a sandwich, and sat at a round table in the middle of the terminal. He sat next to some seniors who left their reading for a few minutes to chat in Spanish with each other. Of course, he didn't understand them. As far as he knew, they were talking about him.

One of the men, with bronzed wrinkling skin and white hair and dressed in a colorful beaded shirt and blue jeans, stood up and walked over to Declan's table.

"Habla Espanol?" he asked.

Declan responded with a smile and even slower, "No...hablo Ingles. Oh, sorry, I mean, no hablo espanol. Hablo Ingles." He laughed at his own lack of proficiency when it came to foreign languages.

"What brings you to our part of the world, friend?" The stranger asked in English, surprising Declan with the clarity of his question.

"Just... sightseeing."

A pause lay still across the table as Declan looked around at the flying whales awkwardly, The old man was looking straight at him. After thirty seconds or so the man finally spoke again.

"Sometimes knowing a truth isn't worth losing one's family, or even one's life. Have you thought through the non-monetary costs before you came here?"

Declan looked around the room again, making sure no one was listening. The table of senior citizens now sat empty, and the airport seemed quieter than it had been before. The man continued after a few seconds.

"It is obvious to many here at the airport why you have come."

"What do you mean?" Declan said defensively. "Is sightseeing a crime now in Chile?"

"I'm your friend, Declan," the stranger said quietly, causing Declan's head to turn quickly toward him. The man kept talking. "I don't want your family in Boston to be without you. They love you. You love them. They need you. They shouldn't lose you... and for what? For some crazy theory you saw somewhere on the internet? That's not science, Declan. That's just craziness. Enjoy your stay here for the next few days. In fact, here's $500 in case you want to get some stuff for the kids and the wife. Although, you two aren't really hanging out much these days, are you? Either way, when you leave here, don't come back, okay?"

"Are you threatening me? Is that what this is? You're threatening me?"

The old man stood slowly, ignoring Declan's question. "This is not America. Your rights are of no consequence here. What is important is that you understand what I am telling you. I am telling you to not come back after you leave. Have an amazing trip, Declan. Enjoy your stay here in Chile."

He walked away. Declan sat gazing at the rafters, dizzy from the conversation. He moved his head slowly down to the $500. The bills were in US denominations, quite a lot of money if he decided to convert them to Chilean Pesos. What kind of person has that kind of money to throw at someone else as a 'kind gesture'? Declan thought. Perhaps the kind of person who could walk up to a 'stranger' and tell him to have a good time and to not come back to this place. A person who had a lot of power here.

Declan reluctantly took the money and walked around the airport for the next few hours, being careful not to go into any unauthorized areas. He realized now that people were watching him. He also noticed how the airport began to fill up again with passengers and customers.

After a few hours of reconnaissance, he walked out of the terminal, hailed a cab, and instructed its driver by saying simply, "Best Western Hotel." A moment later, the car drove away from the airport.

Week 5 and Counting

Declan arrived back in Massachusetts on Saturday and slept for the next two days. He knew he had a long week ahead of him putting his plans together, organizing the team around the information he'd gathered, and taking care of some last minute things at home. But through it all, even his exhaustion, his commitment to truth, knowledge, and controlling his future would lead him to changing the world. Conspiracies and NASA be damned, he would uncover the box of truth for all who were willing to see it. He would ignore the old man from the airport and simply be more careful with their plans.

The long week started with printing out all the pictures Declan took of the airport, which he forced himself to wait until preparing to board for his return trip. He didn't imagine the old man with the money would have appreciated him taking these that first day. He laid them out across the desk and table in the garage office. Then made a list of the plan's important and remaining phases.

*Book hotel in case airplane doesn't show up. Book second hotel room (cash only) as meeting place in case something goes bad.

*Learn about the A321

*Build 2D layout of Punta Arenas and meet with Wolfpack about the plan

*Help Adam find a collection of weapons in Punta Arenas

*Make sure to have everything taken care of here at home

*Find a point person to send info back to the US

*DCF

*Life Insurance

After a search on the internet, He called Hotel Rey Don Felipe and made a reservation for three rooms for Wednesday, November 23rd. He also made reservations for three other rooms in three different hotels using a fake identification card Adam had made in the last few weeks, easily one of his most useful skills up to this point.

He then made three different plane reservations for November 21st. Adam would fly to Buenos Aires, spend a few days at a hotel, then on the 23rd fly into Punta Arenas where he would immediately take a taxi to the Hotel Rey Don Felipe. Ronnie would take Declan's earlier flight path from Logan airport in Boston to Santiago, Chile, then finally to Punta Arenas, meeting Declan and Adam at the hotel on the Wednesday before Thanksgiving. For his part, Declan would drive south to New York City, flying out of JFK to Miami, spend a night, then on the 22nd fly to Mexico City, taking a red eye to Santiago and finally ending up in Punta Arenas on the morning flight. Each of them would head to two different places in the city, then meet in a fourth room Declan booked under another alias. He would need to give his passport at the hotel, but Adam's to-do list required this to be done later this week.

The bang on the outside door surprised Declan as he clicked through the steps needed to get "half way across the world." He opened the garage office slowly, almost expecting the FBI to storm in with battering rams and body gear. Ronnie stood hunched over, however, chewing tobacco and spitting it out at the same moment Declan opened the door.

"What's up, Ronnie? Come in and stop pollutin' my driveway." Declan laughed and motioned to his friend to come in. Ronnie obliged and walked into the garage office wearing a t-shirt with the arms cut off. The screen print on the front advertised a casino. On the back a cartoon layout of the casino showed an crowd of partygoers drinking, gambling, and flirting raucously.

"For a guy who likes to sleep in, you're up early this morning." Declan said, trying to get the conversation started quickly. He needed to get work done and couldn't spend time on a long chat.

"I can't sleep, Declan. I haven't been able to for a long time, and it's starting to affect me."

"Why can't you sleep?" Declan asked.

"Honestly, I'm scared. I don't know if I can do this. I don't know if I can fly that plane, specifically if the Chilean friggin' Air Force is involved, which, why wouldn't they be? I feel like this job is way too big and so outside of my control, there's is no way we're going to be able to make it happen."

"I get it, Ronnie. I really do. I'm scared, too. The details I have to figure out are intense and there are honestly times I don't think we can do it. But the "why" is so important here. We have an opportunity to change the world, to change history and science. Do you wanna be known as the guy who threw dust on fields all his life or one of the team that rewrote textbooks and proved everyone's thoughts on the biggest subject, literally in the world, were completely messed up? Take control of your life, Ronnie. What we're doing..." Declan forced a tear to further his point, while also pausing for effect. "What we're doing is really big. I want you to be a part of it. Do you want to be a part of such a huge change? Can you see our vision, see it being accomplished?"

Ronnie stroked his scruff beard as if he were capable of being deep in thought, but after a short five seconds, he confirmed, "Hell, yeah, I want to be a part of that!"

"Then let's make it happen. Let's not be double minded, as the Bible says in James. Let's make our plans. Execute them. Act as a team. Go through all of the stuff we're going to have to go through. Then our names will be considered alongside the greats, from Christopher Columbus to

Vasco De Gama to Marco Polo, as some of the greatest explorers in history. Does that sound good to you?"

"I don't know who those guys are, but if you have a beer, I'll take it and let's get to work."

"That's the spirit. Only a few weeks until history."

* * *

Grace sat in her apartment fuming at recent events in her life over the last few weeks. She wanted to do the right thing, be a good example for her boys, but every circumstance she found herself in since leaving Declan drove her into deeper waves of self-pity, the likes of which she rarely ever encountered.

Jobless and effectively a single-parent since she walked away, only faith seemed to be driving her decisions. Apparently, however, she forgot to release the emergency brake, because something was stopping her from moving forward. How could she get ahead? Declan had moved on quickly enough, working tireless hours on that stupid project. He was apparently using up every remaining personal and vacation day from school to allow him time to still get paid while being on this bizarre, extended vacation. He should be fired, but instead he thrived, like usual, in whatever he chose to do. Her life, on the other hand, continued to head the wrong direction. She couldn't get past any trial she faced, as if she someone held her down and forced her to stay in some torture chamber when all she had to do was walk out.

She could pray, of course, but her faith felt forced, and rocks of bitterness welled up around her heart. She remembered Marie using the expression, "Fake it till you make it," and decided to pray for the first time in a few weeks. The boys would not be back from school for a few hours, and she needed something, so she awkwardly kneeled in front of the couch and placed her elbows on the navy blue cushions.

She called out to God in tears, begging him to take control of her life. I can't do this, she told him, but I needed your help. After a heartfelt appeal that she was sure God knew anyway, she heard the door knock upstairs, followed by voices speaking to one another. Footsteps headed toward her door. Another knock.

She stood up and walked slowly to the door, drying her tears before opening the door. Pauline introduced her to a lady Grace had never seen before. The woman smiled at her. With the week she was having she half-expected it to be Amber again, so she was somewhat grateful.

"May I help you?" She said, trying to sound as authentic as possible.

"Yes, you are Grace Dumais, correct?" She'd pronounced it wrong, with the Spanish A sound. Except for a somewhat contorted face and an inch or two more height, the woman looked a lot like Grace.

"I am." She said, not wanting to give too much information to someone she didn't know or worse, a saleswoman. She did not intend to purchase cutting knives or a vacuum cleaner or a trip to the third heaven via the Jehovah Witnesses.

"Hi Grace. My name is Mary Belizzi. I'm with the Department of Children and Families. I'm here regarding a complaint that has been made. I cannot disclose who made that complaint. Nevertheless, I need to ask you some questions. Could we chat for a few minutes?"

The room spun a hundred miles per hour as Grace stared at the smiling stranger for at least thirty seconds without speaking. She thought through what was happening and how to respond but couldn't think of what to do. Of course she'd respond kindly, allow this lady who was simply doing her job to come in and ask her questions. And of course she would answer those questions, whatever they may be, with truth and kindness. Of course she would. Then, finally, the room stopped and she was more in control of her senses.

"Of course, you can. I'm... sorry. Come in. Please. Would you like something to drink?" She spoke with as much hospitality as she could manage. She worried she sounded more like a crazy person.

"No, thank you," came the expected response. They both sat down in the sitting area of the basement apartment.

After a slight pause the state worker began the conversation. "So when we have a complaint given to us, we have no choice but to take it seriously. We don't, however, have a presumption of guilt or innocence until we investigate every avenue of the charges...."

"I'm being charged with something?" Grace interrupted defensively.

"No, no, I'm sorry. We use those terms, but we use them differently than the police or the law. A charge is simply a claim that a child is, or might be, in danger. Then we are tasked with the responsibility to assess the risk that the claim is true or not."

"Can you tell me the charges?" Grace inquired.

"Not right away. I understand that is difficult, but I have to investigate initially around the risks and dangers of the children and ultimately I need to do that with as little interference from anyone else as possible."

The implication that Grace would be an "interference in her children's lives" irritated her, but she forced herself to remain silent. Mary continued, "So, today we'll talk, and then I'll leave and write what I believe is an assessment of this visit. I'll probably return with one other person, if everything goes as smoothly as I think it will. Together we'll both write a similar report and sign off that everything is okay. If we see or experience anything that concerns us, depending on what those things are, we might return a few more times."

A sickness gripped Grace. All she wanted was to be left alone with her boys, to get a job and start a new life free of control freaks and painful drama. With this new development, it appeared that might be months. Perhaps faith's journey was simply too grueling. Perhaps it wasn't worth it.

"So... a few questions. And they are going to seem very pointed, but once again, I want you to know I want what's best for you and your family. My goal is not to take your children away from you. My goal is to protect the children of the Commonwealth of Massachusetts and helping you be a better parent allows me to do that.

"My first question is this: do you think your kids are safe in your home?"

"Yes. Absolutely. Honestly, I have no idea why you're even here."

"Ok, that's fair," Mary responded. "But you do want what's best for your kids, right?

"Do you have children, Mary?" Grace asked, clearly irritated.

"I do not yet," Mary said calmly.

"Ok, but let's say you did. Would it mean you didn't want what's best for your kids if you were irritated that a stranger walked up to your door one day out of nowhere and started asking you a bunch of questions to 'protect your kids'?"

"This is where we find ourselves, Grace. I don't know what to tell you. I have the authority of the Commonwealth of Massachusetts, and someone has made a complaint to us. I have to follow up. You can answer my questions, deal with me for a few weeks, and I assume everything will be fine. But right now, I just need you to answer the questions I ask."

"I hope someday you don't have a crazy ex-husband in your life. I'd hate for your co-workers to have to put you through this, too." This was the first time in the conversation she brought up Declan, but she knew it was him the minute Mary introduced herself and where she worked. Mary, for her part, ignored the comment.

"Would you say that recently you have overused alcohol or drugs?"

"I don't ever use drugs that aren't prescribed to me by my doctor, and I rarely drink any alcohol whatsoever. When I do its usually beer or wine." Grace tried hard to not sound agitated. Mary wrote some notes down and continued.

"Those drugs that the doctor prescribes, do you ever take too many? Even accidentally?"

"No."

"Ok, thank you. Recently have you and your kids been a part of any situations that may be described as 'dangerous?'"

"No." Grace said pointedly, realizing she could take an opportunity to explain what she meant and it would be advantageous. "And I don't just mean that in a way where I'm trying not to answer you. It means that in no way, under any circumstances have I ever been in a 'dangerous' situation with my kids, in all of their lives."

"Ok. Thanks for explaining your answer there. I appreciate that." Mary said, and Grace could feel the tides turning. She still fumed, however, at having to go through this process.

"Grace, let's talk about your support system as a single parent. Who do you have in your life that supports you emotionally, if you need to talk to someone, or if there is anything you need help with as a single mom for instance?"

"Well, my mother lives in Keene, New Hampshire and we talk on a regular basis, at least once a week but usually more. My pastor and his wife talk with me several times a week. They are some of my closest friends, and have helped me during the dissolving of my marriage in the last year. I have a few friends I don't necessarily talk to every week, but could call up if I ever needed anything. Also, I have an appointment to meet with a therapist next week. I don't have to, but I realize it is something that will benefit me personally, so I will do it despite the personal cost."

Mary wrote down some notes and after a few more questions she needed to ask to ensure Grace's children were safe, she finished the interview.

"Grace, thank you so much for your time. I realize this probably wasn't what you had in mind today when you woke up, but I appreciate it. I believe your children have a good mother who loves them and protects them and I believe they are safe and there is no risk to their safety at this time. I will be putting that in writing. I will need to return next week randomly for a quick visit as that is our policy, no matter how an interview like this goes."

Mary stood up and Grace couldn't let her walk out without asking another question. "Before you leave," she said, "What if this happens again? What if random people call you and tell you all sorts of things about how what a horrific mother I am?"

"Oh that's easy, Grace," Mary answered her. "We have the name of the person, how they know you, and if they continue to send us your name, eventually they will need to be held accountable to those accusations. But at first, we do have to check on every threat to a child's well-being. Does that make sense?"

"It does. Thank you so much for coming today. Please let me know how I can be of any assistance." She guiding the woman towards the door.

As Mary walked out, Grace stood in shock, feeling too weak and drained to do anything but lay down. Is there anything else, God? she thought. Surely faith in you has to do something for me, because what it's brought me so far is a huge pile of crap.

It feels weird to say this now, but the first day of Thanksgiving week, I jumped out of bed after my latest dream. I had a realization that Grace was struggling intensely with putting her faith in God, and Declan wasn't even trying anymore. The dream worried me enough I decided to call them both on the morning of November 23rd. When I called Grace, she told me her last month had been nightmarish. The trials piled up around her and bullets of discouragement shot through the thin layer of faith her she'd held at the moment. I prayed with her over the phone and reminded her that Marie and I were always there for her. I begged Grace not to let the enemy get the upper hand in her life. She said she would fight, but admitted the more she fought, the harder life came at her.

We hung up the phone, then Marie and I spent some time praying for Grace before I called Declan. I had no idea how he would react to me after the last email blitz, but I honestly felt like he needed me in that moment. To my shock, he picked up the phone after the second ring.

"Hey, Jack!" He answered. "How've you been? Thanks for calling."

"I've been good, Dec! Hadn't heard your voice in a while, so I thought I'd give you a ring and see how you're doing."

"I'm doing so good. Right now I'm in Mexico City."

"Mexico City?!" I couldn't disguise my shock. I hadn't expected him to tell me that. "What are you doing there?"

"Just spending a few days traveling and trying to change the world," he said nonchalantly. "Changing the world is hard work, Jack. I know you're doing a decent job at Apex, but to truly make a dent in the way civilization thinks, you've got to have more than just faith. You need that, yes, but then take the bull by the horns and control it. In other words, if you don't control the things in your life, your faith in that object or person will backfire because they will control you. Then you're finished."

I knew I would regret this, but I had to ask. "Can you give me an example of what you're talking about, Declan? What kinds of things do you have to control before they backfire?"

"My wife, for starters." His breathing sounded labored, as if he was walking and talking at the same time. Now and then I heard a distant car phone. "I was too lenient and she didn't know how to survive without me. Even so, she thought it was a good idea to do her own thing. Fine. We'll see how she likes it. She can't live without me, Jack. Not to mention it's against the Bible to get a divorce."

I didn't know where to start with a response, but I gave it a shot. "Declan, I believe your thinking is off-track. The purpose of faith is not to get your way, or to be successful. The purpose of faith is to help you realize that you can't get your way on your own. There's always a bigger picture that you're not privy to. So, as far as Grace, yes, she'll have some problems on her own. After all, she's got some hefty codependency issues. But if she focuses on faith coupled with hope, she'll be all right. I'm sure of it. And your theology on divorce is a little off, Declan. I was not in support of her leaving you, but when you say things like that, honestly, I wonder if maybe she made the right call."

"Honestly, Jack, I don't give a damn what you think," Declan responded harshly. "You spend all of your time with her and have completely ignored me in the last month. I have no idea why you're taking her side, but I can only imagine."

"Declan, have you been drinking? You're not talking sensibly right now."

"Why, because you're sleeping with my ex? We're not legally divorced, yet, so you're actually sleeping with my wife. That's crazy! Wait till I tell your church about this one. It'll be as bad as when I told DCF Grace was running a whore house out of her new apartment!"

"Are you nuts, Declan?"

"Not in the least, Jack. But I am going to change the world, then you'll see. My name will be up in lights, textbooks, and I'll be in every American talk show. That British guy, Graham Norton will probably have me on his show, too." His voice got louder, and more muffled. I picture him hunched over, pressing his face harder into the phone. I have a vivid imagination sometimes. "Then when I'm on that stage, I'll tell all your secrets, and Grace's. I'm in control now and forever, Jack. So, f-"

I hung up. My relationship with this man was, in this moment, officially over.

* * *

Grace and the boys woke up on Thanksgiving morning feeling anything but thankful. As she drove out of Shrewsbury, the air felt crisp and clouds hovered over the beautiful overcast Fall morning. Suddenly, as if it touched her shoulder, a fog rolled out excitedly from the trees and air and ground. It blanketed her view like a canvas around a covered wagon. Then a disgruntled wind blew and the red, orange, and yellow leaves began to fall gently towards land like snow on Christmas Day. The sun then peeped its head out, staring down at the acres of trees as a proud father to his children and giving the trees a majestic and brilliant and gorgeous appearance. She drove on toward Keene. The scene told her everything would be all right. No matter what came at her, her faith could keep her strong enough to protect through the intensity of the trials.

She was going to spend the day with her mother. Though she held onto a sadness about losing her "family" as it had been, she loved her Mom. Grace understood in many ways she'd followed the woman's footsteps, needing someone who couldn't need or love her back, but she was much younger than her mother when she figured out the problem, and attributed that to her mother's example. Today she would proudly spend a day of gratitude with the woman who raised her and showed her true love.

When they arrived, her mother met them in the same driveway where she watched her father drive away for the last time years before. Neither he nor Declan would be joining the festivities, and she wondered whether or not that was a good thing. She missed Declan. She missed his smile and his initiative. She missed his face and putting her hands on his body.

Mom interrupted her thoughts by opening up the back door of the car for the boys. Her playful impatience showed as she asked them to get out of the car and give their Nana a "super big kiss and a hug." Grace watched them, then climbed out of the car and hugged her mother, who then ran off to kick a soccer ball back and forth with her grandkids. Although the temperature held to just over forty degrees, the sun beat down over the Keene valley, making it feel warmer. The boys eventually went off to play on their own, so Grace and her mother walked into the house she'd grown up in. Everything inside smelled amazing.

They talked while they cooked. Nancy asked Grace to cut up and mash the potatoes. The meal didn't take long to finish as most of the food had been prepared in advance. After an hour or so, the turkey exited the oven and was carved up in edible arrangements amid immense amounts of steam pouring from the sides. The boys came in immediately after they were called to the table and everyone sat down.

Today's Thanksgiving dinner would host only the four of them. Declan was spending Thanksgiving traveling from Mexico City to Santiago, Chile. Grace's brother John couldn't get away from working his big time software job for Google. "Apparently being with your family isn't a high priority for the search engine company," Nancy quipped while setting the table.

Nevertheless, the table sported all the wonderful Thanksgiving-type foods, from a huge juicy herb crusted turkey to Apple sausage stuffing to the "best sweet potato casserole I've ever had," according to Luke. Everyone ate and talked for over an hour. The boys didn't even complain about having to stay at the table for so long. The mood had changed since they began their journey from Shrewsbury to Keene early that morning, and Grace finally began to understand that trials or difficulties didn't have to own her, or even make her into a new person. Her reactions and attitudes in the midst of those trials which would help her become the person she wanted to be.

After dinner and dishes, Nancy and Grace crashed on the couch while the boys watched a Christmas movie. Their eyes fixated on the young curly-haired human who lived at the North Pole and thought he was an elf.

They laughed as he traveled to New York, and on the way was bitten by a raccoon when he tried to kiss it.

Nancy asked Grace, "So how have things been at home? Getting used to single life?"

Grace thought about her mother's words as she slowly sipped her peppermint tea. "I guess I am. Very slowly. I miss him, you know? At the same time, I know I made the right decision. I had to let go, at least for now. It was best for him. And me."

Nancy placed her hand on Grace's knee. "You need to find the whole Grace. The Grace that walked into the house when she was in high school with her head up, knowing half or more of the school wanted to be her or to date her. The Grace who knew who she was, who loved in such a big way, and who confidently walked into a room and was completely okay with every eye being on her." She gave her daughter's knee a pat. "Grace, somewhere along the way, you lost your ability to just be the person God made you to be. I don't know, maybe I showed you a horrible example of needing to have someone in your life, and you carried that out when you walked into that relationship, but now you can and should live in a way God created you, just the way he wanted you. You're unique and special and kind and beautiful. You're a wonderful mother and one of the best daughters I know."

Grace smiled sadly. "How do I become that person again, Mom? I'm so lost. I've traveled so far away from being that young lady. I don't know if I can get back. I depended on him for... for... for everything."

"Grace, do you know why Declan believes the Earth is flat?" Nancy asked with surprising bluntness.

"I didn't even know you knew about that," Grace said, wiping a tear from the corner of eye and sniffling a little.

"Of course, I knew. He couldn't help but talk about it every time we were in the same room together."

"Oh. I guess when he starts talking, I check out of the conversation."

"Yes, you do." Nancy laughed. "But the reason he believes in the flat Earth is because he must live in a world that he can control - everything we see and everything we experience. So, talk of other galaxies and things that can't be explained are unacceptable to him. When it comes to relationships, then, and a woman's mind, specifically yours, he defined it in ways he could understand and, ultimately, control.

"But there is no controlling the mind of a healthy woman. Even the great philosopher Keanu Reeves said, 'It's always wonderful to get to know the mystery and the joy and the depth of a woman.' Men make jokes all the time about understanding them. Listen to them. They make jokes because they don't understand and they can't stand that. So they either attempt to control us with their bodies and their words. Over time, those strong, mysterious, deep, joy-filled women can turn into robots or mere shells of themselves."

She reached out and stroked her daughter's hair. "You have an opportunity now, Grace. You can choose to live life the way you were created to, or live someone else's life, and all the while trying to control the things around that cannot be controlled. Who do you wanna be, Grace?"

Grace was heaving tears of pain and relief that erupted from deepest parts of her soul. Nancy gently lifted helped her to her feet and they walked to Grace's old bedroom where she laid down. She held her daughter and they wept together.

Grace slept soundly on her teenage bed while Nancy crept out of the room and watched the boys for the rest of the day and into the evening. They played games and watched television and ate Nana's homemade pumpkin pie with whipped cream. All the while their mother rested, occasionally coming out of her sleep coma to the sound of laughter and excitement of her Mom playing with the boys.

How could she live without Declan? How could she be her whole self, when she'd lived most of her life as a quarter of the person she'd once been? For most of the next day and a half, Grace slept. It felt as if she was giving her old self a funeral. Eventually, her new self rose again, confident and sure about who she was, and trusting God to take care of her family.

* * *

Grace woke up the next Saturday morning refreshed, invigorated, the old rusty thermometer outside of her window read a balmy thirty-four degrees. The sun beamed heavily into the room, causing her to linger an extra few minutes in its heated path.

When she did walk out the bedroom into the living room, her boys barely turned around. Clearly Nana had taught Luke how to turn on Mickey Mouse by himself. Not even the Mom they hadn't seen for more than a day would turn them away from this new addiction. She wondered why her mother wasn't out of bed yet, but figured that a day with the boys probably tired her out more than usual.

Grace decided to make breakfast for everyone. Opening one cupboard, Grace reached up and grabbed her mother's old recipe box, searching for a specific recipe that made her mouth water thinking of it. Finally she found the words "Baked Apple French Toast Casserole" written on a tattered white 3x5 card, smiled, and went to work creating her masterpiece.

She knew her mother was going to want coffee as soon as she woke up so she made a pot of Dunkin' Donuts morning blend Nancy had stashed away in her pantry.

An hour passed and she called the boys away from the TV to the table. She told Luke to go wake up his Nana, an errand he was happy to oblige. He returned minutes later saying she wouldn't wake up. That was curious, seeing as how Nancy was such a morning person. Grace would wake her after breakfast. A post-Thanksgiving breakfast, even if a day late, brought good memories for this family of three.

They ate and discussed Mickey Mouse, turkeys and why people ate them, and their desire to have a trampoline to jump on as soon as possible. They wanted to talk to Santa about that. The food melted in their mouths. Afterwards, Grace realized she ate too much. The food coma was real. The hangover would be worse.

After she cleaned up breakfast, she sent the boys out to play and walked into her mother's room. She slowly opened the door, a slow methodical creepy creak playing from its hinges. She expected Nancy to be looking up at her smiling, having smelled the coffee and breakfast she knew waited for her. But as she entered the room, a still silence hung in the air, and the blankets did not move.

"Mom, it'a time to wake up, sleepy head." She whispered loudly. "Mom?"

Moving across the room to the side of Nancy's bed, Grace lifted her mother's comforter away from her neck. A ghastly whiteness laid across her wrinkled face. Horror struck as Grace knew immediately that her mom had breathed her last breath hours before.

More tears. She could handle losing her job and Declan's passive aggressive attacks on her motherhood, but she feared this loss was more than she could handle.

Grace called out for her Mom to wake up a dozen more times in the midst of her wails until she eventually laid her head on Nancy's body. This time her Mom would not wake up, and in the midst of this room with her best friend, she never felt so lonely.

Week 3 and Counting

Declan boarded the plane to Punta Arenas with a small suitcase and a backpack that held his laptop and a few papers with coded information he didn't want to exist on any digital medium. The time had arrived, feeling like it did in school on his way to a wrestling meet, or every time he met up with Grace in their first few months dating.

Those were good days, and he'd tried to save them as life progressed and their marriage fell apart but for whatever reason, she continued doing everything she could to destroy the relationship. The cycle needed to be broken. Surely if she'd left the fixing of their marriage to him, he would have saved it. After all, he loved to fix things.

Declan had enjoyed his few days in Mexico City, but his troubled mind fixated on both proving to the world the error of their ways and somehow working things out with Grace. He knew things could get better. She only needed to listen and help him work on certain aspects of their lives. Her constant habits of ignoring details, spending too much and wanting the attention of others drowned out their ability to create compatibility. The world acted similarly, ignoring clear evidence before them that the Earth was not round, nor did life exist outside of our planet.

Declan was going to detonate a truth bomb. His knowledge, research, and leadership would change the face of education. For the first time in months, he prayed.

God, when I get off this plane, I'm in your hands. I have planned, persisted, and am trying to prove your truth. There are many doubters, but I know you will use me to reveal this vicious lie. They don't want others to know you created the earth as a table. Your table. A tabled canvas where your creation launched nearly 7000 years ago. Right now, God, protect Adam and Ronnie and I and help us to finish this! We just want your truth to be known.

And God, please be with my family. Forgive Grace and her desire to divide what you have put together. Protect our children from her inability to parent.

And through all of this, God, I know that you are with me. Great things will be done in your name! I'm getting excited just thinking about it. Truth first, God. Truth first. Amen.

As the plane took off and the pilot and flight attendants spoke their instructions in Spanish, he laid his head down and ran through the plan in his mind until he traveled to dreamland, skipping the snacks and meals and movies. Declan knew when he woke up, he would be taking the ride of his life.

"Bienvenidos a Punta Arenas," announced the pilot a minute and a half after the wheels of the plane touched the ground, waking Declan from his slumber. "Hace trece grados centígrados en Punta Arenas, Chile. ¡Disfruten de su estancia aquí y que tengan un buen día!"

The travelers slowly exited the plane. Declan, with his small bag and backpack, headed straight for the exit and taxi area. During this visit he would not loiter in the terminal for surveillance. Instead he visited a few prearranged sights, spending a few minutes at each location before heading toward the place they would meet and spend a few minutes together before the next morning at 9:30 when they would enact their plan with a flight scheduled for Buenos Aires. He quickly looked on his phone to make sure that flight's status was currently "on time." Check. Hailing a taxi, he jumped into the car and simply said, "Straights of Magellan."

Along the drive he noticed the beauty of Punta Arenas. Monstrous mountains hovered over the city and its neighboring water channels. Declan thought of the joke about the "idiots that believe this all happened on accident." Breathtaking scenes covered every landscape, and he pondered reasons more people didn't consider moving here, to the southernmost city in Chile and South America. This was the most beautiful place he'd ever seen. Of course, this balmy fifty-six degrees was the warmest this city would see all year. In the winter months of June, July, and August, it wasn't quite so comfortable. As the car drove, his eyes shifted from the majestic mountains of Patagonia to the crystal waters that laid between him and Antarctica right now. This place would be the subject of a Hallmark Christmas movie, if Santa had been from the South Pole instead of its northern rival.

Eventually the taxi dropped him off on a street next to the water. Declan paid the fare and stretched himself out of the small car. He smelled the clean mountain air, and noticed immediately there was something special about this place. God created the world to feel this way. Minimal human touch kept it all clean and natural.

Declan walked to where boats floated in and out of the harbor. He read a sign that said, barcos en alquiler, Isla Magdalena. Moving that direction, to a small shack where a wrinkled brown-skinned man with black and gray hair greeted him with a smile.

"Puedo viajar en barco a la isla?" Declan asked in a slow pattern. The vendor realized immediately he was speaking with an American.

"Si. Veinte cinco peso, Por favor. Salimos en diez minutos," the man replied slowly to ensure Declan understood.

Declan took out his wallet and handed him twenty five Chilean pesos he'd exchanged at a Worcester bank before he left. He didn't want to spend too much time in the airport when he arrived, remembering his government "friend" on the last surveillance trip, so planned appropriately for anything he needed before he left.

Ten minutes later, the man motioned for him to board the mid-sized yellow motorboat. As the lone passenger, he picked a padded seat to choose from at the front of the boat. Quickly the captain backed out of its mooring spot at the pier and picked up speed, moving toward the small island. They were headed away from Antarctica, and for now that was okay.

Gray clouds covered the sky. The waters beneath mirrored the color as the boat slid across the waves. The man mentioned something about twenty miles, so Declan figured that was the distance they would travel on this trip. As the boat approached the island, he noticed a lighthouse on the top of the tallest hill this side of landfall. Painted white with a few red strips around its circumference, Declan assumed the building acted as a research hub for the penguins rumored to waddle around their uninhabited home.

The boat pulled up to a rickety red dock. He jumped out onto the unstable platform. The creaking sound he made upon stepping on the dock scared him a bit, but Declan figured if the dock was going to fail, the chances of it failing now were slim to none. Onward he traversed.

Around the coast of the island laid large rocks. Certainly this was no beach resort, as children would not be able to handle the rocky interior. Not that there were any children here to begin with, he laughed to himself. On the other side set a more smooth, sandy layer, but still with small rocks. Still not Cape Cod.

As Declan moved to the interior, he encountered dozens and dozens of penguins strolling and playing across the landscape. Rope corridors kept visitors to a certain path leading toward the Lighthouse, so he stayed on that path alone. There was no one else here except the captain of the boat who remained at the dock. Anyone in the lighthouse likely stayed inside its warm walls. The penguins playfully wobbled over to him, curious as to what type of creature they were seeing. All around were small tunnels in the dirt which housed the beautiful birds.

Black and white and gray and all sorts of different colors and shapes were represented as the penguins clapped at their new friend visiting them. For a few minutes Declan talked to his aquatic flightless friends, until he got bored of their refusal to answer, stood straighter and, this time, instead of praying like normal, decided to have a real conversation with God.

"So God. Here I am. At the edge of your whole created earth. Crazy huh?"

As he asked the question, he heard a quiet whisper blow through the wind that brushed his face. A voice that said, "You can't control me."

"God," he laughed to himself, "I don't want to control you. I'm just trying to control the things you've given me power to control. That's all, I promise. I want truth. I want things to be right. So that's what I'm doing. You gave me my brain for a reason, right?"

Again the wind picked up and this time blew harder. He heard the voice again, as clear as day saying to him, "You can't control me."

As the wind continued to strengthen, the penguins grew agitated around him and started clapping harder against his legs and themselves, but not in a festive way. They moved around one another and started hitting the ground and those around them. The birds called to one another loudly and angrily. The wind gusts slammed against his body and one penguin in particular stepped toward him, as if he brought the wind with him.

Declan turned around and walked back towards the boat still waiting for him on the rickety red dock. He said out loud, "God, I don't know what you're saying to me. Here I am, just doing what I think you want me to do. That's all I've ever done. Are you telling me to stop? Are you telling me to turn around? Certainly you want people to know the truth. That's what I'm here to give to you."

He walked faster now, as the sound of the penguin's feet moving toward him patting against the ground. Then, quicker than it all had started, as he stepped onto the dock the sound and press of the wind and the frenzy of the penguins came to a stop. There was only silence. In that silence, he heard a voice say, "Declan, don't try to control me."

The waves gently brushed against the dock. Declan looked across the Strait of Magellan, at the mountains miles away on the other side of Punta Arenas, and the clouds giving way to the beginning of a stunning sunset shot through with rays of light in yellow and red and orange. Declan climbed back onto the boat and nodded to the captain who'd patiently been waiting for his return. The boat backed away from the dock and once again moved across the waves.

Declan's heart pounded. Whatever God was trying to tell him, he would continue on with his plans. He was a lot of things, but one of them was not a quitter.

* * *

The following Thursday Grace woke up with the same deep sadness she'd carried all week. She hoped it would soon go away. She knew she needed to be strong today for her sons, only one of whom truly understood what had happened to their Nana a few days earlier.

Grace showered and made a cup of coffee, followed by bowls of Lucky Charms for the boys. Brandon and Luke ate together in silence.

Usually she asked them questions and tried to inject them with some energy in the mornings, but today the silence made her feel better.

She wanted Declan to be sitting at the table with her right now, letting her weep into his shoulder. During times of pain, she knew the ease with which people reverted back to those things that are the worst for them. She also knew this was why she wanted him here, but didn't care. Like food to a glutton or a cigarette to a chain smoker, right then she needed the thing she most craved. She'd called him, but heard only his voicemail.

For the last several months, Grace had let go of things that caused her to worry or even controlled her. She was never big on controlling her own life, but also never had the faith to let God do it either. No, that was what Declan was for. He controlled. She obeyed. Until the night she let him go. Since then, everything was going to hell in her life and she blamed God for all those one way trips. As the problems began to pile up with each passing day she wondered whether or not her faith would ever show evidence that what she hoped for would happen. After all, Scripture said that faith was supposed to show the reality of what one hoped for, that it was the evidence of things we cannot see. Where was this evidence?

If someone would ask her right now what her specific hope was, she wouldn't be able to answer. Did she have none? Was there anything?

She had hope in God, yes, but what the hell did she have to hope for in regards to her life? Heaven? Her mother walked – no, skipped - even now down the streets of gold. But she died too young, and Grace certainly wasn't itching to walk or skip down those same streets any time soon.

She hoped... she hoped... she hoped that the only person she would ever allow to control her from now on was her God. She hoped that with the talents he gave her and the children he gave her, she could walk through life peacefully with full knowledge that where she walked he went with her, protecting her, where her worry was simply an overreaction to believing one could control everything.

And, she hoped that the things or people in life trying to control her - the worry, the men, the women, the food, the "leaders" or any number of addictions that wanted to wrap their tentacles around her, body and soul - would fall prey to the strength of her trust. For too long Grace placed her confidence in this person or that need, but if she'd learned anything during this tumultuous time, it was to counteract all of these storms with nothing but hope.

Take a deep breath. Focus on the solution. Let go of the bitterness and pain. No Human, food, or pill will make you feel better. Walk through the issues. Thank God he brought you through it. Hope he will continue to do so.

Today, she would need that mantra more than ever. She told the boys to put on the clothes she'd placed on their beds then got dressed herself. Her mother wouldn't have wanted anyone in today's service to wear black, but Grace couldn't bring herself to "celebrate" like it was Cinco de Mayo or something. She put on one of her favorite, more celebratory black dresses, and felt good about her decision.

Her cell phone rang. Grace looked at the screen but didn't recognize the number. She didn't know why, but she answered it. When she heard who it was she regretted it.

"Hello," she said. "This is Grace."

"Hi Grace, this is Mary Belizzi from the Department of Children and Families."

"Mary, this is not a great time ,or even a great day. Could we talk some other time?"

"Of course, Grace, but I did just want to tell you that we won't need to talk any more, unless you want to. I've signed off on the case and DCF will no longer be looking into any of the allegations. I wanted to thank you for cooperating and wish you well on your future. Thanks so much, Grace."

"I don't know what to say," Grace replied, tears welling up in her eyes. It would be a day full of tears and she wanted to save them. "Thank you, Mary. You have no idea how much that means to me. Have a great day." She put down the phone and smiled, both on her face and in her heart. Things would turn around. She just needed to get through the rest of the day.

* * *

Marie and I picked Grace and the boys up at her mom's house at 9:15 am. Fletcher's Funeral Home of Keene had asked her and the boys, if she wished, to be there by 9:30. We arrived early and stood around, trying to pump ourselves up like we were about to play basketball. There is no emotional preparation for a funeral, especially the receiving line. People walk through the line, greet you and say how wonderful the person was, followed by how sorry they are for you and your loss. Many of the people you know, some you don't, but the common thread of the line communicates vividly that you are not better off having lost the person being memorialized. The line not only reminds you of this fact, but represents it.

Marie and I positioned ourselves in between Grace and a few of her aunts at her behest to keep the line moving in the event if anyone "got stuck" in front of her. Thankfully the mourners moved swiftly. Apparently most people dislike the tradition as much as those on the receiving end.

The walk-through began around 10:00 am, with a steady stream of people flowing in and out until the service began at noon.

The day went mostly smooth. Her mother was well-liked. The only two bits of drama Grace mentioned was her Aunt Lois' constant moaning that she never "made up" with her sister after a fight they'd had three months earlier. The fight had centered around the celebration house their families would spend Christmas this year. As usual, Nancy made her own family a priority, while Lois wanted to bring everyone together. Lois had hung up on Nancy, as was her usual custom in tense situations. Nancy's other two sisters handled this problem by reminding Lois that this funeral was not to mourn their relationship, but to remember Nancy only. It wasn't about her. This shut Lois up for the better part of the morning.

The second bit of drama revolved around a white haired man no one knew, or understood why he was there. He walked in quietly, not speaking to anyone for a while, then moved through the line greeting only Grace. He was well-spoken with a clear British accent as he told her how sorry he was, and that he would be praying for her and the boys. He then walked away from the line and out of the room. He called himself Adam, and said he knew Nancy from years before. Grace fixated on the man for the rest of the day. Before he left the funeral home, he handed her an envelope. She thanked him but did not open it immediately, instead placed it on the small table behind her with a few other sympathy cards. After he walked away, Grace asked Marie and I and the rest of her family if anyone knew the man. Everyone told her they did not but promised to try to remember. How anyone would remember something they don't know in the first place, I don't know, but this was the promise.

Grace had recognized him from somewhere, and it bothered her. After an hour of trying to remember where she'd seen him she moved on. In some ways, the diversion was welcome from the miserable nature of the funeral. It certainly helped Grace push through the day. A few days later she went through the pile of envelopes and came to the one the stranger had given her. She found $20,000 inside and a letter inside.

* * *

The plan the next morning started with the three men meeting in the extra hotel room Declan had reserved at 4:00 am, then leaving separately for the airport. As things tend to do, however, the plans immediately needed to be altered.

He opened the door and stepped into the hotel room which would host their meeting in five minutes, turning on the lights. A stench of stale air hovered in the cool room, and he walked inside with a black duffel bag and his personal backpack. Inside this was only his laptop. The duffel held a change of clothes from the company that hosted vending and janitorial services for the Punta Arenas airport, and a variety of first aid items for cold weather climates.

His anticipation caused him to feel like his entire body was about to burst. Declan placed his bags on the bed, walked to the cloth chair on the other side of the room, and sat down. He noticed a piece of paper from the hotel's stationary on the desk next to the chair. He picked it up when he realized his name was written at the top of the sheet.

"Declan, sorry, man. I can't do this. I don't think we can make it happen, and I'm not ready to do this. I hope you understand. Ronnie."

What the hell! Declan thought to himself, crumbling the paper up and throwing it in the trash." How long ago had Ronnie left this? He looked closer at the handwriting. The script was far neat to have written by him. Adam is not going to be furious.

As if that was its cue, Declan's phone went off. Adam's name displayed on the screen. He was video FaceTiming.

"Hey, Adam." Declan calmly answered the phone. He didn't want to appear worried, this project was too important.

"Hi, Dec!" Adam responded in an unusually cheerful voice. From the his screen, it was apparent that Adam wasn't anywhere near the hotel.

"Where you at?"

"I'll get right to the point, Declan. I'm not coming."

"What do you mean you're not coming? We have a job to do!"

"Dec, you have a job to do. I never intended to come. I do appreciate you flying me to Buenos Aires, though. I will have a wonderful vacation! However, like I'd planned from the start, instead of flying to Punta Arenas, I changed my ticket to better suit my current needs and schedule. Oh, I also talked Ronnie out of coming. I told him he would die and there was no way for us to be successful with any of this. He agreed, so I had someone - a friend - deliver his message to the room last night."

"Why, Adam?! Why would you do this? We could have proven that the world was flat together! I can't believe this. This is the lowest of the low! You are disloyal! You are double minded. You have no honor, you scared little piece of crap!"

Adam laughed and laughed on the video screen and when he responded, he did so calmly. "Declan, Declan, Declan. You are such an ignorant bloke. You call me low and disloyal? What about leaving my group and sleeping with my daughter? You call me double minded? What about your wife, Declan? You could be with her right now, but instead you chose this path over her. Why? Because you can't control her anymore, can you? You say I have no honor? You had an affair, then after your wife found out, you could have stopped it. Instead you continued to try to take advantage of my daughter for your own personal gratification. If Amber hadn't put a stop to it, you'd probably have brought her along on this little trip of yours because you need to control everything in your life." He leaned forward, closer to his phone. "But here's the thing. You can't control me. I am in control right now. And I, too, am walking away."

"I'll do this without you, Adam! I'll do this and my name will be in lights and you'll be out in the cold. You will have nothing! In fact, I'll find a way to use my success to rid the world of you, be sure of that." Adam's image pulled away, as if he was beginning to grow tired of holding his phone. A heavy weight grew in Declan's belly, feeling his final chance was about to leave him here, alone.

"In some ways," Adam said, "I just feel sorry for you, Dec. Either way, though, if I were you, I wouldn't try it by yourself." He shrugged. "Maybe you can find yourself a new Wolfpack. Maybe you can find some other old guy's daughter to fool around with? It doesn't matter to me. I'll be here, in America, remembering your reaction to us dissing out on you. In a few minutes I'll be going back to bed, my own bed. Again, I do look forward to Buenos Aires. Have you been to Argentina, Declan? It is beautiful this time of year. Have a great day, my old friend! Enjoy Chile, and talk soon, OK?" He gave a curt smile and a passing wave. Then the screen went blank.

Declan threw his phone on his bed in disbelief. He hit the bed several times as hard as he could, angrily cursing God for what just happened.

"I can control you!" Declan yelled. "I can control anything I want and I will still make this happen. I am my own destiny!"

After the funeral and the reception where family and church friends gathered to eat and celebrate her mother's life, Grace finally rested back at Nancy's house. She gave the boys a bath, read them a Magic Tree House chapter book, then sent them off to dreamland, hopefully not thinking about the day's events.

Marie and I spent a few minutes with her after the kids went to bed. We didn't, however, hover too long. People have a tendency to make funerals about themselves and the way that the deceased fit into their own lives. We only wanted to help Grace however we could. If she needed something, we'd be there for her. If not, we'd leave. She was tired, and we took the hint.

Grace had no idea what she was going to do for the rest of her life, only that she needed to take it one step at a time, and always be very careful where she put her faith. She'd realized in the last four weeks that she didn't need anyone. Having spent her entire life believing she needed her boyfriends or her Dad or her Mom or finally Declan, now she understood the meaning of faith in its true form. While she needed everyone God put in her life, she didn't need any of them to complete her. God created her to be complete on her own. With Him she was whole. She was enough.

There would be no more wishing she was someone else. Out of the entire universe - all of the planets and all life on earth and everywhere else - there was only one Grace Ann Miller. God made her, and as she accepted herself and the circumstances God allowed in her life, she felt content with the life He gave her.

For the first time since she arrived home after the funeral, Grace turned on her phone. She had a voicemail.

"Hi Grace, my name is Tom Dancy. I work with the Department of Children and Families here in Massachusetts. Mary Belizzi shared with me her report, and of course as you know by now, that's been taken care of. She also told me a little about your background and your interview. She and I talked for a while, and we'd love it if you would be interested in applying for a job with us here at DCF. I know, I know, it seems odd given the circumstances you found yourself in the last few weeks, but after we'd done our research and conducted your interviews, and to be honest our employment needs here in Central Mass, we'd love it if you'd be interested in at least applying, maybe coming in for an interview with us in the near future. Maybe we could get something done before the new year? No promises, but if you're still looking for work, we'd like to see if there's a mutually agreeable solution.

"Thanks so much for your time, Grace. My number is 508-929-2000, ext. 722. I look forward to hearing from you. Hope you're having a great day!"

Grace smiled, then laid quietly in her mother's bed thinking about the woman's last words to her. You have an opportunity now, Grace. You can choose to live life the way you were created to, or live someone else's life, and all the while trying to control the things around that cannot be controlled. Who do you wanna be, Grace?

"Thanks, Mom," she whispered into the air. "I choose my own life. I choose joy. I choose hope and love. I choose faith. I choose me."

* * *

A week after the initial launch of the Flat Earth project that never actually happened, Declan woke up at 3:30 am to begin the final event which would change the science textbooks, but this time as a solo project. He felt confident and ready, yet unsettled in his spirit. Since things changed, there were a few "black holes" of information he needed to fill. The problem was he didn't know whether or not he could ever uncover that information. So, going in blind, mainly because of finances, was his best option now.

In the last week, he'd studied online how to start and fly a commercial airliner, secured a handheld firearm from a contact of his in the states, and found an employee on the janitorial staff of the airport who was stupid enough to allow Declan to steal his access card. They looked similar, so if Declan stayed away from everyone he could for the few minutes it would take to get into the airport.

Since last week's change - not a setback, merely a change - happened, he decided to walk out of the hotel in a t-shirt and shorts, then change in a crowded parking lot into the janitor's uniform. He'd been watching one specific man, Carlos Alvarez, several times in the last week until he worked out his routine. There were some holes there, too, since he was never able to get into the other side of the door. He would have only one chance when he did that, and that was on game day.

Security in the Punta Arenas Airport looked very different than any in the US. There seemed to be a laid back attitude from just about everyone he saw during surveillance. This was going to help him accomplish his task. Declan hoped that beyond the janitor's door, the badge would grant him the access he needed, including to a plane.

Most often he found Carlos cleaning bathrooms in the general area of the airport. The major black hole of information in front of him was whether or not Mr. Alvarez could walk anywhere he wanted, in any terminal, to clean. If so, then this plan would work. If not, Declan would be apprehended very quickly.

By 4:00 am, Declan had walked out of the back stairway in the hotel and into an alley he knew there were no cameras. Not being seen early on was instrumental to his plan. He caught a bus to the airport in front of a different hotel. Soon enough the airport lights glowed before him. All of his study and preparation led to this moment. He controlled his own destiny now, and the world was going to look forever different.

Then the bus continued towards the terminals for another few minutes, then turned away down another road - still part of the airport but leading towards a large hangar. Declan glanced around and realized he was the only passenger. He wished he'd noticed that earlier. He slowly reached his hand inside the bag and grabbed the loaded Glock 19. He didn't take it out because he still wasn't sure what was happened. He needed to be ready, however, for whatever came next.

As the bus pulled into the hangar, Declan noticed the official seal of the Chilean Air Force on the door. His heart pounded faster and the started to sweat. From the bus's overhead speaker came a familiar voice.

"Declan, I warned you to stay at home and not to come back. You obviously didn't think I was serious. That's OK. I understand guys like you. But here's the deal. You're done here in Chile. The next thing you do is going to forecast your future."

Declan pictured the man from the airport on his first visit. He had been purposefully keeping an eye out for him whenever he entered the airport in the past week, but had not seen him. The man continued, "You can place your hands above your head, completely up, in a surrender position. Leave everything you have on your seat, walk straight to the front of the bus, step out of the bus, and lay down next to the bus. If you do that, and only that, you will be temporarily detained, but eventually sent back to the United States, and all rights to ever visit Chile ,or Argentina, suspended for the rest of your life."

Declan wondered if this was a two way conversation. "And what if I don't?"

"There is no other decision, Declan. That is the choice you will make."

Declan thought about life back in the United States. He had no family, no friends, and no job. He'd invested everything he had into this venture. Consequently, he had nothing or no one he could go home to. And here was some idiot who thought he could control him now. All his life people tried to control him, but Declan found ways to wrestle it back from them all. High risk, high reward.

Why should this guy, as far as Declan knew he was only one guy, keep the truth from coming out for the entire world to know?

No. He would not be controlled. He would finish what he started. He had too much pride and too much at stake to stop now.

Declan slowly lifted his hands up in the air, but as he did, he grabbed the Glock with his left hand, then leapt up and ran to the front of the bus. The driver's seat was empty. He jumped into it and turned the key. He never noticed the laser pointing at his temple. At 4:17 am in the Chilean Air Force side of the Presidente Carlos Ibanez Del Campo International Airport, as the bus engine turned over, a .308 Winchester sniper bullet entered and exited Declan Dumais' skull.

The Final Week

The Christmas season moved slowly from calendar day to calendar day for Grace. She liked it that way during this time of the year. She felt lonely without her mom or Declan around the house or to talk to on the phone, but she held closely her time with the boys, even deciding to bring them with her as she Christmas shopped. Her new habit was to shop at the malls to see what she wanted to get them, then buy the gifts on Amazon. The world changed around her and she didn't want to be left behind.

She'd worked on her resume and sent it in to the Department of Children and Families. After careful research of what they really did, she realized what a responsibility the Commonwealth had in taking care of hurting children. Her own, personal case had been so rare that she felt bad for Mary who'd come to interview her that day. Grace wanted to make a difference, and the more she looked into it, the more she understood that working at DCF could make a huge impact in the lives of hundreds, maybe even thousands of children. They'd scheduled her first interview for the week after Christmas, and she couldn't be more excited about it.

Declan would have been upset at her for working as a "slave to the state," but at this point she didn't care. She felt good about being the person she was now and carried so much joy everywhere she went, that people in her life saw the difference.

One evening, while she sat quietly in front of the fireplace sipping hot chocolate, the boys having gone to bed a half hour earlier, Grace received a phone call from a number she didn't recognize. Usually she ignored those, but because she it might be DCF, she answered.

"Hello."

A deep voice with a slightly Spanish accent said, "Hello, is this Grace O'Neil?"

"Well, no, my name is Grace, but my last name isn't O'Neil. How can I help you? Is this a telemarketer?"

"No ma'am. My name is Franco, and I'm with a local government in the southern tip of Argentina, a place called Isle Grande de Tierra del Fuego. Do you know of this place?"

"I don't, no. My husband, or my ex-husband has been somewhere down there recently. But I though it he was in Chile though, not Argentina."

"Okay, okay. May I ask your husband's or excuse me, your ex husband's name, Grace?"

"His name is Declan. Why do you ask?"

"Oh ma'am, I am sorry to tell you this. A man who referred to himself as Declan O'Neill has been found dead on this island. Could O'Neil be an alias?"

Grace sat silently soaking in the news. She knew it was him, it had to be. Oddly, she didn't feel any shock, or happiness, at the news. Her first feeling was of being lost, but she didn't want to feel that. So she processed and prayed for the next few seconds while the man on the other end waited.

After the pause, she asked, "Franco, may I ask how he passed away? Do you know that?"

"Oh, yes, ma'am," he responded. "Declan was attacked by a puma. These are usually non-violent animals, but apparently something caught this one off-guard and it attacked him. I am so sorry to have to tell you this. My deepest condolences to you and your family."

"Thank you," Grace said calmly and hung up the phone.

She walked to the fireplace, threw a log in, and lit a match to start the fire. Minutes later, the fire roared, tag teaming with her hot chocolate to warm her on this cold New England evening. She stared at the fire and thought about the difference between a fire in a fireplace and a raging firestorm in the middle of the woods. Natural occurrences in one place could be safe, in another they could destroy people's lives.

Grace thought about Declan and cried. Not because she loved him in any type of romantic way any longer. She knew better than that now and no longer needed him. She cried because, instead of allowing curiosity to well up inside himself and let truth come to light naturally, he chose instead to prove everyone else was wrong, simply so he could be right. In the end, that was why he went to South America. Not to prove some sort of truth, but so he could be right.

Grace stood up from the couch and walked to her mother's backyard patio. Soon she would travel back home but in this particular valley with mountains surrounding her, she looked up gazing at the brilliant stars draped across the sky. Her breath escaped her mouth as it merged with the cold temperatures. And with moist eyes, she smiled.

"I love you Declan," she spoke in a regular voice, not caring if anyone heard. "I hope you found what you were looking for. I hope... well, I hope that before you died, you found hope, trust, faith. And I hope you basked in it, if only for a moment."

Acknowledgments

I have so many people to thank for helping me to write this book. It's been a dream of mine to write a novel, and alas, here it is, and I trust you've enjoyed it. I'd like to thank Dan Keohane first for his mentorship and guidance in helping me finish "Flat Earth". Literally this book would not be finished without you Dan, so thank you. Also, your editing is fantastic.

I'd also like to thank George Lippert for his amazing work on the book cover. I've always looked up to you, George, and now I hope many others can do the same. If you're reading this, you really need to immediately google Dan and George's names, because they are both extremely talented authors with several books I've enjoyed. But if you're wondering, I recommend "The Riverhouse" by G. Norman Lippert, or "Plague of Darkness" by Daniel Keohane.

Thank you to Spencer Mclennan, for your guidance and help with flight paths and Samantha VanRiper for talking me through a life of those who work for the Department of Children and Families in Massachusetts. Thanks also to Andrea Maile for reading my second to last draft. Because of your thoughts, the last draft changed dramatically.

I'd also like to thank Clint and Pablo, who started this crazy story by sitting on a couch with me in 2017 in New Hampshire and waxing eloquently about the flat earth videos you watched. That three hour conversation led to this story.

Thank you also to the amazing people of Valencia, Spain, who housed my family for a month and showed us how truly wonderful Spain can be. I wrote more than half of this book there, and I hope to write more there in the future.

Finally, thank you to those who take the time to review my book on Kindle or Apple Books and also to those who share this novel with others! I greatly appreciate it.